DEAD LEVEL

DEAD LEVEL

A
Home Repair Is Homicide
Mystery

SARAH GRAVES

BANTAM BOOKS   NEW YORK

Copyright © 2011 by Sarah Graves

Published in the United States by Bantam Books, an imprint of The Random House Publishing Group, a division of Random House, Inc., New York.

BANTAM BOOKS and the rooster colophon are registered trademarks of Random House, Inc.

Library of Congress Cataloging-in-Publication Data
Graves, Sarah.
Dead level : a home repair is homicide mystery / Sarah Graves.
p. cm.
ISBN 978-0-553-80790-5 (acid-free paper)
eBook ISBN 978-0-345-53456-9
1. Tiptree, Jacobia (Fictitious character)—Fiction. 2. Women detectives—Fiction. 3. Dwellings—Maintenance and repair—Fiction. 4. Eastport (Me.)—Fiction. I. Title.
PS3557.R2897D43 2012
813'.54—dc23   2011035914

Printed in the United States of America on acid-free paper

www.bantamdell.com

2 4 6 8 9 7 5 3 1

First Edition

Book design by Karin Batten

DEAD LEVEL

PROLOGUE

Hours after inmate Dewey Hooper, seven years into a twenty-year sentence for manslaughter, escaped from the prison system's medium-security facility at Lakesmith, Maine, guard Jeff Rohrbach got his orders. He was to collect up all of Hooper's personal belongings, including books, papers, writings, drawings, and anything else that might give a hint as to the missing man's whereabouts.

Yeah, Rohrbach thought scornfully. *Like that's gonna happen. Guy decides to pull a runner, he's gonna leave clues. Little map, maybe, X marks the spot on it. Jeeze, you'd think some of these supervisors had never seen the inside of a prison before. But:*

Mine is not to reason why, Rohrbach told himself resignedly, stopping at the door to "D" corridor and turning his face up so that the guy watching the surveillance camera could see him. The locked corridor, called a pod, held a group of a dozen cells that constituted a prisoner's neighborhood.

While he was here, Hooper had been a good citizen of his neighborhood, or at least a relatively trouble-free one. Took his orders without backchat, no fights, no contraband discoveries. It was as if Hooper had been relieved, really, to have someone else telling him what to do for a change. Arriving for his shift this morning, Rohrbach had been amazed to hear that Hooper had taken the initiative to attempt an escape; that the inmate had actually made it out Rohrbach thought was just short of miraculous.

He waited patiently while the guard monitoring the camera opened the pod door's electronic lock: *ka-click!* when it opened, *ka-click!* again when it closed behind him.

Inside, the brightly lit corridor featured identical doors, each pierced with a small window. At this hour of the morning, the cells were empty, their occupants all out at various scheduled activities: work, school, exercise, and so on. Except for Hooper; what activity he might be engaged in this fine morning was still anyone's guess.

Rohrbach entered Hooper's cell, which looked just like all the others: a ten-by-fourteen-foot cubicle with white walls, a white linoleum floor, and a slot window too narrow for a man to get even half his face through, much less his body. The bed was a shelf built into the wall; the combination washstand and toilet was brushed steel, also built in. A desk-shelf with a molded plastic chair tucked under it was the only other furniture. The mattress on the bed was a thin blue plastic pad.

Brackets in the wall above the bed showed where another bunk could be hung, if necessary. There was nothing else in the room: no books, no pictures on the wall, no calendar. A blanket and a towel, neatly folded, were on the neatly made bed, atop Hooper's pillow. Cell and corridor smelled the same, like Clorox, sweeping compound, cheap air freshener, and men's sweat.

The cell's stark impersonality came as no surprise. Others on the corridor, in defiance of regulations, had taped clippings of newspaper stories, their kids' artwork, and other items that were personally important to them on the walls. But Hooper had been, Rohrbach recalled again grimly, a model prisoner, and when the order came down that all prisoner belongings should be stowed in footlockers, not displayed on the walls as if these were college dorm rooms, Hooper, unlike most of the other inmates, had complied at once.

Rohrbach thought the regulation was stupid. A comfortable inmate was a calm inmate, and a calm inmate was a safe inmate, in his opinion. And unlike the administrators who sat on their butts all day thinking up ways to make Rohrbach's job harder, when you worked among guys whose nerves were already severely on edge, the last thing you wanted was to make them even more angry, agitated, and resentful.

But that wasn't Rohrbach's call to make, either. His job was to root through that footlocker, dig out whatever Hooper-locating secrets it might hold. The idea that Hooper might've left a trail of breadcrumbs in the form of a map or a diary was still stupid; hell, the guy was barely literate, as far as Rohrbach could tell.

On the other hand, it wasn't like they had anything else to go on. The prisoner had simply evaporated. Gone like a fart in the wind, as the onetime head of another Maine prison had been known to say.

Rohrbach pulled the gray molded-plastic box from under the bed. Inmates couldn't have locks, so it opened easily. *Might as well ask a Ouija board where Dewey Hooper is,* Rohrbach thought. But when he looked inside the box . . .

"Holy mackerel," he breathed. Notebooks. The footlocker was filled to the top with notebooks, the kind prisoners were allowed to buy with their small work-detail earnings: tape bindings, no plastic or metal, cardboard covers removed in case weapons might somehow be fashioned from them.

Alert for sharp objects that might be rusty or contaminated—some inmates hid blades, needles, and other dangerous things in footlockers, and although he didn't expect any such problem from Hooper's belongings, you never knew—Rohrbach removed one of the notebooks and opened it.

A limp four-leaf clover fluttered out; as it fell to the floor Rohrbach recalled Hooper's only idiosyncrasy: superstition. You could make the guy turn his cell into a plain white box, no problem, but don't try to make him walk under a ladder. Then, as what he was seeing sank in:

"Man, oh, man," Rohrbach said to himself, recalling again the passive little guy who'd seemed to live only for work detail, his eagerness for new assignments seeming to suggest he was enrolled in a training program for running a prison, not confined in one.

Rohrbach flipped quickly through the pages, then slowed, turning them wonderingly:

They were all the same. Page after page, over and over . . .

Day after day. Year after year. Hundreds of times, thousands of times . . . *I guess still waters really do run deep,* Rohrbach thought, and then a sound from the corridor made him turn.

It was Charlie Theriault, here for armed robbery, nine years into a seven-to-fifteen. "Hey," Charlie said.

"Hey," Rohrbach greeted the man in return. Charlie was all right. A little moody but not a problem. The inmate entered his cell, came out with his towel.

Rohrbach looked back down at the notebooks. "Charlie," he said, "do you recall her name? Hooper's wife, the one he—"

Killed. Beat to death. He didn't want to say it, though. Putting violent images in an inmate's head was never a good idea. And as it turned out, he didn't have to; Charlie remembered.

"Marianne," said Charlie, confirming what Rohrbach thought.

As he had expected, the notebooks gave no clue as to Hooper's whereabouts. What had been on his mind, though, through all those quiet years of him being a model prisoner—

Oh, that was crystal clear. *Marianne Marianne,* read the first line of the first notebook in childishly rounded cursive script, like the writing of a small boy. And the next line and the next, on both sides of the page.

Marianne Marianne Marianne . . .

Page after page, notebook after notebook. Year after year:

Marianne.

CHAPTER 1

To remove screws easily, use a
screwdriver bit and the "reverse"
setting on your electric drill.
—Tiptree's Tips

Harold had Facebook, and LiveJournal, and Twitter. He had a BlackBerry, an iPad, an iPod, and a third-generation Kindle.

He had a pain, mild but constant, a fluttery twinge in the soft tissue just above his left eye, deep in the hollow where you'd put your thumb if you were going to try lifting him by his cranium. Sometimes late at night, in his tiny apartment in a grimly forgotten, perpetually unfashionable corner of Lower Manhattan, he would find himself Googling: *twinge, eye, flutter.* Or: *thumb, skull.*

When it occurred to him what that last pair rhymed with— *numbskull*—he stopped Googling it. But he couldn't forget.

Each weekday, Harold took the subway to his job at a video store a few blocks from Ground Zero, a place with a sale bin out front and a sputtery neon sign in the grimy window. Once it had thrived, but the only videos people rented nowadays were ones they wouldn't dare view on the Internet for fear of prison time.

The films didn't have brightly illustrated cardboard sleeves, or even titles. Furtive men—no women, in Harold's depressingly extensive experience—entered the store with money in hand, and asked without looking up at Harold for number 19, or number 204.

Harold wondered if they were ashamed of themselves, or if maybe they just didn't like seeing his eye twitch. If maybe *they* were creeped out by *him*. What he didn't wonder was what kind of unspeakably sordid images the videos contained; he needed the job too much for that.

But after three years in the store—the sputtering neon sign, the nagging eye pain, the worn black plastic cassettes or clear jewel cases that he wiped thoroughly with spray cleaner anytime one of them got returned—he also needed a vacation. So when the store's owner laid Harold off for two weeks due to cash-flow problems, he decided to go to Maine.

He'd never been, just seen pictures of the place. Probably Maine colors weren't as bright as they looked in the pages of magazines, with lighthouses as red-and-white-striped as new candy canes, and water as blue as . . . well, nothing in this life was ever really that blue, Harold felt sure.

But it didn't matter what it was like there. It was the *idea* of Maine that attracted him: clean air, not too many people. Forests you could walk into and not find your way out again, mineral-clear lakes, numbingly cold, where you could wade in and dissolve with a sigh, like a fizzy lozenge.

Not that he meant to; wade into one of those lakes, that is, and never wade out. But the idea of such wilderness—of surfaces that hadn't been handled and breathed on, or even looked at, by millions of people—spoke deeply to him, somehow, even though he had never experienced any such place himself.

So Harold left all his electronic gadgets at home and took a bus from Port Authority to Bangor, Maine, then a smaller one whose seats were made of hard plastic. As they wound out of Bangor, the driver drank Diet Coke and blared Top Forty on the radio propped up on the cluttered dashboard while the bus juddered along the twisty, crumbling two-lane blacktop.

Hours passed while Harold stared out the window at a world growing steadily more rural and less like anything he'd ever seen before: small wooden houses with garishly colored plastic toys in their rough yards, lobster traps stacked along unpaved driveways, boats sagging on trailers. Next came lengthy stretches where it seemed no one at all lived, the unfenced fields high and boulder-studded and the forests appearing darkly impenetrable.

At last they reached a small, desolate-looking intersection marked by an out-of-business gas station and convenience store. No sign, but the driver said it was the right place; hoisting his backpack, Harold got out and the bus trundled away, leaving him alone on the gravel shoulder, which was littered with hundreds of old and new filtered cigarette butts.

All around him loomed giant evergreens, their pointed tops etched on a fiercely blue sky. A big white-headed bird—a bald eagle, Harold realized; he'd never seen one of those before, either—sailed above.

The roar of a diesel engine shattered the silence as a log truck loaded with forty-foot tree trunks hurtled past, the smell of fresh pine sap sharp in its wake. Watching it go, he felt a sudden, drowning sense of isolation and loss, as if his old life had been torn away and had yet to be replaced by anything.

If it would be. Abruptly, he wished he hadn't come. Back in the city, he was always so surrounded and assaulted by crowds and clamor, it was easy there to pretend that he wasn't alone.

Here it was different. Turning, he heard the gravel crunch loudly beneath his feet. A big dog barked, somewhere on the other side of a line of trees. From the rotting eaves of the boarded-up convenience store, wasps drifted, each one materializing in the gloom at the nest's entrance, then launching itself.

Harold wondered suddenly what it was like in that nest, in the insectile dark. But he didn't think he'd better try to find out. Just then a car pulled up to where the gas pumps used to be.

"You waitin' for a ride?" The car was an old, dark blue Monte Carlo with the word TAXI inexpertly stenciled on it in white.

The driver, a large, whiskery man wearing a fedora, chewed a cigar stub. Harold did not recall any cabdriver back in the city ever waiting so patiently or looking at him so frankly, as if genuinely engaged in this interaction and curious about Harold's reply.

Harold hefted his backpack, which he had let down onto the cracked concrete pad that the absent gas pumps had once stood on. Ten minutes later, after crossing a causeway and traversing some of the most astonishingly beautiful geography he'd ever seen—trees, a long beach with legions of small birds striding stick-legged on it, a wide expanse of water, then more trees and water again—he reached the island city of Eastport, Maine.

"Here you go. That'll be seven bucks. A buck a mile," the taxi man explained around the cigar stub.

Harold blinked, still stunned by the beauty and variety of the fields, forested land, and reedy marshes he'd been whisked through, the ponds, pools, and tidal inlets he'd passed over.

Chomping the cigar, the driver eyed him wisely. "City boy, eh? Don't worry. You stay here, you'll get over it. Eventually," he added with a wink, taking the ten Harold handed him.

"Keep the change," said Harold. The Monte pulled away in a belch of gray exhaust fumes that the breeze, smelling strongly of salt water and creosote, snatched up and dispersed.

Leaving him alone, again, though here at least there were people going about their business: into the hardware store, the pizza shop, and the T-shirt-and-souvenir store all located in the three-story red-brick buildings directly before him. To his left loomed another brick edifice, an old bank now repurposed into an art gallery, with a fountain and a small terrace in front of it. There was an ornate metal park bench placed on the terrace, which he thought was a nice touch.

Right behind him was an old-fashioned diner. Through a small screened front window, he saw a long Formica counter and a series of red leatherette booths, and suddenly realized he was starving. He'd been on the road almost two days with only snacks and small bottles of juice to eat and drink, from the vending machines in various bus stations.

Turning to enter the diner, he got his first view of the bay, which even after all of the water he'd already crossed he hadn't realized was so very near. Seeing it on a map had been one thing, the letters printed over it spelling out *Passamaquoddy Bay,* which he guessed must be a Native American name. But being right next to it was another thing, especially since there was no one on it.

Or almost no one; dark blue with flocks of gulls hovering over it, the bay was narrow and extended a long way to his left and right, which he recalled from the map were north and south. A few fishing boats puttered, their wakes boiling white, engines puffing up clouds of diesel. The bay itself looked serene, though, not like the busy, commerce-clogged waterways at home.

He gazed for another moment, inhaling the salty air. But more delay than that, the pangs of his appetite would not allow. A whiff of grilled bacon drifted sweetly out of the diner's screen window, seized him by the nose, and drew him hungrily in.

Half an hour later he was sopping up the last bit of egg yolk with his last corner of buttered toast. The waitress was so free with the coffee refills, he thought she'd have left the pot if he'd asked. He washed the delicious mouthful down with a sip from his freshly topped-up cup and, sighing, leaned back.

He'd made it. He'd gotten here, all the long way to Maine's

downeast coast, so far from the island of Manhattan and, as he had already begun realizing, so utterly different from it.

And he felt . . . fine. Scared, a little, and still not sure how he was getting away with such an adventurous, such a previously unthought-of, expedition. He didn't quite trust his success yet, he guessed. But so far, so good.

Two men slid onto stools at the counter. They were in their sixties, maybe, Harold thought from their work-bent postures, and they were similarly dressed in jeans, boots, and faded plaid shirts, with Red Sox ball caps on their heads. When they spoke, continuing a conversation that had evidently begun outside, their accents amazed Harold.

"Pretty fah from heah." The first man stirred sugar into his coffee.

"Fah," the second man agreed. "Nawt thet fah, tho."

They were saying that something was only somewhat far from here, Harold realized. He listened some more.

"State prison's just a hop, skip, and a jump from here, if you've got a car once you make it outside the fences." *Cah.*

"They didn't say he's got a car. In the newspaper."

Paypah. "Maybe he didn't. Not then. He might by now, though. Have one, that is."

The second man drank coffee, then added, "He's not coming here, though. I know, I know"—he put his work-worn hands up to ward off objections—"this's where he's from originally. Killer like that, though, he does a runner"—*runnah*—"he'll hightail it to somewhere else, prob'ly. Somewhere he can blend in."

Somewheyah. "Prob'ly," the first man agreed, nodding sagely. "Like New York City. Hell, I guess most anyone you'd meet out on the street might be a killer, there."

You've got that right, Harold thought wryly, gathering from what he'd just overheard that a convicted murderer had recently escaped from the state prison and was on the loose. But that had nothing to do with him, he told himself reassuringly. All he wanted was a walk in the woods, and there was certainly nothing there, he felt sure, to appeal to a prison escapee.

He got up from his booth. The men had turned to discussing a hunter who'd gone out three days ago and hadn't returned. Old Bentley, they called him. Bentley Hodell; had heart trouble, poor guy. Had an attack out there, maybe—*mebbe*—out in the woods.

"Excuse me," Harold cut in. "Could either of you tell me a good place for a fellow to take a hike? Like, out in the forest?"

The men, who when they turned he saw to his surprise were not in their sixties at all, but closer to his own age, perhaps in their mid-thirties or even younger, gazed silently at him for a moment. During it, Harold saw traces of the fresh-faced boys they had been before hard work began taking its toll: bright blue eyes, open expressions, regular features.

"Not in a park, though," Harold added. "I want to hike in the real Maine backcountry."

The men looked communicatively at each other as if silently agreeing on a place to recommend. Then they told Harold about it, even borrowing the waitress's ballpoint to draw him a rough map on a paper napkin from the bright metal dispenser on the counter.

"Watch out for the killer," they added, but laughingly, and Harold decided that if they weren't worried, he wasn't, either.

Killah.

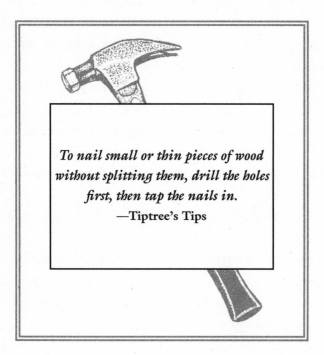

CHAPTER 2

> *To nail small or thin pieces of wood*
> *without splitting them, drill the holes*
> *first, then tap the nails in.*
> —Tiptree's Tips

My name is Jacobia Tiptree–Jake, to my friends–and when I first came to Eastport I thought I'd never get rid of my awful ex-husband, Victor. After our divorce, he'd followed me here for the express purpose of annoying my wits out, and then he did so: earnestly, diligently, and unceasingly, displaying in the process a sly creativity he'd previously shown only while cheating on me.

That was a dozen years ago; now fast-forward six years, to him in a rented hospital bed in the guest room of my antique, ramshackle house on Key Street. Victor was dying, and he said he was doing it at my place because nobody else would have him.

Which under the sad circumstances of course I denied, but he was right. Cross a good-looking, smart-as-a-whip slime toad with a pit viper and presto, you'd have Victor; by the time the brain tumor showed up on his head scans, the only personal-relationship bridges he hadn't burned were the ones he'd dynamited.

Still, he was my son Sam's father, so we took care of him.

And then we buried him, which at least solved the getting-rid-of-him problem . . . or so I believed then.

Fast-forward once more, though, to just recently, and to me in that very same big old house. It was a bright, breezy morning in mid-October, six years to the day since Victor had died; his death-iversary, Sam always called it. Busy trying to prepare for a trip, I was getting a few towels out of the linen closet in the upstairs hall when someone spoke to me, the familiar voice saying my name faintly but distinctly.

Instantly the hairs rose on my arms. "Victor?" I whispered. Which was ridiculous. And yet . . .

Glancing nervously around, I even scanned the hall's pressed-tin ceiling and crown moldings, two of the many antique features—a fireplace in every room, hardwood floors aged to the glowing amber of good whiskey—that had attracted me when I'd first seen the two-hundred-year-old dwelling.

But of course no one was there. The hall window looked out toward Passamaquoddy Bay, a long, narrow body of water that separates Moose Island—the two-by-seven-mile chunk of granite where Eastport, population 1,545, is located—from the Canadian island of Campobello.

Directly across, I could see the huge shoreline estate where the Roosevelts spent summers back in the 1940s. From the rambling shingled mansion with its wide swath of grass sloping down to the beach, they swam and sailed, played croquet, and walked the windswept shore as if they were any other vacationing family.

Nowadays the estate is a park; thousands of people visit it. But the voice I'd heard couldn't have come from over there, either. A storm had washed every hint of haze out to sea just the night before, and even though the razor-bright fall air made the island look near enough to step practically out my front hall window onto, it was really almost two miles distant.

"Jake." Again, more insistently this time. Telling myself it must be what Sam would've called a Fig Newton of my imagination, I tried to ignore it, instead letting my gaze wander down to Key Street, where a double row of maple trees lining the thoroughfare glowed reddish gold in the morning sun.

Behind them, antique clapboard houses like my own presided over autumn lawns; in the gardens, the last straggling asters and chrysanthemums flung their bright heads this way and that in the breeze. Beyond, a jumble of downtown roofs jutted at angles, soft charcoal scribbles of woodsmoke blowing horizontally out of their chimneys.

Then came the bay itself, still choppy after the chaotic squalls of the night before. A little red scallop dragger bobbed energetically on the flowing tide.

"Jake." The window was open, gauzy white curtains billowing, but the only sound coming from there was the growl of a nearby leaf blower. Frowning, I glanced up the stairs to the third floor, where a framed-in hatch led higher still, to the attic.

But that area couldn't possibly be occupied. Days earlier, I'd taken the stepladder from its usual place propped against the hatch, hauling it downstairs to patch the trim around the leaded-glass fanlight over the front door.

And so far I'd neglected to haul it back up again. Besides, I knew that voice, and its owner couldn't be talking: not to me, not to anyone.

Not even on his deathiversary. But there was no denying that I *thought* I'd heard him, and when the phone rang I jumped a foot.

Answering distractedly, I was still busy trying to convince myself that what just happened couldn't have. Because first of all, there was the whole thing about him being dead, a condition that I firmly believed impeded even the most determined attempts at communication. And anyway, what would Victor have to say after six whole years?

He'd said it all—the good, the bad, the deeply, hideously atrocious—

back when he was alive. That, however, didn't seem to matter to the hairs on my neck, which had taken a cue from the ones still bristling on my arms.

Meanwhile, on the telephone, Dan Weatherston—the editor of our local newspaper, the *Quoddy Tides*—was trying to persuade me of something. "Sure, Dan," I heard myself replying. "No problem."

Ordinarily I'd have cheerfully agreed to get my thumbnails yanked out rather than tell anyone that I would write five thousand words about anything, and before I'd have said I would do it by the following Friday I'd have pulled them out myself with pliers. But at the time, I barely heard what the *Tides* editor was saying, still too preoccupied by what had—or hadn't—just occurred, so I answered him without thinking.

After I hung up, though, it hit me: what I'd promised, and what I would have to do to fulfill that promise. Downstairs in the kitchen, in a full-on bout of knuckles-to-the-front-teeth horror more chilling than anything my ghastly—and now possibly also ghostly—ex-husband could inspire, I considered calling the editor back to say I'd developed a case of dyslexia. Or maybe a brain tumor; after all, Sam suffered from the former ailment and Victor had died of the latter one, so I could plausibly pretend to have either.

Not that I'd have tempted fate that way . . . I think. But why, *why* had I agreed to write a newspaper column?

"Jake?" The voice came suddenly from behind me and this time it definitely didn't belong to my dead ex-husband.

Well, of course it didn't, I told myself sternly; it hadn't been his the first time, either. Also, it hadn't been his face in the bathroom mirror that morning, in the steam from the shower I had taken. And once the face was gone, dissolved all at once like a magic trick, the droplets trickling on the mirror's still-foggy surface absolutely had *not* been trying to form words. . . .

"Jake?" Again, but now instead of being scared speechless, I was too stunned by the pickle I'd gotten myself into to reply.

All Dan Weatherston wanted was an article about old-house fix-up tips and tricks, which was what I'd been doing pretty much nonstop since I came here from New York. But while many of the tasks I'd done were standard—window salvage, falling-plaster rejuvenation, doorknob rejiggering, and the ever-popular old-plumbing rescue maneuver (consisting of [a] know where the water main is and [b] shut it off), my methods usually weren't.

Standard, I mean. Just for starters, I almost always broke something while trying to repair some other thing, and no home-repair book that I've ever read recommends this. Then there was the parts problem; modern plumbing, for example, is done with space-age glue, PVC pipe, and hard plastic connectors, whereas in 1823, when my house was built, the plumbing consisted entirely of a cast-iron hand pump, plus buckets.

Later upgrades—pipes, faucets, a drainage system that didn't rely heavily on one of those buckets—hadn't been exactly space-age, either, unless you count *Sputnik*. The most recent refit of anything mechanical in the whole place, in fact, was back in the sixties when they reluctantly got rid of the coal furnace.

As a result, trying to get replacement parts for my old house was nearly impossible, or if they were available they were wildly expensive. I could tell you what an early-nineteenth-century brass window latch costs at a salvage warehouse, for instance, but if I did I'd have to start taking blood-pressure pills.

So—and perhaps also, as my son Sam has suggested, because I enjoy a battle—I'd gotten into the habit of improvising. A strip of Teflon tape applied to the threads of an antique screw, for example, can make it seat securely in an old threaded fitting that is otherwise too stripped to be of any further use. Or a piece of a rubber glove, say, wrapped tightly around a leaking pipe and then C-clamped above and below the leaky place, can ward off a flood if despite my advice of earlier you (a) don't know where the main valve is or (b) it breaks off when you try turning it. (Don't ask me how I know that last part; see *pills,* above.)

But none of that is my point: not my methods, or even that I'd learned them mostly by doing. It's that in the process, I'd found that keeping an antique dwelling in even halfway decent shape had more to do with Rube Goldberg and the less-mentally-well-balanced characters from Looney Tunes than with anything in any how-to book, other than maybe the one about how to drive yourself . . . well, loony.

Which was how I felt, just thinking about trying to write anything about any of it.

"*Jake.*" Looking impatient and a little worried, my friend Ellie White touched my shoulder, then shook it gently. "Earth to Jake. Is everything all right?"

"What? Oh. Fine," I managed at last. "Just distracted, is all." Which was putting it mildly: an impossible voice, an even more impossible project . . .

Turning, I focused on her striking presence: red hair, pale skin with a scattering of gold freckles across a face that belonged on an old-fashioned storybook princess, plus a flair for the dramatic–also to put it mildly–in matters of costume. For our planned outing today, she wore a canary-yellow peasant blouse with red rickrack around the neckline, a turquoise skirt with patch pockets in vivid orange and green, and purple leggings plus leather sandals with bright brass buckles.

On anyone else it would've looked as if the color wheel from the paint store had collided with a truck hauling fireworks, but Ellie's outfit matched her outlook perfectly. "So, are you ready?" she wanted to know. "Because by now I thought you'd be–"

Yeah, ready. I looked around a little wildly. Nearly noon; how had it gotten so late?

"Almost," I lied unashamedly, waving at the stuff I'd piled up on the kitchen table. When other people went to a lake for a week, they took swimsuits and suntan oil, fishing gear and light reading material.

"See? We're practically on our way," I said, indicating what I was bringing instead: sacks of galvanized nails, work gloves and safety glasses, a T square, a carpenter's level, and a box of carriage bolts big enough to use for fixing the Brooklyn Bridge. The gasoline-powered chain saw and cordless drill, which, as its name suggested, ran on a battery, were already in the pickup truck, along with three huge coolers loaded with food, drinks, and ice; I'd been making progress before the phone interrupted me.

And before that damned voice. "Hmm," Ellie said skeptically, noting the absence of suntan oil, etc. "No frivolity for you, I gather." But the cottage we were going to belonged to my current husband, Wade Sorenson—it had been in his family for decades—and this was supposed to be a *working* trip.

During it I intended to finish the deck we'd been building all summer, yet another thing I'd said I would accomplish that I was beginning to regret. But there was no help for it; a few days earlier, I'd foolishly bet Wade a hundred bucks that I could complete the project this week: the steps, the railings, and most of all, the decking boards, dozens of narrow planks that had to be nailed down, one by one, to form the deck's floor.

And time, as Ellie had so pointedly reminded me, was a-wasting. "Just let me make sure I've got everything," I said.

Once we were there, a trip back to the hardware store could take up the entire morning. "Chisel, claw hammer . . ."

While I examined the heaps of stuff I'd already assembled, Ellie picked up the *Bangor Daily News* lying on the table by the carpentry supplies. *Escaped Killer Avoids Capture,* the headline blared.

Ellie scanned the article. "Wow," she said, and then began reading aloud about a convict who'd sneaked out of the Maine State Prison by the astonishing method of (1) removing the body of a newly deceased prisoner from a body bag, (2) placing himself in it, and (3) hopping out once the body bag got to the hospital morgue.

Then came the kicker; they'd put the "who" at the beginning of the second sentence. "Dewey Hooper," Ellie said, looking up.

She rarely read the paper at home, too busy with a house, two gardens, a coop full of hens, enough anonymous good deeds to win the Nobel Peace Prize if they ever became known, and a five-year-old daughter, Lee, so active and energetic that even when she was a tiny infant, we'd had to tie a badminton net over her crib.

Ellie frowned at the *BDN*'s front page again. "He's the one who . . ."

I zipped a canvas carryall open. "I remember." How could I forget? "Seven years ago. Strangled his wife, over in Perry."

It was a small rural town on the mainland, about ten miles distant. "Said she deserved it," I went on, stuffing the bag of galvanized nails, the carriage bolts, and carpenter's level into the carryall, "because she couldn't make good coffee."

Of course, the fact that, according to the coroner, Marianne Hooper had been regularly kept chained to a post in the cellar of the shack they had lived in might've had something to do with that. The filthy bandanna her husband had kept tied over her eyes could have been partly behind her inability to brew decent java, too.

There was also the possibility that he wouldn't have known a good cup of coffee if it bit him in the elbow, but never mind.

"He put her body outside in the middle of a blizzard; guess he figured it would keep until spring, when he could bury her," I recalled, sorting through more tools on the table.

Unfortunately for Dewey Hooper, though, a January thaw had coincided with a visit from some leaflet-distributing Jehovah's Witnesses, and even with their attention mostly focused on their list of local heathens in need of salvation, they noticed that one of the logs peeking through the melting snow on the woodpile was wearing a blue housedress.

"Hooper," I continued, "was a nutball with a mean streak a mile wide. And I'm betting he still is."

I dropped the T square, a retractable tape measure, some pencils, and a pencil sharpener into the carryall. "But at least he's not headed this way."

I knew this because there was a picture of Hooper under the headline: low forehead, heavy eyebrows, wide, smirking mouth.

The moment I'd seen it, just to be on the safe side I'd called up Bob Arnold, Eastport's police chief.

"And he says," I reported now to Ellie, "that there've been recent developments."

I tossed some duct tape into the carryall. "According to the state police, the latest thinking is that Hooper stole a car in Lewiston, another in Portland, and a third in Scarborough."

A car, a van, and a delivery truck, actually, stealing items and cash from each. Ellie nodded, relieved.

"So he's headed south, toward the big cities. More people, more places to hide . . . that makes sense."

But then she tipped her head assessingly at me. "How're you feeling about it, though? Him being out at all, I mean."

"Me? I'm fine. Why wouldn't I be?"

"Oh, I don't know," she replied, imitating my brisk tone. "Maybe because you testified against him."

I stuffed another roll of duct tape into the bag; you can never tell when you might need more duct tape.

"Or maybe," Ellie went on, apparently thinking I might like a change of subject, and she was right, the day I'd gone on the stand against Dewey Hooper had been one of the most upsetting of my whole life–

"Maybe it's because in the paper back then, there was a picture of her from before she married him. Marianne Hooper, and when we saw it we both said–"

"Right, that she looked like you." In fact, before Hooper got hold of her, Marianne had been the spitting image of Ellie: that hair, that face. That is, before the fractured cheekbones, split lips, and other injuries they found at autopsy.

"That's still no reason for me to feel anything about it now, though," I countered.

Ellie lifted the carryall I'd been filling, unfazed by its weight. Her slender build and fine features made her look as fragile as a china figurine, but she was an Eastport girl born and bred.

So under all that extravagant prettiness of hers, she was as tough as an old boot. "Right." She drew the word out skeptically.

The resemblance, she knew, had bothered me a lot back then, as if just looking so much like the dead woman might put Ellie in danger. But that was clearly unreasonable, *and* Hooper was now headed directly away from our area, which as Ellie had said made sense; he was crazy, not stupid, and people around here knew him by sight. So we dropped the subject, and she went out to the backyard with my two dogs, Monday the old black Lab and Prill the Doberman.

Through the kitchen window, I watched the animals dancing around her in anticipation, just in case she should accidentally drop any biscuits. Which—accidentally, of course, from one of those patchwork pockets that just happened always to be full of them—she did. Next came her laughter, and the dogs speaking for treats, a trick they would do only at her expert command.

Listening, I suddenly felt very grateful for her. She'd been my friend since practically the day I arrived in Eastport, still shell-shocked from a divorce battle so vicious that it might as well have been fought with rocket launchers, and accompanied by a teenaged son so rebellious and moody I'd been tempted to make him ride in the car's trunk. In fact, back then Sam had hated me so much, he'd probably have preferred the trunk. Also it was dark in there, and all the recreational drugs he was hooked on at the time had made his eyes sensitive.

But now everything was different. Ellie and I had been pals for a dozen years. She had a daughter, Sam was a clean and sober young man—I'd been a *very* youthful mom—and Victor was gone.

He *was,* damn it, I told myself again. *Gone . . .*

But not forgotten, apparently. "Okay, so *now* are you all ready?" Ellie wanted to know, coming back into my big, bright kitchen with its tall pine wainscoting, high, bare windows, and scuffed wooden floor.

"Well. There is one other thing." Swiftly I told her about Dan Weatherston's call, during which he had been able to make an outrageously impossible task sound doable.

"He wants me to write down how I transformed a two-centuries-old Federal-style house with three full floors plus an attic, forty-eight antique double-hung windows, three brick chimneys, and a bathroom so primitive it belonged in the House of Usher . . ."

I took a breath. "Into one that's at least not immediately likely to fall down on your head," I finished.

The key word there being, of course, "immediately." What the house might do next week I had no idea; only the fact that it had lasted nearly two hundred years already gave me any confidence at all in its standing-upright potential.

At least the bathroom didn't still look like Edgar Allan Poe would feel right at home in it; maybe if I kept on being able to communicate with ghosts, I thought, I could get *him* to write a newspaper column about it.

"Oh, Ellie, I can't believe I told Dan I would . . ."

"Never mind. Sit." It sounded like one of her dog commands; reflexively, I obeyed.

"Now, as I understand it," she said, "first you and I are going to drive up to the cottage."

At the old soapstone sink, she ran a glass of cold water and handed it to me. I drank it to humor her, and also because I felt faint again about what I'd promised to the *Tides* editor.

"Five thousand words," I managed. The *Tides* would run it in sections, but the editor wanted to see the whole thing all at once, right up front. "About rehabilitating an old—"

"Where," she went on, ignoring me, "after spending the day with you, I'm going to leave you there, along with the supplies you need to stay there for a week."

Her tone conveyed what she still thought of that idea. The cottage we were headed for was a remote, rustic lakeside cabin thirty miles distant, at the end of a dirt road with no running water, no TV or Internet connection, and just enough solar power from the collecting panels propped on the outhouse roof to run a reading lamp in the evening.

"Alone," she added, leaving me no doubt about her opinion of that part of the plan, either.

The truth was, I felt a little hesitant about it myself. I'd never spent so much time there alone before, and the deck job was a sizable one even though most of the heavy work was already finished; only the bet I'd lose if I didn't do it spurred me on.

Although now that I'd cleverly arranged to have a writing assignment hanging over my head, too, what I really felt like doing was leaving the country. Or maybe the planet.

"Ellie," I began again, annoyed with myself now, "every bit of this is absolutely my own—"

Fault, I was about to say, ignoring Ellie's try at breaking it all down into bite-sized chunks so it didn't seem so bad. The no-plumbing part, especially, was starting to weigh on me; in the wake of last night's storm, colder air had begun rushing down from Canada, and when it was frosty outside, a late-night trip to the facilities could put, as Sam had once expressed it so vividly, an icicle on your bicycle.

In fact, the whole project was beginning to seem the exact opposite of the lighthearted lark that I'd imagined it would be, back when I was just planning to do it. Despite my wager, I was about to ask Ellie how she thought I might bail out of it even halfway honorably, but just then my live-in housekeeper, Bella Diamond, hustled in, hauling a rented rug shampooer.

Rawboned and hatchet-faced, with dark henna-red hair skinned so tightly back into a rubber band that her eyes pulled sideways, she wore a navy blue sweatshirt with the Maine Maritime Academy's gold anchor emblem on the front of it, jeans whose fraying knees were heavily patched with darned-on squares of red plaid, and an expression that suggested she was experiencing the pleasure of a mouthful of lemon juice.

"Hello," she uttered, wrestling the rug machine on into the dining room, where I knew she intended to do battle with a stain on the carpet. But she said nothing more, except for a muttered oath when the rug machine ran over her sneakered toe; Ellie and I rolled our eyes at each other and kept prudently silent.

Grouchy, Ellie mouthed. *Supremely,* I agreed, wondering if maybe a week up at the cabin wasn't a good idea after all. Bella had recently married my father, becoming my mother-in-law as well as my employee; the combination had created a domestic situation that, for its yield of hilarious scenes centered on our differing opinions on household hygiene—Bella was a clean freak right down to the molecular level, me not so much—I'd actually come to enjoy.

Only not lately. Something was eating Bella, and she wouldn't say what. "You still here?" She came back for the bag of rug-shampooing attachments; Ellie moved toward the door. "Because I don't want to start on this until after you've gone."

"Almost," I told Ellie, meaning I wasn't quite ready to go yet.

"Yes," I told Bella, meaning the obvious. "I am still here. But start whenever you want."

"Hmph," said Bella, going out again. Grumbling, she hauled the bag into the dining room; a moment later I heard her dump the attachments unceremoniously out.

"What's with her?" Ellie asked.

"No idea. I'm hoping while I'm gone she'll get over it."

We got busy hauling the bags of supplies; in the driveway my husband, Wade, had just finished checking the oil and tire pressure in the pickup truck.

"You *sure* you want to do this alone?" he asked, wiping his hands on a rag as he dropped the hood.

Wade was tall and broad shouldered, with blond, brush-cut hair, a square jaw, and pale, intelligent eyes that were blue or gray depending on the weather. Stuffing the rag into the back pocket of his Levi's, he strolled toward me.

"You're the one who bet me a hundred bucks I wouldn't be able to," I retorted. "So it's all your fault."

Working together on weekends all summer, Wade and I had cut up all the broken sections of the old deck and hauled them away. We'd dug new foundation holes, filled them with gravel, then set in concrete blocks and bolted a half-dozen upright posts to them. Finally, we'd built the frame and fastened in the joists, which were the crosspieces all the decking boards would get nailed to.

By me, and I didn't like the pockmarks the nail gun made, so I'd be hammering them in by hand; my arm hurt already, just thinking about it. But I'd made that bet, and now I was stuck with it.

"Well, yeah," Wade said, meaning the all-his-fault part; he was generous that way. "But honestly, Jake, I didn't think you'd take me up on it. Your judgment," he added delicately, "may have been clouded at the time, besides."

What he meant was that while we discussed it he'd made me a quince margarita, a drink that for firepower belongs right up there beside an AK-47. "I think," he murmured into my ear, "I'm going to mix that drink for you more often."

"Fine," I said into the sweet-smelling flannel of his shirt. As Eastport's harbor pilot, Wade guided big cargo ships into the freighter terminal, through the wild tides and contrary currents of our local waters. When not doing that, he repaired antique guns here at home in his workshop.

"But for now," I added, stepping from his embrace, "the bet is still on."

Having Wade's arms around me generally makes me forget any other plans I may be pursuing. But I'd gotten my gumption back now, and I was determined: "I'm going, and I'm doing it." The deck, I meant, *and* the newspaper column; the day was crisp and bright, the air tangy with sea salt, chamomile, and beach roses.

So why not? Let them all be amazed, I thought, when I came back next week—my laptop, whose battery could be charged off the truck's battery, was in my pack—having finished the project *and* written five thousand publishable words.

I certainly would be. "I'll say goodbye to Sam and your dad for you," Wade said as he walked around the truck one last time, eye-balling the tires and peering under it for fluid leaks.

"Thanks." I swung up into the cab. My son, no longer a sour-pussed little renegade but an accomplished, pleasant-to-be-around young fellow now that he wasn't drinking, had gone to the boatyard earlier to try helping a guy with a sailboat.

Sam said the boat had a few problems but at least it hadn't sunk yet, which he thought was a good sign. Meanwhile, my dad was spending mornings downtown lately at the woodworking shop he shared with a couple of other older Eastport gentlemen; thinking of him made me hope Bella's bad mood wasn't marriage-related.

But even if it was, I couldn't do anything about it. Ahead, Ellie pulled out in her own small sedan; I followed, pausing at the end of the driveway to look back at the house. With its neat white clapboards and forest-green shutters, red-brick chimneys, and porch flanked by pots of blooming geraniums, it looked solid and safe, like the kind of place I'd always wanted to live in.

It looked like home. But then on impulse I glanced up, just in time to glimpse the faint, stealthy twitch of a curtain at one of the attic windows. *If you go, you might never see any of this again,* that furtive curtain-twitch seemed to signal.

And that really was silly, I scolded myself. Maybe the deathiver-sary was preying on my emotions even more than I'd thought; even now, it seemed that my deceased ex-husband, Victor, had retained his talent for making me feel bad.

That is, unless I stopped letting him, by going about my business as planned. And anyway, with Wade waving behind me and Ellie al-ready pulling out ahead, I didn't have much choice.

So, swallowing the sudden lump in my throat, I set off down Key Street in the pickup truck. After all, there was that deck to complete, and a newspaper column to write—or try to.

Besides, the lake was beautiful this time of year, with cool brilliant days whose sunshine was pale as champagne, night skies full of stars glittering like ice chips. It was quiet, too, now that the summer visitors had mostly gone home, the only sounds in the surrounding forest made by the wind and wildlife.

If nothing else, I would have a peaceful time there.

Yeah, sure I would.

Once Jake and Ellie had left for the lake, Bella finished shampooing the carpet. She brought the rented rug shampoo machine back to the store, then managed to kill a little more time by mopping the kitchen floor, scrubbing all the knobs on the front of the stove with Comet cleanser and a toothbrush, and dusting the parlor piano, then polishing it with her secret mixture of lemon juice, olive oil, a drop of rosewater, and beeswax.

But her real task for the day still waited, and although she had been dreading it for weeks, she couldn't put it off forever. Once each year, rain or shine . . . So with her kit of cleaning gear she trudged upstairs to the guest bedroom.

Still and silent, the room had a double bed in a spare maple frame, two matching maple bedside tables, and woven throw rugs. A roller shade and a pair of plain white cotton curtains hung at each of the two windows; a small television, never turned on that Bella could recall, stood on the maple dresser.

Don't be silly, she scolded herself as, after hesitating in the doorway a moment, she went in. After all, just because a person had died in a room didn't mean it was haunted, she decided as she took down the curtains, pulled the sheets, the pillowcases, and the white chenille bedspread into a pile, and rolled up the throw rugs. If it did, the whole house would be thronged with ghosts.

But this was not a thought she wanted to pursue while alone in the old dwelling, and especially not here, in the room where Dr. Tiptree had breathed his last. Grimly she removed her shoes, then stepped up onto the mattress; from there she could reach the overhead light fixture and the ornate glass shade covering it.

A dead spider inside the shade lay with his legs curled up tightly over his body as if trying to protect himself. *I know how you feel,* she thought, brushing the poor creature's husk out onto the floor where she could get it later with the vacuum cleaner.

Right now, in fact, she felt the same way, hollowed out by anxiety, wishing she could wrap her own arms around her body and curl up into a ball, as if that might hold the fright off. But it wouldn't, any more than it had held off death for the spider.

Or for Dr. Tiptree, either, whose presence she still felt in the room even after all this time. Replacing the glass shade, she stepped down with a sigh of relief from the mattress that he had spent his final days on.

Foolish, she scolded herself. *You're just a superstitious old scaredy-cat, that's all.*

But she wasn't. Only in the past few weeks, as the date of his death approached, had she felt some new, unpleasant sense of here-I-am-ness from the deceased man, as if what Jake called his deathiversary were summoning him back for a reenactment. From a faint, easily dismissed notion of some . . . some *otherness,* there and gone like a whiff of perfume or a few barely heard signature notes of an old, half-remembered melody, the uneasy feeling had grown until it was all she could do not to shout, sometimes, with the dreadful anxiety it produced in her.

And that, Bella knew, was ridiculous. First because ghosts couldn't hurt you, and even more important, because as everyone knew, there was no such thing as them.

Thinking this, she turned with the bottle of Windex to the mirror over the bedroom dresser and gasped with shock at the face hovering in it, just behind her. But in the next instant, she let her breath out; it was only the dust rag hung on the bedpost, its shape curved by shadows and her imagination into a pair of eyes, a twisted nose, and a soft, drooping grin.

Angrily she swiped dust from the mirror, wiped off all the baseboards, brushed fluff from the corners. The closet door stood open a crack; yanking it the rest of the way, she forced herself to look inside. . . .

Nothing. *Well, of course there isn't,* she told herself as she damp-mopped the hardwood floor. The window shade slipped from her fingers and flew upward with a bang; her hand went to her throat. But she composed herself, and began wiping the top edge of the old window sash, then opening it an inch to air the room. *Which could use freshening,* she thought, *because it smells like . . .*

Cologne. She recognized it at once: the expensive, dryly witchhazel-scented stuff that Dr. Tiptree had always used before he started smelling like pain medicine.

And later, like pain. Bella stepped back from the window, caught in a moment of memory so clear it was like diving into a pool. He'd walked into this room and stood for a second, looking at the bed. Knowing, she supposed now, that he would die in it.

But not how soon. Awful, that final illness of his, seeking whom it might devour. At the time, though, she'd merely come up with some fresh towels, and when he saw her in the doorway, he'd thanked her.

For, he'd said, making it all so pleasant. He'd smiled at the flowers she'd put into a bowl on the dresser; peonies, she recalled.

"Jake always says what a genius you are," he'd told her as he sat down on the bed.

Testing it, she supposed: Good to lie in? To die in? "I see now that Jake was right," he'd said, and even then she'd thought his eyes looked a little sunken in, his lips a little blue. Maybe that had been the light, because the windows in here faced north.

Or maybe not, because he'd leaned down to unlace his shoes—it was then that she'd smelled cologne, the clean astringency of a prosperous, well-barbered man—and as far as she could recall, she'd never seen him wear them ever again.

Bella had other memories of him in this room, but none she wanted to recall. He'd died three weeks later. Lips pursed, she bent to gather up the bedspread and linens into her arms. Then, turning with them, she glanced once more into the mirror on the dresser, and her arms tightened reflexively around the bundle she held.

Bella. That voice, that cologne whiff, that *face* . . .

Not a dust cloth this time, or anything else she could blame it on, either. Squeezing her eyes shut, she tightened her fists, shook her head in mute rejection and denial, mingled with bone-deep fright. *Please. Go away,* she thought.

Just go away, and—

And when she opened her eyes again, he had.

CHAPTER 3

To repair pitted metal surfaces,
apply a "liquid metal" product,
let dry, and sand smooth.
—Tiptree's Tips

"Hurry," said the young man anxiously pacing the launching ramp at the boatyard, a mile outside Eastport on Deep Cove Road.

The young man's name was Richard Stedman, and at his panicky phone call a couple of hours earlier Sam Tiptree had gotten there as fast as he could, unfazed by the crack-of-dawn summons or the short notice. Both were part of the job; after working on and off at the boat-yard for nearly a dozen years, he'd long since become the go-to guy for all kinds of problems among boat owners.

Not that Sam himself was impressed by that fact; boats always had some new challenge to throw at you, and past successes were no protection from future failure where they were concerned. All a guy could do was pay attention to what a vessel was telling him, he reminded himself as Richard Stedman gazed beseechingly at him, then be ready to try answering in some way that was at least halfway useful.

"Okay, let's just see what the trouble is," he told Richard, now hurrying ahead down the boat ramp.

"I already know what the trouble is." Richard's rubber flip-flops slap-slapped the ramp's grooved granite-slab surface. "Damn thing's capsizing."

"Yeah, well," Sam replied, unwilling to commit himself any further than that without more information, and not about to take Richard's word for anything, either. Because on the one hand, Richard Stedman so far had been good-humored, a hard worker, and most important, willing to listen, a trio of qualities that in Sam's experience was uncommon among boatyard customers.

On the other hand, though, here Richard was, running around practically barefoot in the middle of October. *So we'll see,* Sam thought, still keeping an open mind about the fellow trotting ahead of him between the dock pilings.

Here on the windy side of the island, the water bounced with a light chop, the greenish froth-topped waves still racing in the aftermath of the storm the night before. But the sky overhead was blue, only the dark gray mounds of the low-pressure system's trailing cloud bank showing like foothills of a mountain range, to the east.

"Just take it easy," Sam told the worried boat owner. "So far, we don't know anything."

"Yeah, yeah," Richard groused, but amicably enough under the circumstances. "You mean *you* don't know."

Fair comment; *Courtesan* was tied up outside the farthest corner of the long T-shaped dock. Sam hadn't seen her since the last time Richard had dragged him down here, four hours earlier.

What he did know, though, was that it made him happy to be here at all: on or near the water, among the boats and even among their be-leaguered owners. It was a knowledge he'd gone through a lot to obtain, trying and failing at college, trade schools, even online corre-spondence courses.

But none of them had worked, and he'd drifted aimlessly and un-happily for a while before realizing: he could do *this*. And not only could he *do* it, but he was *good* at it. The only thing wrong with living and working right here in Eastport, in fact, was the lack of female companionship; most of the women his age were taken, and of the ones who weren't, either they didn't want him or he didn't want them.

"See?" Richard said, pointing. "She's going down."

"Huh," Sam replied, understanding now as he caught fresh sight of Richard's recently purchased vessel at last. The way she moved in the water, sluggish and tubby looking, contrasted sharply with her bright, jaunty attitude of earlier in the day. And her rail, riding a foot or so closer to the waves than it had been . . .

"Oh, yeah, that's . . ." *Bad.* His voice trailed off as he sized up the situation and realized that it was dire.

"Going down," Richard repeated gloomily. "Isn't she?"

In his late twenties, he was about five-eight and compactly built, with small but solid-looking muscles, thick, curly yellow hair, and the deeply tanned complexion of a man with the freedom to have spent much of the previous summer outdoors.

Not exactly a veteran sailor, Sam had already decided, but Richard was definitely correct about one thing: from the look of her at the mo-ment, his boat was about to become an underwater activity.

"Yeah," Sam conceded. "You've got problems, all right."

He strode farther along the dock, then knelt on it, peering over *Courtesan*'s rail and into her hatch. The twenty-four-foot fiberglass yawl Richard had bought used a few days before floated parallel to the dock—if you could call what she was doing floating.

Even *capsizing* wasn't the right word; *sinking,* actually, was more like it. Sam stood and thought for a moment, gazing back toward shore.

Now at low tide, the storm-scoured beach extending a quarter mile on either side of the dock was a curving crescent of smooth, gleaming stones.

But at high tide, the water had been twenty feet higher, leftover waves from last night's big blow swamping the dock and tossing thick mats of seaweed and driftwood right up into the boatyard's gravel parking lot. Which meant that now the water was getting deeper again as the tide came back in.

Richard shot Sam a hopeful glance. "I figured you'd know what to do," he ventured.

Sam didn't reply. Five years ago he'd have enjoyed the flattery, even milked Richard for more. But back then he'd been a twenty-year-old kid whose youthful energy and odd natural talent for boats were getting submerged in a sea of alcohol.

Not that he'd lacked excuses: years before that, his mom had been a financial manager on Wall Street, with little time—or natural talent, either—for chasing after a small boy. Her own upbringing had been nightmare material, too, so had it been any wonder she'd had no idea how to raise her own kid?

Meanwhile, his dad had been a well-respected brain surgeon, the kind you went to when all the other brain surgeons started talking to you about hospice. As a surgeon he was the equivalent of a tightly focused, freakishly accurate laser. But as a dad he'd been more like a brick through a plate-glass window, when he was around at all.

In the end, Sam's father had died of an octopus-shaped mass that he'd joked must have formed inside his skull as revenge for the many other tumors he'd killed—that is, before he became unable to joke at all. Sam sometimes wondered if he would ever be able to forgive his dad, or if instead he would carry the memory of Victor's long-term neglect mingled with his own helpless love for the man, like an albatross around his neck forever.

Today, he realized; *today's his deathiversary.* "Sam?"

The voice jerked Sam back to the present, and to Richard Stedman still standing there looking at him like a puppy hoping not to be kicked.

"So what do you think?" Richard asked. His voice didn't sound hopeful. Not that it should have, even if his boat hadn't been on its way down to Davy Jones's locker.

Hope, Sam knew, was a feeling reserved for the boat-buying process and its immediate, euphoric aftermath. Once the deal was done, other emotions kicked in: rage, sorrow, despair. If a new boat-owner was lucky and had any skill, his feelings didn't end up includ-ing the gut-twisting terror that accompanied drowning.

"Not sure," Sam temporized, reluctant to voice the bad news. Richard had hauled the boat down here to the slip he'd rented, he'd told Sam, to get her shipshape while enjoying the natural surround-ings: granite cliffs, a thickly forested shore, and the rocky beaches that were all you could see from the dock, plus of course the water itself.

Courtesan wasn't quite ready to sail, Richard had admitted, but he'd thought that he could motor her around in calm weather, using the seven-and-a-half-horse Evinrude on her transom. Now, though . . .

"Doomed, isn't she?" Richard repeated.

Sam had liked the look of *Courtesan,* even at first sight. A lot of used boats had sat unloved in someone's backyard for too long, their decks showing the imprints of the autumn leaves left to pile up on them and their teak trim cracked with neglect.

But *Courtesan* had been well kept, and she'd floated when she slid off the trailer Richard had bought for her; some preowned vessels didn't. Sam had congratulated the new skipper on the deal he'd made, suggesting that if Richard needed any help getting her seaworthy, Sam and the boatyard equipment were available.

Then he'd handed Richard his card, not expecting to hear any more about it. The urgent call this morning had been a surprise, but also a false alarm; bilges were supposed to have water in them, Sam had informed an embarrassed Richard.

But a little while ago when Sam's cellphone rang again up at the boatyard office, Richard had sounded like the world was ending, and now his face sagged with dismay. And this time the alarm was well founded. Sam turned to gauge how difficult it might be to get *Courte-san* out of here, if she could be rescued at all.

Set on poured concrete pilings, the dock stuck out from the boat ramp a hundred yards into Deep Cove, another pair of floating T-sections extending left and right from the end of the main pier. The floating sections were tied to the main structure by a series of heavy chains secured around steel posts, so the floats could rise and fall with the tide.

Metal gangs led down to the weathered wooden decking on the floats, all bouncing rhythmically with a soft musical clanking of their chains and creak of wood rubbing against wet wood. For boats that were operating properly, the whole setup worked conveniently and well. But when they weren't, obstacles posed by the dock's various elements got problematic.

Like now; Sam stepped aboard the distressed sailboat, unable to help seeing a cartoon dialogue balloon floating over her.

Glub, glub, the dialogue in the balloon said. "Except for my little bilge-water scare, she was okay when I got down here this morning. But now . . ." Richard spread his hands.

Yeah, *now* was the problem. The bad feeling Sam already had got worse once he was aboard. Even if she hadn't been riding so low—wallowing like a sow, as the older guys at the boatyard would've put it—the way she felt under his feet would've told him at once that she was ailing.

A boat this size ought to have a brisk, lively feel to her, the sense that she could lift up and skim, almost like a kite, if given the opportunity in the form of wind. But this one felt duly reluctant, as if she had a bad headache.

Or was filling up with seawater. Sam wondered if the rain squalls embedded in the recent storm had flooded *Courtesan*—say, if her hatch had leaked via a bad seal, or hadn't been secured properly. Or, alternatively, if just possibly her new owner had damaged her somehow while trying to work on her.

It happened. "Pump?" Sam asked. He carefully kept any hint of criticism out of his voice.

Richard looked away. Out on the water a barge chugged toward the Canadian island of Campobello, loaded with fish-food pellets for the salmon-farming operation over there.

"I think the pump's okay. Battery's dead, though. It was all right last night when I left, but . . ."

No need for comment; Richard's face said he already knew that if the pump had been hooked to a working battery, it would not have mattered how much water *Courtesan* took on. The pump's motor would've switched on automatically when the flooding rose enough to activate it, and pumped the boat out.

"Yeah, well. It happens." Pumps had a way of failing just when you needed them. "Water under the bridge now," Sam said. Or in this case, in the boat. He peered down through the hatch into the boat's tiny cabin, which, like her exterior, was in need of some cosmetics: patching and painting, mostly. Then from the new life vest, foam cooler, and gas can that Richard had left aboard overnight, Sam got a clue, especially as he thought about what he would want to do if he were Richard and he had just put *Courtesan* in the water.

"So you were going to take her out? Motor around the cove a little, maybe?"

"If I could get the engine running," Richard agreed glumly. "But as it turned out, I never even got that far. Couldn't get the centerboard down."

In the floor of the cabin gaped an opening, awash with oily water. Down in the hole, hung on a sort of hinge and not visible from above, was *Courtesan*'s centerboard, like a big fin that stuck down from the bottom of the hull. The centerboard gave the craft stability by lowering her center of gravity; it kept the boat on course when she was headed upwind.

But sometimes you wanted to raise the centerboard; when, for instance, you were motoring into some shallow harbor, sailing downwind, or pulling her on a trailer as Richard had, to get her here. The centerboard would've been up then, and although you could motor around fine without it, Richard hadn't known that.

"So you haven't had the centerboard down at all?" A stuck centerboard was a common occurrence in a boat that had sat for a while. The board itself could warp or swell, and bind inside its housing, or the lever it moved on could get jammed.

"No. Couldn't budge it," Richard said.

A sudden roar from a slip at the far end of the dock cut through the morning calm; steady boatyard client Bud Underwood was out there, starting up the nifty little Cessna 150 two-seater he'd recently converted to a floatplane. As the aircraft pulled away from the dock pilings she'd been tethered to, Sam had a moment to wish very hard that he was on it; this day was going downhill even faster than Bud took off, soaring over the cove.

Then Sam noticed more stuff lying on the dock. While Sam had been examining the deck and cabin, Richard had apparently run all the way up to his car, where it was parked in the boatyard lot, and returned with a wet suit, swim fins, and a snorkel mask.

"I was thinking that I'd go down and check the hull," Richard explained. Underwater, he meant, and at this time of year the water here was about fifty-five degrees, a bone-chilling temperature that even the wet suit wouldn't do a lot to temper.

Sam eyed Richard with new respect. The unhappy would-be sailor might be new at this, but he had game and he'd definitely brought it with him today. So Sam hated to disappoint him.

But he had no choice. "Listen, when you were trying to get the centerboard free, did you poke anything down there? A pole, a stick, anything?"

People did. A frozen centerboard could be so infuriating, it was tempting to drop a stick of dynamite down there, sometimes. Sam thought that might end up being the cheapest solution to the difficulty, in the present case; just not right here by the dock.

Richard's pale skin flushed. "Yeah. An iron rod. I thought if I smacked the centerboard mechanism hard enough, I could—" His face changed, sudden understanding flooding it. "I did it, didn't I? I poked a hole through. Right through the—"

"Through the hull, yeah." An expression of such misery washed over Richard's face that Sam had to add, "Look, you didn't know."

Richard's shoulders sagged under his U. Michigan T-shirt. He looked for a moment as if he might cry. But then, to his credit, he straightened. "Okay, so what do I do about it?"

Again, he hadn't asked Sam what *he* was going to do; instead he'd taken it on himself. But his rough-and-ready attitude wasn't going to keep the boat afloat unless they both took fast action.

And maybe not even then. Sam guessed that *Courtesan,* her mast up but her sails at least hauled and stowed, had about an hour before the water she was taking on sank her.

But that wasn't the worst of it. "We need to get her back up on land right away," he said.

Because the tide was still rising, twenty feet of it at its highest point. Which meant that *Courtesan* could end up submerged completely, only her mast jutting up through the waves to mark where she'd sunk. "Like, pulled out of here."

Richard gave him a look: *No kidding.* "How?" he asked, not to Sam but to the rising sea, the dark stones gleaming on the beach, and the sky arcing over their heads like a blue bowl.

Now you're getting it, Sam thought, because owning a boat meant being at the mercy of those things.

"I'm still not sure. What you should do now, though, is go up to the boatyard office, tell them we have a bit of trouble down here."

Which, Sam thought, was probably the kind of understatement his dad used to come out with when some poor guy he was operating on started bleeding or having seizures or some other complication that was almost surely catastrophic: *a bit of trouble.*

Richard didn't know it yet, but he was in serious danger of spending a whole lot of money in a very short time, in the very immediate future, because a water-filled sailboat was not a cheap thing to drag up out of the drink. The crane alone ran a hundred and fifty an hour.

"You go, will you?" Richard was pulling on his dive gear. "I still just want to have a look."

Sam understood. Richard hoped that below *Courtesan's* steadily lowering waterline, he might find something less disastrous than a breached hull. Given the history Richard had described, that was unlikely, but Sam supposed that if it were his boat he'd want to go down there, too, just to see for himself what was what.

He also supposed that most of Richard's previous diving had been in warmer water. But at least he wasn't being a crybaby about it, and anyway, Sam had no business trying to stop him.

Thinking this, Sam sprinted away up the dock toward the parking lot. Straight ahead lay the whole boat school campus, a sprawling collection of low metal Quonsets housing classrooms interspersed with gigantic garage-like structures where all kinds of vessels were built and repaired, plus a wide paved parking lot. To his right stretched the big evergreen-forested peninsula of Shackford Head State Park.

To his left, a hundred yards distant on the other side of Deep Cove Road, stood the boatyard office, surrounded by boats of all sizes in every condition, from old wooden hulks rotting where they stood to factory-fresh cruisers, their oiled trim glinting expensively and polished brightwork gleaming in the sun. The office, a low frame structure whose paint needed refreshing, bore a hand-lettered sign: "No Cash, No Splash."

As he trotted toward it, thinking that he'd better alert the crew that the boat-lifting crane was probably going to be needed this morning, a girl exited the office and began running his way.

The girl wore a blue striped top, cargo shorts, and white sneakers over those short cotton socks with the little pink yarn bobbles at the heels. Long legs running easily, dark glossy ponytail–

She was, Sam saw as the distance between them diminished quickly, a really beautiful girl. "I'm Carol, Richard Stedman's sister," she said when she got nearer. "Where is he?"

·   ·   ·

"He's done it before," I told Ellie. "Shown up, that is." Victor, I meant. "Right after he died, he sort of . . . appeared to me."

Because of course I was still thinking about what had happened—if it had—earlier that morning. Having an ex-husband start talking to you six years after you buried him . . . it leaves an impression.

"What do you suppose he wants?" Ellie asked.

"No idea." Which was no big surprise; I hadn't had any when he was alive, either. But then, neither had he most of the time.

"I thought when he first did it, what with his death still being so recent and all, that maybe it was just, like, '*Sayonara.*'"

A final farewell, his apparition more the product of my own imagination than anything else . . . it was the theory I'd come up with back then when his recent funeral made it more believable.

But now I didn't know what to believe. "Anyway, let's go," I told Ellie.

After the half-hour trip up Route 1, I'd followed Ellie's small sedan onto a narrow lane that dead-ended at a grassy turnaround. The rest of the way in to the cottage was a dirt track punctuated by rocks, ruts, washouts, gulleys, and the occasional blown-down tree trunk; her car would never make it, so once we'd parked, we'd moved all the supplies from it over into my pickup truck.

Now we got in, too, and began jouncing into the woods. The terrain was so wild, it looked almost prehistoric: plants and animals aplenty, but no people. "Do you think he'll come back?" Ellie asked after a while.

"Beats me." On either side, fragrant pine groves alternated with birches and aspens. Dragonflies buzzed at the windshield and sparkled in the open truck windows as if curious about us.

"I hope not," I added, as a partridge ran onto the road, froze, then flew with a whirring of wings back into the brush. Ellie said something, but I didn't hear it.

"What?" Gripping the wheel, I steered the truck along the narrow dirt track between a pair of massive old broken-off tree trunks. Brushy red-leafed sumac with fruit like lush purple pinecones crowded up against the road on either side.

"I said, it's the anniversary." Of his death, she meant.

I eased us around a rut so deep that it would have taken the muffler off the truck and then come back for the transmission.

"I hadn't thought about it," I lied, swinging the steering wheel the other way.

The road into camp was a good-news/bad-news kind of thing, unmarked and primitive enough to keep vandals and party animals at a distance but hard on us, too. To reach the cottage, you had to know where you were going *and* want very badly to get there.

A rock I hadn't noticed bonked the truck's underside as Ellie looked wisely sideways at me. "Oh, you haven't, huh? Guess somebody else must've put those flowers on his grave, then."

We reached the beaver pond, flat calm with clumps of reeds sticking up from it. A culvert was supposed to drain the pond so it didn't flood the road, but the beaver enjoyed plugging the big pipe with grass and branches, so after last night's storm the backed-up water had overflowed, running over the dirt track in a widening trickle.

"I don't know what you're talking about," I retorted. But she was right; I visited the cemetery every year, because although my ex-husband was a skirt-chasing villain and a lying son of a bitch besides, he was dead now, and also he was Sam's dad.

Besides, after he'd followed us here to Maine and lived in Eastport for a while, he'd mellowed considerably. "Yeah, it was me," I admitted finally. It felt strange, missing someone I had fought with so viciously. "What can I say? Victor's a lot easier to get along with now that he's in his grave."

Or he would be if he'd only maintain the silence generally associated with that location. "Stop here a minute," said Ellie, and when I did she jumped down from the truck.

By the time I'd set the emergency brake and got out, too, she was kneeling on the exposed end of the big, corrugated metal culvert running under the dirt road. The culvert sent the water from the beaver pond on one side of the road to an outflow stream on the other side.

That is, it was meant to. Peering over into the plugged-up culvert's end, Ellie began yanking with both hands on the reeds, moss, grass, branches, and leaves that the beaver had stuffed in there.

"Oof!" she said, hauling mightily. But it was no good. Using only their tails and their curious little handlike paws, the beavers had stuffed that culvert so solidly full, a bomb might be the only good way to demolish it.

And putting explosives in the culvert would unblock it, all right, but it would also destroy the road. "We'll need to get the boys down here with some power tools soon," she said.

"Right." Ellie and I could do it, of course, but culvert clearing was just the sort of big, mucky job all the men in our families enjoyed and we didn't, so we left it to them.

I knelt beside her. The pond's bottom was silty and gray-green from all the gunk that the beaver had dug up while engaged in his construction project. Small, shiny insects skated on the water's surface while more dragonflies zipped through jagged midair acrobatics, snapping up mosquitoes.

"Hey." Ellie looked puzzled, peering down at the rugged pond bottom. "Where'd that big rock come from?" she said, pointing.

The water was four feet or so deep everywhere else. But directly below us, it got suddenly a lot shallower because of a round, domed rock, at least two feet across and covered with the same gray-green silt that lay on the pond's bottom.

"I don't remember such a big rock here before," I began. "Maybe someone threw it in here, and . . . whoa!"

At the rock's unexpected movement, I reared back so fast, I nearly fell off the culvert, which would've been too bad, since the huge thing lurking down there wasn't a rock at all. It was a snapping turtle, its thick, hook-nosed head poking out suddenly from its shell while its fat, black-clawed legs thrust sideways, lazily but purposefully.

Then its *eyes* opened, two round, shiny black orbs glowering dourly up through the water at us as if to say what were *we* doing here, and would we like to get eaten? Grabbed and dragged under the water to drown and then *devoured*?

Because if so, the huge snapping turtle's cold, black stare said very clearly, it would be happy to oblige.

"Yikes." Ellie stood and tiptoed back to the dirt road, her look startled but delighted; she adored wildlife.

Me too, actually, but those thick-clawed legs looked strong, and if the thing heaved itself up onto the bank and came at us—never mind what they say about turtles, they're fast enough, and you don't get that big by being an unskilled predator—I didn't know what I'd do.

Run, for one thing. Scream, for another. "Ellie, come on. It's way past noon and it'll get dark early tonight." Cold, too, so I wanted to get more firewood in and the solar panels wiped off and adjusted.

"Oh, all right," Ellie said, though I could already see her plotting to return, probably to try feeding the thing in the pond pieces of lettuce.

The only use that monster had for lettuce, I thought as we hopped back into the truck, was as a garnish for our fingers. But I didn't say so as with relief—at least on my part—we left the beaver-blocked culvert and its prehistoric-looking guardian behind.

A few minutes later we were unchaining the gate across the last half mile of the cottage road. Through the trees I caught glimpses of the lake, the water level higher than I'd ever seen it before, and thought uneasily of the pond; if it did overflow, we'd be stuck here.

Then Ellie spoke up: "Jake, you don't think that guy who escaped might be heading this way, do you? Dewey Hooper?"

It was what the monster turtle had reminded me of, too: cold, black eyes, and the flatly predatory look in them as it watched us.

"No," I reassured her. "I really don't." We drove in, the truck rolling silently over a thick mat of fallen pine needles. Huge hoofprints showed where a moose had walked on them not long ago, but nothing else disturbed them.

Not, for instance, human footprints left by a whacked-out wife killer. "He's hundreds of miles from here by now."

I hoped. Somehow Bob Arnold's reassurances weren't quite as comforting as they had been back when we were in town. Here, we were on our own.

"I know," Ellie replied. "Of course he is. But . . . look, it's really not just that she looked so much like me, is it? That's bothering you, I mean. It's that . . ."

I got out and closed the gate behind us and put the padlock back through the chain that held it shut. "Yeah," I said when we were rolling again. "Yeah, it is something else."

Because it was true, her own resemblance to the murdered woman wasn't the real problem; Hooper wasn't even aware of it, as far as we knew. It was what that remarkable likeness reminded me of:

Seven years earlier, Hooper had let his wife, Marianne, out of the cellar—he'd done that sometimes—then taken offense at a remark she made. About him always being drunk, or never finding a job, or not taking a shower more than once a month, maybe.

Whatever; evidence found later said he'd wiped the floor with her numerous times before, but he hadn't managed to kill her fiery spirit. So she'd said something sassy to him, no one knew exactly what, and all he'd done was backhand her across the face in reply, which was how he explained it in court against the advice of his attorney, who hadn't wanted him to testify at all.

So was it his fault, Hooper had inquired very reasonably of the jury, that when she fell, she hit her head on a corner of the kitchen counter and died?

Whereupon it had fallen to me to explain, under oath, about the many times she'd come to me—back when he was still letting her not only out of the house but off the property and even into town—bruised from yet another session of being Dewey's punching bag, and how I'd told her to get out, to come anytime and stay at my house for as long as she liked.

Which pretty much put paid to Dewey's tale about how it had been just the once that he'd hit her. The M.E.'s testimony about a fractured hyoid bone, a classic hallmark of a strangling, hadn't helped him, either, and as a result, Dewey was convicted of aggravated manslaughter and sent away to prison for twenty years.

Dewey, of course, thought that this was unjust, and at the time he'd made no secret of his anger at everyone involved. But now, seven years later, most people's memories of him had faded.

Just not mine. If I'd had it to do over again, I would have gotten Marianne Hooper out of there by whatever means necessary.

But then—like everyone, I guessed—in my life there were a lot of things I'd like to have done over again.

"Look, the Portland and points-south sightings of Hooper still make sense. He's a day's drive away at least. And even if he weren't, he doesn't know about this cottage."

Bottom line, there wasn't a much safer place than a cottage in the Maine woods. Still . . . "Open the glove box," I told Ellie.

Putting the truck in reverse and twisting the wheel hard, I backed in the last hundred yards, with pine boughs brushing the fenders on both sides. When the way behind us opened up, we were in a clearing with sheds on one side, the cottage on the other.

Downhill between the trees the lake glittered, brilliant blue and white-ruffled with a breeze, the little waves slopping at least two feet higher up on shore than the last time I'd been out here.

"Oh," Ellie said softly into the silence when I'd turned off the truck engine.

In the glove compartment lay a Bisley .45 six-shot revolver, its blued-steel barrel glinting darkly and its figured rosewood grip gleaming like good old furniture. Beside it, I'd tucked in a box of Buffalo Bore cartridges, but I doubted I would need them; the weapon was already loaded, and if anything came up that took more than six shots to settle, I was probably done for anyway.

And I still didn't think anything would. "I don't know what Wade was thinking of, Jake, teaching you to shoot a weapon that size."

Smiling as I recalled the answer to this, I got out of the truck. He'd been thinking of marrying me, actually, courting me on the same gun range where police chief Bob Arnold spent a lot of his spare time, because, as Bob said, it might only pay off once, but that once was plenty.

It was also where I'd taken a shine to target shooting and to Wade in the same breathless moment of recognition. I'm not sure which I liked first, the man or the smell of gunpowder, but the combination turned out to be potent and we had been setting off small, interesting explosions ever since.

"You've got your cellphone, too, right?" she added.

"Yes, Ellie." It had been all I could do to talk her into leaving me here alone, even before Hooper's escape; she believed that the presence of a mild-mannered but combustibly tempered redhead was an advantage in just about any circumstance.

But one of the reasons I wanted to be out here was for the solitude. Maybe it was the dustups I'd been having with Bella, or maybe the deathiversary really had gotten to me, and the hints of haunting in the old house really were psychological, not supernatural.

Or maybe my loner nature was just poking its head up and taking itself out for a little airing, as it had done a few other times over the years. For whatever reason, though, a long silence sounded like heaven to me. While I was here, I didn't even plan to turn on the radio.

Meanwhile, the fresh pile of boards at the edge of the truck turnaround reminded me of something I *did* mean to do: that deck.

"Come on, let's get the supplies inside," I told Ellie.

For the next half hour, we worked steadily, transferring the tools, the coolers, the dry goods, and my clothes and toiletries into the cottage, a sixty-by-eighty-foot post-and-beam building with a sharply peaked roof, shingled outside and pine-paneled inside.

The main floor was one big room with a woodstove situated dead center in it, an open galley kitchen with a gas stove and propane refrigerator, and a living area with bright braided rugs, big overstuffed chairs, and a round wooden table plus a pair of daybeds for lying around on, reading and relaxing.

Not that much of that went on at the cabin, though, since a few feet downhill was the lake. A long wooden dock ran out into it, and when we weren't working on the camp—a surprising amount of labor went into just keeping the place in running order—we were swimming, fishing, floating in inner tubes, or just messing around in boats.

"Oof." Ellie set the last canvas bags of supplies on the kitchen counter. "It's like you're staying for a month."

I put the gasoline-powered chain saw down. Most of the deck work that remained could be built with a handsaw, a hammer and nails, and a battery-driven drill equipped with wickedly long bits that looked like parts of a spearfishing kit, for drilling the holes the carriage bolts went into, to attach the steps and railings.

But I did still have to cut the posts for the railings that would run alongside the steps, and I had no intention of trying to do that by hand. The posts would be made of six-by-six-inch pressure-treated lumber, and pressure-treating doesn't just force anti-rot chemicals in; it also makes the wood a lot harder. So I'd bought myself a new sixteen-inch gas-powered Stihl: big enough for the job, light enough for me to handle well, and best of all, an easy starter.

"I mean—" Ellie pulled things at random out of the food satchel. "Pistachios? And a garlic press?"

"Well, I don't want to be eating entirely out of cans while I'm here." Crouching by the chimney, I opened its square, cast-iron cleanout hatch and angled a small hand mirror up into it.

Deviled ham on toast would be fun once or twice. But after that I meant to enjoy foods no one else in my family tolerated: a brussels sprouts quiche one night, for instance, rice with black beans another. Having to go back down that bumpy dirt road for a spice or condiment was not in my game plan, either.

"A nutmeg scraper," Ellie said, marveling.

Tipping the mirror one way, then the other, I tried to look up the massive stone chimney the woodstove was piped into. But as I did, something fell *down* the chimney, landing on the ledge at the bottom of the hatch with a sooty thud.

"Uh-oh." It was a dead bird.

Ellie knelt beside me to see, and I felt her recoil just the tiniest bit before she repressed a shudder, because of course she was not superstitious and neither was I, and never mind the odd, Victor-ish events that had gone on at my house that morning.

But anyone with half a brain knows dead birds are bad luck. I mean, have you ever looked at a dead bird—some poor floppy, limp-necked thing that's smacked into a plate-glass window and bounced off, and now has two little cartoon x's where its eyes used to be—have you ever looked closely at one of those and thought, *Oh, great, this means I'm in for some* good *luck?*

I lifted the thing from the cleanout hatch with a garden spade from the toolshed, and flung its sooty body into the trees where the wood ashes that permeated its feathers meant that it wouldn't even get eaten by animals, or anyway not very soon. So I flung it *hard,* wanting its sad, forlorn carcass as far away as I could get it.

Just then another dragonfly zipped by, brushing me with its wings; from high overhead a woodpecker set up a fast, chattery rat-a-tat. A fish jumped, landing with an extravagant splash down in the lake, and the sweet, sappy-sharp perfume of fresh lumber drifted up, waiting for me and Ellie to get to work on the deck.

Off the end of the dock, a long ripple extended fast, heading for the other side of the lake. A small golden-brown head at the ripple's tip belonged to a familiar creature:

"Hey, Ellie! Cheezil's here!" I called. It was our name for the weasel-like animal—thus his name, Cheezil the Weasel—who lived down by the dock somewhere; we hadn't seen him all summer.

Hurrying down the gravel path toward the dock, I watched him swim energetically away toward the far side of our small cove, feeling that the lithe, furry animal counteracted the dead bird's influence at least a little bit. When he reached shore, I could just make out his slender form, scampering between the rocks and up toward a tiny log cabin, past a canoe that was overturned onto concrete blocks to keep snow from filling it up over the winter.

Then he was gone, intent on some wild, weasel errand that only he knew; so maybe things weren't so bad after all, I thought, and when I got back to the clearing Ellie was setting up the barbecue equipment.

"Lunch in twenty minutes," she said. Lowering the truck's tailgate, she arranged hot dogs, buns, and the barbecue fork in a neat row on it, then lit the grill. "I'm starved, aren't you?"

And just like that, everything was all right again. We were here, we were fine, and I was going to get a lot done while also having a good time during my week of solitude, deep in the Maine woods.

And mostly, I was going to get the deck done. Dead bird or no dead bird, five-thousand-word essay or no five-thousand-word essay . . .

Victor's ghost, I added firmly to myself, or no Victor's ghost.

Harold got a motel room, then set about pursuing his hiking plan right away; after the long bus ride, his legs needed a good stretching out anyway, and the four or five miles the guys in the diner had described sounded fine to him.

So only a little over an hour after he'd arrived in Eastport, the same taxi driver who'd brought him there helped Harold unload his hiking gear from the trunk of the cab, then left him standing at the dead end of a paved road.

Ahead, a dirt track curved into the woods; the guys in the diner had said it led to a lake, and past that to an old dam and a granite quarry. Harold could hike in the two miles to the lake, they'd said, glancing without comment at his footgear—black socks and walking sandals that he'd bought especially for this trip—take a swim if he wanted, then continue on to the quarry and past it to another paved road leading back to the highway. If he started soon and kept moving right along, they'd told him, he could be in Eastport again by dark, and the cabbie had agreed.

As for the return trip, just stick your thumb out when you get back to the main road, the cabbie had advised. Someone'll be along. Hitchhike, the driver meant, causing Harold to realize again how different everything was here. In the city, sticking his thumb out might've gotten him a ride, but it could also have (a) gotten him murdered, or (b) made someone else think they were in danger of being murdered, if they picked him up.

A chipmunk scampered across the road, pausing to rear up on its back legs to scold Harold. A bird sang; he didn't know what kind, only that its song was about the prettiest sound he'd ever heard. When it stopped, the silence was so complete that his ears rang, and the smell of this place . . . pine sap, warm dust slaked with the recent rain, and some kind of pungently aromatic herbal fragrance. It gave him a burst of energy, just inhaling it.

He stepped onto the dirt road with his pack straps weighing pleasantly on his shoulders. A canteen of water, some sandwiches from the diner, and a chocolate brownie were in the pack. He'd bought a compass, too, and an emergency flare from the hardware store in Eastport.

Also, he had a gun, a .22 pistol he'd borrowed from behind the counter of the video store, on his way out. The owner kept it in case of robbery, but there hadn't been one in all the time Harold worked there. He would return the weapon before the owner even missed it, Harold felt confident; meanwhile, he kept it in his jacket pocket.

A hundred yards in, the dirt road curved sharply again, so that when he turned to look back all he could see were the trees, some evergreen and others bearing reddish or silver-green leaves. He walked on, passing through a swamp where black tree skeletons jutted from black, algae-covered water.

Startled by his footsteps, a huge frog jumped from the road into the water with a plop that made Harold jump, too. *Silly. There's nobody here. No one to be scared of, or mad at, to resent or be repulsed by.*

One thing about solitude, it didn't make you feel as if you were being rejected. Like somehow, everyone else had grabbed a brass ring and you'd missed yours. Here, Harold felt . . . normal, as if he fit in, just another creature among many.

Like a natural man, he thought, savoring the idea. Ahead, the road's damp tan surface was a bright ribbon reflecting the sun. It was a lot warmer here than in Eastport, just the exertion of walking with the pack on making him sweat. He stopped to pull off his jacket and sweater, leaving on only his T-shirt.

God, it was beautiful out here. If he'd brought along his cellphone, he could've taken pictures with it, but he hadn't; besides, he had no one to call: no relatives, a few acquaintances but no real friends . . . a loner even as a child, with his parents now passed away he had even fewer people to miss him.

None, actually, he admitted frankly to himself. When his bus had pulled out of Port Authority, he'd thought forlornly that if he never returned, no one would care. His boss would get a new guy to rent porn. Everything would go on as if he'd never existed. But now . . .

Suddenly, Harold didn't feel lonely at all. This world, full of birds and trees, grasses and insects, a blue sky overhead, sun shining and a little breeze blowing so it wasn't too hot . . . it was enough. He stopped, feeling his shoulders straighten pleasantly and the tension in his neck vanish.

More than enough. Maybe he wouldn't even go back. It was just a thought, not a plan or even a real possibility yet. But hey, it was a free country.

A free world, and he was a free—a *naturally* free—man. Hiking the pack up onto his shoulders again—happily, he realized with a tiny shock of wonder—he looked down the road ahead of him, suddenly seeing something about it that he hadn't noticed before.

There were marks in the damp tan dirt, not just tire tracks from whatever vehicles were sturdy enough to be driven in here—one set of those, he noted, looked quite recent—but a double line of smaller ones, too. Harold squinted at them, recalling a joke about three not-very-bright country boys out hunting, who'd fallen to arguing about what kind of tracks they were following.

Bear tracks, said one. Moose tracks, said his brother. Deer tracks, insisted the third stubborn hunter. And while they were arguing over what kind of tracks they were, the train came along and hit them.

Pursing his lips thoughtfully, Harold began walking again. The marks went on down the dusty road for a quarter mile or so until they veered off onto an even smaller, grass-covered trail that led into the woods.

Puckerbrush, the taxi man had called the thick undergrowth between the trees. Don't get lost in it, the driver had advised, and Harold had promised not to. Now he crouched, peering at the marks where they left the road.

But then it hit him, how ridiculous he was being. Who did he think he was, anyway, Daniel Boone? The only tracking he'd ever tried doing was of customers who didn't bring video rentals back on time, via the phone numbers (usually fake) and email addresses (likewise) they'd given at the time of their first transactions.

Even Harold could identify these tracks, though. He followed the grassy trail with his eyes until it bent between an enormous tree stump, twenty feet tall at least, and a moss-covered boulder that was even bigger, lunging up from the earth.

Then he eyed the marks in the road again, seeing that they obscured small, round pockmarks and runnels that must have been left by last night's storm; the cabdriver had talked about it. And these other prints he'd been following were on top of the storm traces; that must mean they were more recent.

From this morning, then. *Huh,* Harold thought, a prickle of unease shifting the hairs on his neck. He wasn't as alone out here as he'd thought. Because these prints leading off into the woods weren't deer tracks, or moose tracks, or even train tracks.

They were boot prints.

Marianne . . . Striding down the trail just off the dirt road leading to the lake, escaped prison inmate Dewey Hooper scowled ferociously as the thought of her hit him yet again.

She'd put a spell on him, that was the trouble. A hex that kept him thinking about her. Back in prison, he'd been crazy with it: her name, day and night, filling his head, drowning all other thought. Writing it down helped, like emptying a pitcher.

But it always came back; that, and the memory of her face . . . He shook his head angrily, forced himself to think of something else. Like freedom, for instance: now that he wasn't locked in there like some zoo animal, things would surely be better.

As if to prove it, his right palm began itching. That was a good sign; everyone knew an itchy right hand meant you were going to get money. He was right-handed, too; that doubled the luck and was appropriate for him, besides.

Right for spite, the old saying went, and he was full of that, wasn't he? Always had been, but at the moment just being free felt so good, he wasn't dwelling much on that, either.

He spotted an acorn on the leaf-mold-covered earth under an oak tree and snatched it up. An acorn in your pocket brought long life, and if, as he fully expected, he found a place to sleep indoors tonight, it would keep lightning out. Now if he would only see two crows, or three butterflies . . .

He'd always been superstitious. Even in prison, if anyone spilled salt in the lunchroom, Dewey got some and flung it over his left shoulder. It drove the guards nuts, because some of the guys were so strung out, they'd go off on you for looking cross-eyed at them, never mind taking what they imagined belonged to them, even salt.

A grin twisted his lips as he continued along the trail, still thinking of them back there: the night-shift guards, their skin the color of dried paste and their guts hanging over their belts on account of all the junk food they gobbled, the sunlight and fresh air they never got. The day-shift officers, stringy as beef jerky and doing their time just as surely as the inmates were, ugly and dead-eyed.

And the support staff; oh, they were the worst. His smile tightened to a grimace as he recalled the parade of mealymouthed social workers, pinch-faced nurses, and snot-nosed so-called teachers, all bent on improving Dewey whether he liked it or not.

Scowling at the memory, he spied some apples dangling from an old tree. The land around here had been hardscrabble farms once, small homesteads each with a herd and a henhouse, hayfields and a garden, plus an orchard for pies and applejack. Here and there you'd find a row of those trees still standing, but mostly now it was only a singleton that survived, like this one here.

He climbed the tree, snatched one fruit plus another for his pocket, and jumped down. The apple in his hand was wormy but what the hell; biting into it, he imagined turning a flamethrower full blast on the prison social workers, crisping them where they sat.

When he first got there, he'd have done it if only he'd had the flames. But soon he'd had something better: a plan, which he'd begun working on constantly, in part to try keeping thoughts of Marianne out of his head. Meanwhile, he'd been careful to keep his good luck polished up, too, always choosing the chair that was facing a door, for example, stealing a bit of parsley for his pocket when the cooks weren't looking—by then, he had a kitchen job—knocking wood every chance he got.

And now his planning and polishing had finally paid off: he was back in his own familiar territory of downeast Maine, hundreds of miles from where the cops were looking for him.

He was, he congratulated himself, so smart and lucky that he could hardly stand it. *Free,* he thought with a burst of delighted exhilaration. *No one telling me what to do anymore, or how and when to do it.* When you were behind bars, you could barely blow your nose without somebody trying to give you static about it.

He could hardly believe the pleasure of just being out of there, as if he'd been inside a pressure cooker and someone had taken the lid off. No more orders, no more work duty, no more pretending to be a good little boy. *Free* . . .

But he was also hungry, thirsty, and in need of a warm, dry place,

free of insects, field mice, and any other pesky wildlife that might pre-
vent him from getting a decent night's sleep.

Fortunately, though, he knew how to take care of all these needs.
He'd grown up hunting and fishing here, and he knew every path,
trail, and road in Washington County, not to mention every house,
garage, and backyard clothesline in the area.

These new jeans he wore, for instance: he'd had to roll the cuffs up
and cinch the waist with a length of wild grapevine, but otherwise
they weren't bad. His boots, too, were stolen off a back step; no doubt
they'd been left there by some poor guy whose shrewish wife nagged
him about mud in the house.

Women, Dewey thought, tossing the apple core away. Somehow
they always managed to mess up a man's life. But then the memory of
how clever he'd been returned: his jacket and sweatshirt, too, were
pinched from different places. That way no one would twig to the notion that someone had stolen a whole outfit.

So now a bunch of pudgy, limp-spined husbands were going to
come home from their stupid office jobs, Dewey imagined, and want
to know where their stuff was, and when their wives didn't have an
answer for them maybe they'd grow a pair, find the nerve to smack
the women upside the head a few times. It was the only way to handle
them, Dewey knew, and the sooner a guy manned up to it, the better.

And if he went too far, it was the woman's own fault, Dewey
thought as he stepped over a log, up onto a rock, and sideways off the
path to avoid a muddy patch. Tracks on the dirt road were one thing;
people walked or drove there a lot.

Back here, though, he didn't want anyone getting any ideas, like
maybe that the famous prison escapee, Dewey Hooper, wasn't really
headed south out of Portland, hundreds of miles and a whole world
away from the backwoods of downeast Maine.

That instead, he'd deliberately stolen three cars and then crashed
or abandoned them one after the other on purpose, like dropping a
trail of breadcrumbs. A trail for the cops, who had fallen for it, at least

from what Dewey had read in the newspaper he'd fished out of a trash barrel that morning.

The grassy path narrowed between a pair of massive boulders that stuck up like the two sides of a doorway. Beyond them, the thicket of mostly brush and saplings he had been walking through darkened to mature woodland, a patch of it that two centuries of loggers had not yet quite gotten to.

The forest canopy spread green and fragrant over his head, a few patches of blue poking through and the air cooling suddenly. Dewey felt his neck and shoulders relaxing for the first time in years. A couple of miles ahead, the lake's few rustic shoreline cabins were mostly empty now that the summer season was over.

But in them there would be firewood and drinking water—you couldn't drink out of the lake unless you wanted a nasty gut bug called beaver fever—plus coffee and food, mostly canned stuff left by the summer people. At least one would have a rowboat or a canoe he could use, too, and he might even find some guns.

By tonight, Dewey would be tucked up snugly in one of those cabins, with a fire going in the woodstove and beef stew from one of those cans warming in a kettle on it, coffee in a percolator, maybe even biscuits if they'd left biscuit mix. He'd be warm and toasty, with not a soul suspecting he was nearby.

And even if anyone spotted, say, the smoke from the chimney or light from a window, he might still be okay. This time of year it was mostly only hunters who came out here: good old boys, many of whom wouldn't tell on him, he felt certain.

Because Dewey wasn't the only guy who'd ever wanted to slap some mouthy broad halfway to kingdom come, that much he knew for a fact. And it wasn't his fault, either, that instead of halfway, as it had always been before when he'd needed to teach Marianne a lesson, that last time it was all the way.

He plucked the other apple from his pocket. Biting in, he let the sweet juice and pulp dribble down his lips.

That last time, he'd actually killed her. And no good-luck charm in the world could do a thing about that.

Not that he cared, he told himself firmly. *Boohoo,* he thought as he made his way through the forest toward the nearest of the lakeside cottages. *Boohoo with a freakin' cherry on it . . .*

But then he stopped. Directly ahead, the trail continued uphill between more boulders; he knew the way, having been here before many times, hunting and trapping.

To his left, though, the land sloped down into a hollow with what remained of a long-dead tree sticking up out of it: a twisty gray trunk denuded of bark and aged to a silvery sheen with sharp daggers of broken-off branches stabbing out in all directions.

Dewey stared at the tree, or rather, at what was under it. A circle of stones marked where someone had built a fire of sticks very near the tree trunk. From its lower branches hung pieces of clothing: shirt, pants, jacket. A pair of boots stood with toes nearly touching the charred campfire remnants.

To Dewey, the scene described disaster: someone had gotten wet, fallen into the lake, maybe. Maybe it was late, and as cold out here as an October night in the Maine woods could be; getting back out again in wet clothes had looked iffy. Starting the fire, drying the clothes, and waiting until it was light had looked better to someone.

But the tactic hadn't worked, and now as he approached the dead fire, Dewey saw who that someone was.

Well, I'll be damned. Bentley Hodell, you old son of a bitch. Ain't seen you in a dog's age.

The man's nearly naked body lay where it had fallen, half in and half out of the fire circle. Dewey recognized the short braid of frizzy gray hair, the hooked nose, and most of all the big gold signet ring on the right hand, stretched out as if grasping for something it could never reach.

Not in this world, anyway. Bentley had won that ring in a card game, Dewey recalled. He'd been there when it happened, in the back room of the Happy Crab sports bar in downtown Eastport. Afterwards, Bentley had bought everyone a drink, then given Dewey a ride home.

And now here he was, naked to the elements. Or nearly; Dewey couldn't remember when he'd seen a man so pitifully exposed. From the looks of things, Bentley must've been out here bird hunting; a shotgun lay broken open on the ground a ways back from the fire circle. But then something more happened; heart attack, maybe.

Something fast, it looked like to Dewey, and that, anyway, was a blessing. Bentley had been a good guy. He didn't deserve to be lying out here in just his skivvies.

On the other hand, the jacket he'd been wearing looked good and warm. Carhartt, it was, blue denim with a red wool lining. A pair of truly sturdy boots would be better than the cheap ones Dewey had on, and even the pants hanging from the dead tree's branch had flannel in them; Dewey could see it where Bentley had rolled the cuffs up, to make the pants as short as his legs.

But they would fit Dewey just fine. *Sorry, buddy,* he thought at Bentley, reaching for them—then drew his hand back as a pang of uncertainty struck him; this making-his-own-decisions stuff was *hard.*

If he took the clothes, he'd have to leave Bentley out here naked, and that idea rubbed him the wrong way. Not that he felt any more responsibility for old Bentley than he did for anyone else; it just felt like bad luck, was all. He couldn't put the stolen clothes he was wearing on the other man's body, though, because sooner or later, Bentley would get found.

Maybe not this year, or even next year or the year after. No doubt a search party had already gone by; it was a lot harder finding a lost guy out here than a person might think, especially if the guy wasn't moving or making noise due to being dead.

First, snow would cover him. Then, when spring came, weeds and bushes would leaf out, hiding this dead-tree hollow.

On the other hand, some other bird hunter could wander out here tomorrow and happen across him, and if that occurred Dewey didn't want Bentley's body to be wearing a set of stolen clothes. Chances were slim that anyone would recognize the outfit.

But they weren't *none.* So Dewey faced a choice: leave his old pal here bare naked, or nearly so. Or leave a fine, heavy jacket and pair of trousers—and boots, don't forget the boots—for a corpse who couldn't get any good out of them.

Damn, Dewey thought, because he sure as hell was going to put something on old Bentley; if nothing else, simple modesty demanded it. Dewey wanted the pants, boots, and jacket, but if their situations were reversed, he knew Bentley would do it for him, not leave his skinny shanks lying all which-a-way on the cold forest floor. Poor guy looked like a plucked chicken left sitting in the icebox, Dewey thought with a rare twinge of pity, and leaving him that way was . . . well, it was unmanly, somehow. It was the kind of thing a real dirtball type of guy would do.

And Dewey certainly didn't think he was one of those. So he had no choice. He could take the jacket, but the rest was going to have to go back on Bentley, and what a delightful chore *that* was going to be, Dewey thought resignedly. Pulling the shirt and pants from the branch where poor Bentley had hung them to dry, Dewey approached the body and crouched by it, wondering where to start.

First he lifted an arm by gingerly encircling the cold, blue wrist with his thumb and forefinger. Then he did the same with a leg, discovering that at least Bentley wasn't stiff anymore. Bad luck about the clothes, but . . .

A sound came from the vicinity of the trail. Dewey couldn't believe it at first, but bad luck came in threes, didn't it? And if poor Bentley being dead at all was one, and his clothes being off-limits to Dewey was two, then . . .

Whistling. Somebody over there was approaching slowly along the trail, crunching through fallen leaves, stopping and starting and making all the noise in the world, and on top of it—

"Yankee Doodle." Some damn fool was strolling along, whistling it,

like it was the Fourth of July or something. And if there was one thing he hadn't wanted out here, it was company. He glanced at Bentley's shotgun, but he could see it wasn't loaded, and anyway, after lying out here in the elements, who knew if it would even fire?

Maybe whoever it was would go on by, he thought hopefully. Or— but then suddenly Dewey knew just what to do, to solve his visitor problem *and* his clothes problem.

Hustling to the base of the dead tree, he hoisted himself up by using old branch stubs as handholds, stabbing himself twice on their sharp ends in his hurry but not caring. When he got up high enough, he eased around the trunk until it hid him.

The visitor was still loitering along, whistling. Leaning around the tree's trunk, Dewey cupped his hand to his mouth and called out just loudly enough to be heard:

"Hey! Hey, you! C'mere!"

Looking puzzled but unsuspecting, the visitor obeyed, while peering around unsuccessfully to find where the voice had come from and instead spotting Bentley Hodell's body with the shirt and pants lying next to it.

"Psst!" Dewey eased out to the front of the tree again, and the visitor—youngish guy, backpack, stupid clothes, sandals, for God's sakes—turned and came toward him, looking shocked.

"There's a . . . there's a . . . dead man," the visitor managed, pointing a shaky finger, and when he got close enough Dewey leapt on him.

CHAPTER 4

The more washing a surface will need (i.e., kitchen cabinets, door frames, etc.), the glossier the paint on it should be.
—Tiptree's Tips

If he hadn't been a brain surgeon, my ex-husband, Victor, could've been a top-notch salesman. Never mind ice at the North Pole; Victor could sell you on the idea that he had warm blood in his veins, instead of embalming fluid so cold it was practically turning to slush.

Back when he was alive, I mean, before he really did have embalming fluid in them.

Ellie shot me a look. "You don't have to hide it from me, Jake, I know you're thinking about him. And why shouldn't you be? It's his deathiversary, for heaven's sake, and that's probably why you thought you heard his voice, too. So why not admit it?"

Lunch had been delayed; in the cool breeze off the lake, our little gas grill was taking its time heating up. Meanwhile, I was making the day-bed, using the flannel sheets I'd brought from the linen closet at home.

And I didn't think I'd imagined hearing him. But: "After all," she went on, "he was your husband, and Sam's dad. It's not wrong or disloyal to remember him, especially now."

I made a hospital corner, folding the flannel tightly under the mattress as if I were packaging it for airmailing. We had no mice here, thanks to Bella; all summer she'd been obsessive about setting mouse-traps, so that whenever we stayed overnight we'd be woken by the *whap! whap!* of tiny necks being snapped.

But at last they'd wised up about big, murderous mammals bearing treats. It got so just opening the cottage door alerted them; the last time I was here, I'd walked in, set my bag down on the floor, and immediately spotted a mother mouse streaking for the exit with a pink, hairless baby the size of a lima bean in her mouth.

Still, I didn't want even a chance of one burrowing under the covers with me tonight; I gave the sheet an extra tug before spreading the down comforter over it, then turned to Ellie.

"You're right." About one thing, anyway. She'd always been able to see past my stiff upper lip. "I am thinking of him."

On the morning he died, the only phrase I'd been able to summon was *Thank God.* For my sake and his; even with a team of hospice nurses who had, I still firmly believe, floated straight down from heaven, plus enough morphine to stun a horse (but none for me, unfortunately), those last few days had been horrible.

"Right now, mostly I'm thinking about the time he hit me."

Ellie looked up from where she crouched before the old wood-stove, feeding it small lengths of split birch. From her face, you'd think I'd said he'd poisoned me with strychnine. "He *what*?"

I mumbled something into the pillow I was fluffing. She must have heard it as "Never mind," because she tactfully went back to working on the fire; she was good that way, never prying, always ready to listen if I wanted to talk. But what I'd really said was "I went blind."

Which I had, right after it happened. I don't even recall now what Victor and I had been arguing over, but it was probably a woman; there'd been so many of them by then that the nurses at the hospital where he worked nicknamed him "Vlad the Impaler."

Anyway, I'd been screaming something profane at him when his fist shot out and slammed the side of my head. Immediately, my vision had blurred, but I could see well enough to watch him look down at his hand as if it had just done something utterly outside his control, like the disembodied hand of the murdered pianist in one of the old horror movies my son, Sam, still likes so much.

Only instead of walking crabwise and lopped-off-at-the-wrist onto the keys of a grand piano, it had hauled off and slugged me. Then my vision darkened, and I passed out.

In the ambulance when I woke, I could see again, and Victor was with me as we screamed in and out of city traffic. After a moment I closed my eyes; he hadn't known I was watching him.

A few hours later, after I got my head examined at the hospital, they released me. He'd told them I'd slipped on a throw rug, a story that was apparently believable—especially coming from him—and one I never bothered correcting.

As for why I didn't leave him, I would have, except for what I'd seen in the ambulance. He'd been weeping with his face in his hands and his shoulders heaving.

"Please be okay," he'd been whispering. "I'm so very sorry, please let her be okay."

And that was the scene I just couldn't get out of my mind on this gorgeous October afternoon more than two decades later. Like I said: a salesman. Or maybe not; even now I wasn't sure what I'd decided about it.

"Time for lunch at last," Ellie announced as I finished making up the bed by folding the red plaid wool lap robe over it, on top of the flannel sheets and down comforter. Fall days at the lake were chilly enough, but once evening arrived it was going to get downright nippy.

Dark, too, like somebody shutting off a switch. While Ellie prepped buns for toasting and started the hot dogs cooking on the grill, I went around testing propane lamps. Their harsh overhead glare cast no shadow, and everyone lit by them looked dead; even Sam, never a connoisseur of atmospheric lighting effects, said those gas lamps made him feel as if we all might start shambling around any minute, hungry for brai-ai-ains.

But I did want them working in case the solar power failed somehow, so just to make sure at least one of them did, I held a lighter to the small sack of white netting covering its gas jet. Turning the gas-flow lever, I heard the soft pop of ignition and after an initial greenish flare watched the mantle heat swiftly, from dark red to blinding yellowish white.

Satisfied, I blinked the intense light-blast from my retinas just in time to see Ellie come in with a platter of sizzling hot dogs, each resting in a perfectly toasted hot dog bun.

On the table already were condiments, napkins, and glasses of sweet, minty iced tea; we feasted like queens while the radio played the third of Vivaldi's *Four Seasons* and the woodstove took the last of the cottage's closed-up chilliness away.

"He never did it again, though," I said after I'd eaten my first hot dog. "Victor never hit me after that one single time."

It was the other reason I hadn't left him, or not over that, anyway. In the end, the medical secretary I discovered in our bed one day accomplished what his clenched fist hadn't been able to.

"Right," said Ellie, fishing a dill pickle out of the jar. "Somehow I didn't think he could've."

She ate the pickle. "Of course, that's what everybody says, that they won't. That's what she said, Dewey Hooper's wife."

"How do you know that?" Ellie had never mentioned knowing anyone connected with the case, at the time or since.

She got up to feed our paper plates to the stove. "I never met her myself, or Dewey, either. But George is cousins with one of their neighbors."

Her husband, George Valentine, she meant, and since he was related to almost everyone in downeast Maine, I wasn't surprised.

"After it was all over, the neighbor said Marianne used to come over crying a couple of times a month. Black eye, split lip—you name it."

"Same with me. Coming over, I mean. Did George's cousin give Marianne the same advice I did?" That she should leave, I meant. Get out, while the getting was good.

Ellie nodded solemnly.

"But she never did," I mused aloud. "Or called the cops."

Even as I said it, though, I understood why. Once I got home from the hospital after Victor punched me, I'd been okay except for the lump on my head; that took a week to flatten.

Emotionally, though, I'd felt winded, as if I were on my knees and couldn't quite summon the strength to stand up again, or even figure out how. What would I have done, I wondered—what would I have been able to do—if there'd been a second time, and after that a third one and a fourth?

Plenty, you'd think, with all the resources I'd had. Back then I was a successful money manager with clients so well-to-do, they bought new shoes when the soles of the old ones got scuffed. I'd had an Upper East Side apartment in a building so exclusive that getting into Fort Knox was easier, not to mention a husband who was such a dog, I could have had Howdy Doody for a divorce lawyer and still walked away richer than half my customers.

Still, it was humiliating to admit that your husband smacked you around. Marianne had felt that, also, I knew; it's why she'd begged me not to tell anyone.

So I hadn't, and I'd regretted it ever since. Now Ellie took the lemonade glasses into the kitchenette, behind an L-shaped counter dividing it from the rest of the room. A pump brought up lake water; we boiled it on the gas stove to kill germs but even then we used it only for cleaning and doing dishes.

Drinking water we hauled from home in plastic jugs, six of which now stood lined up on the counter. "So, no showers on this trip?" asked Ellie, seeing me eyeing the jugs.

"Nope." Ordinarily we hauled water for bathing, too, but the outdoor shower setup had sprung a leak. "I'll take a soap swim," I said.

This late in the year, about the only other visitors this far out in the woods were bird hunters, more interested in bagging their limit of pah-tritch than in me, dog-paddling around nude with a bar of soap.

"Good luck with that," Ellie said; the lake was already so chilly you could cool nuclear reactor rods in it. "If I were you, I think I might just decide to stay grimy."

"Moi?" I asked in mock astonishment. In reply she tossed me a small gingham bag tied with a ribbon, which turned out to be full of miniature toiletries: fancy lotions, cleansing towelettes, and tiny scented soaps, perfect for a sponge bath with a basin of hot water and a terry washcloth.

One of those was in the gift bag, too: a brand-new one with my name embroidered on it in blue. "Aw, you shouldn't have."

In general, the closest I get to a fancy lotion is Jergens, and if a bar of soap makes lather I'm good with it. But looking at these things made me feel all bubble-bath-y.

Briskly she wiped the countertop. "Sure I should. Grimy's okay, but I refuse to let you be uncomfortable."

Or unloved. And that in a nutshell was Ellie.

Later, we sat on a pair of lawn chairs set up in the narrow space between the truck and the shed. "So how's Wade?" she asked.

Not that she needed an answer. She just wanted to distract me from the subject of Dewey Hooper's dead wife, and even more so from what was really on my mind that day: memories of Victor.

"Wade's fine," I said, appreciating her effort. But then I got up, unable to avoid seeing the huge pile of fresh lumber at the edge of the clearing, waiting to get turned into a deck.

And guess who had been elected to do it? Or rather, had elected herself in a fit of what now felt like way, way too much self-confidence?

Correctamundo, as my son, Sam, would have answered. Sighing,

I rolled up my sweatshirt sleeves, settled my ball cap on my head, and pulled on the pair of thick elasticized work gloves that Sam had given me the previous Christmas.

At the same time, I gave up all hope of any non-aching muscles for the next week or so. But that was okay, or anyway it was only to be expected during a work trip. Maybe if I worked hard enough, I could get rid of something else, too: the memory of Victor in his last, terribly sad hours, a recollection that had been clinging to me all day.

As I thought this a tiny shiver went through me, and when I looked down at my bare arms above the cuffs of the work gloves, I saw that I had goose bumps.

"Wait!" Sam Tiptree sprinted after Richard Stedman's sister, Carol, down the boat ramp toward where Richard's twenty-four-foot sailboat *Courtesan* floated at the dock.

Or rather, didn't float. Several hours had passed since Carol had arrived, and for most of them Richard had been fairly calm. He had asked Sam to hold off on the crane, deciding instead (and against Sam's advice) to let the bilge pump attached to a new battery battle the seawater pouring into her.

But now with the tide rising higher and the wind shifting as afternoon came on, Richard had changed his mind, as it grew clear that the pump wouldn't be enough. Gallons of water *out* weren't keeping up with the number of gallons flowing *in*.

Result: *Courtesan* was still sinking, faster now with a big load of water weight still inside her, listing to port a little more each time one of the big, green waves still churning in from last night's storm hit her like a fist. And instead of letting Sam put a second pump down there, Richard had ignored Sam's urging again and then lost patience, jumping over the rail with his goggles and wet suit on into water so cold that it would chill you to your hipbones if you just stood ankle-deep in it.

"Wait," Sam panted, catching up for the second time that day with the slim, dark-haired girl running toward her brother's vessel. Now she was pulling her sneakers off, hopping first on one foot and then the other, the little pink bobbles on her socklets bouncing.

"I already called," he told her. The second battery and pump were coming. Either they would save *Courtesan* or they wouldn't; Sam still thought it was time for the crane.

But Carol wasn't listening. Instead she was scouring the surface of the water with her eyes. "Do something, for God's sake. He's down there!"

Then, without waiting for his reply, and just as it suddenly occurred to Sam that in fact he hadn't seen Richard in a while, she dove, kicking hard and disappearing under the waves.

Oh, holy criminy, Sam thought, and was pulling his own dock shoes off when brother and sister surfaced together.

"Go!" Richard shouted at his sister, and without even looking at Sam, Carol scrambled up the dock ladder, yanked her sneakers back on, and ran uphill toward the boatyard's parking lot. Not only was she beautiful, Sam thought, but he couldn't recall ever seeing a woman so athletic before, at least not in real life.

"Back the trailer down here!" Richard yelled after her. "Do it now, Carol, I haven't got much time!"

It was worse even than he'd thought, Sam realized; just as Richard finished shouting out instructions, *Courtesan* heeled over sharply, as if at any moment the vessel might capsize right onto Richard's head.

Richard, though, seemed oblivious to the danger his boat now posed to his own safety, or maybe he was past caring. Instead he seemed to be trying to walk her in, up to his neck in the salt water with his shoulder hard against her, inch by hard-won inch.

A pickup truck pulling a boat trailer roared over the crest of the hill, charging down at them. At the bottom it swung around, slammed into reverse, and began backing the trailer down the boat ramp a lot faster than Sam ever liked seeing.

Well, except for right now, because apparently this girl really knew how to back up a boat trailer; bing, bang, boom and it was hubs-deep in the murky shallows at the foot of the ramp. The brake lights flashed and she leaned out the truck's driver's-side door, questioningly.

"A little more!" Richard yelled. For a guy who hadn't seemed to have a clue what to do half an hour ago, he was a dynamo now. Back then he hadn't had a plan, though, and now he clearly did.

But what? Sam wondered as Carol kept backing the truck up until little wavelets began kissing the tread in the vehicle's oversized rear tires. The brake lights flared again, and the truck belched exhaust; *Courtesan* shivered minutely, as if she were deciding whether or not she had the will to go on floating at all any longer.

For the moment, the answer seemed to be *yes*. And the truck was no dinky little Bondo-and-baling-wire vehicle, either, but a brand-new Silverado HD, the one with the Duramax diesel V8 and ten tons of towing power. Even that wasn't big enough to pull a twenty-four-foot boat out of the cove, though, when she was full of water.

Just getting her onto the trailer at all looked impossible. You could float an ordinary boat partway on, and crank her the rest of the way; people did it all the time. But *Courtesan* was so nearly capsized, her rail came within inches of the waves. By this time she was as heavy as the equivalent volume of concrete.

Thinking this, Sam glimpsed a sledgehammer in Richard's hand, and where had *that* come from? Richard must've scrambled back aboard his vessel, grabbed the tool, and jumped into the water again. He had an inner tube with him now, too, the kind little kids floated on; the big water toy had the words *River Rat* painted on it, and Richard was sitting in it, kicking his feet and paddling determinedly toward *Courtesan*'s stern.

What the hell was he up to? "Wait," Sam began, hoping to hell the crew he'd summoned to come down from the boatyard office and help would hurry up and get here. Richard looked cold, his hands and feet fishbelly-white, his face reddened with exertion.

But he also looked angry, his teeth gritted in a blue-lipped snarl that said he'd get *Courtesan* out of the trouble she was in or die trying, which if he stayed in that cold water much longer was also a possibility.

And what was the sledgehammer for? Sam wondered again, but before he could ask, two more guys from the boatyard sprinted over the hilltop: Nathan Brown and Nathan Durrell. One lugged a fresh battery, the other a portable bilge pump. After that, Nathan Frank appeared with a coil of hose on his shoulder; "the three Nathans," everyone called them, like "the Three Musketeers."

Or in their case more like the Three Blind Mice; none of the Nathans was exactly known for smarts or efficiency. What they did have, though, was strength. Reaching the dock, the trio of burly men threw down their loads and craned their muscular necks around as if searching for concrete blocks to head-butt into fragments, or some walnuts to crack in their bowling-ball-shaped biceps.

"Hey, guys, over here!" Sam waved, directing two Nathans into the water where Richard floated on the River Rat, then sending Nathan Frank onto the dock.

Two big splashes and a couple of very Nathan-like wolf howls at the cold water later, they were all in position. The men in the water with Richard shoved ham-sized hands against *Courtesan's* listing side, trying to help hold her upright.

On the dock, the third Nathan waited while Sam hopped aboard the ailing vessel. Swiftly he fastened the thick lines to her bow and stern and scampered back over onto the dock, where he tossed one of the lines to his muscle-bound helper while keeping the other.

Then on Sam's signal they *pulled,* trying to keep the boat level while the water inside her sloshed around trying to capsize her. The line tore Sam's hands as waves buffeted *Courtesan.* He fought for his grip and his balance while the ocean shoved the boat this way and that; out of sight on the far side of the boat, the other men cursed in alarm as *Courtesan* leaned . . . then somehow righted herself once more.

"Okay!" Richard shouted to Carol as, madly paddling and then jumping entirely out of the River Rat, he ran up the boat ramp to the truck, grabbed the winch hook on the trailer, and hauled the winch line out by dragging the hook down to the boat again.

Moments later he'd snapped it to her bow. "Okay, now, when I tell you to, hit the winch switch, but leave it on 'low'!"

She stuck her head out the truck's window. "But don't you want to get her out of there as fast as . . . ?"

"Do what I say!" He threw himself back onto the inner tube. "Now heave!" he yelled at the Nathans, and in response, the two in the water put the flats of their hands to her hull, their big shoulder muscles bulging, while the one above hauled.

Sam jumped aboard once more, meaning to take her mast down. But Richard had something else in mind. "Below!" he ordered, his voice now thinned nearly to a whisper with cold and exertion.

And desperation. "Put your ear down by the bilge, tell me if you hear any water running out," Richard yelled. Then with a painful-sounding whoop of a gasped-in breath, he swung the big hammer.

"Richard, no!" Sam yelled, realizing suddenly what Richard had in mind, but too late. When the hammer hit *Courtesan*'s stern, a sickening crunch of fracturing fiberglass reverberated through the boat, up through the soles of Sam's wet boat shoes. *Courtesan* inched forward, reluctant as a tub of mud, at the urging of the Nathans; as her prow nosed up to the trailer, they muscled her on center relative to the trailer's wheels; even if that was as far as they ever got her, Sam thought, it was a miracle.

But the hardest part was still to come. "Now!" Richard yelled to the girl in the truck. "Easy, easy . . ."

The winch engaged, reeling slack out of the line. But when *Courtesan*'s weight hit the motor, it began screaming with strain.

"Stop, stop!" Richard yelled through the motor's howl. It cut off sharply, the winch's heavy cable thrumming with tautness. *Courtesan* wallowed like a way-too-big fish on a too-light line, unable to free herself but still too heavy to be reeled in.

From out of sight below the stern came the crash of Richard's hammer smashing into the fiberglass again, then his shout: "Push! Push! If we can get her aimed uphill . . ."

Richard's plan was simple, Sam realized, but desperately risky. With her prow hauled up onto the trailer, which itself was perched on the slanted ramp, *Courtesan*'s prow would be angled up enough so that water could drain downhill, out the holes Richard put in her stern.

It wasn't an elegant rescue method, and not one Sam would've advised. But it was too late now, and—

Sam, someone said. He looked around. No one was there but the muscle-bound man hauling on a second line, up toward the prow.

"Sam!" Richard's voice this time. "Do you hear . . . ?"

By now Richard Stedman looked as if he needed saving even more than his vessel did. His face was milk-white with a slash of blue lips cut into it as if with a scalpel; the hands sticking out from his black wet-suit sleeves were purplish red from cold.

Sam jumped down through the hatch to the below-decks cabin. He leaned down over the hole in the floor that Richard had rammed the fatal iron rod into while trying to free the centerboard. The hole, awash in black, oily water, looked as if the wet, scaly arm of a science-fiction monster might shoot suddenly up out of it.

Sam. That voice again. But—his gaze flickered around the cabin's neglected interior—there wasn't anyone here, either.

What the . . . ? Sam backed up the three rubber-treaded hatchway steps to the deck. He could lean over from there and hear better, without the waves slap-slapping the outside of the hull on either side of him.

Richard hit the boat with his hammer yet again; in response the stern dropped noticeably, way too fast for Sam's taste. The whole idea was for water to run out of the boat, not in. But if Richard wasn't careful, he'd sink *Courtesan* while trying to save her.

And then, astonishingly: *Sam. How they hangin', buddy?*

Which was when he knew he was losing it. Brain-damaged, the way his mother always said he would be if he kept on drinking and drugging. Or maybe he had a tumor, just like . . .

The phrase had always been his dad's weird, awkward way of trying to be a buddy to Sam. *But there's no such thing as ghosts,* he thought, and even if there were, why here?

Why now? Disbelievingly, he crept forward toward the hatch leading to the hole in the cabin floor, roiling with dark water.

Somewhere above, outside, far away, Richard bashed his boat again with the sledgehammer; Carol revved the truck's engine; a winch motor whined. The Nathans groaned, heaving the vessel forward; Sam felt it tilt up beneath him, its prow lifting as the Nathans shoved it and the winch howled its distress.

"Sam? What's happening? Talk to me, pal, can you hear any water going out?"

Richard's rasping voice hauled Sam back to himself. A loud gushing sound was indeed coming from *Courtesan*'s punctured stern; she'd gotten up onto the trailer enough so gravity was emptying her at least a little bit, as Richard had hoped. Turning from the gurgle of flowing water, Sam shouted encouragingly.

"Yeah! Keep her stern low, let it run awhile before you—"

Winch it anymore, he'd been about to say, because the motor with all that weight on the winch line still sounded overloaded. Once *Courtesan* was lighter, they could pull her higher onto the trailer, let even more of what she'd taken on drain out.

Or that was the plan, anyway. Out of the blue, though, Sam recalled his own thought of earlier, that a boat always had some new curve to throw at you. No sense getting too confident . . .

Sam. Down here. A thrill of real fear went through him: the voice wasn't in his head anymore.

No, it was coming up out of that hole in the cabin's floor, definitely. A *familiar* voice . . . but that was impossible. That was *crazy.* . . .

His dad's voice. Slowly, Sam turned from the hatch opening where he'd been about to go back up on deck. Instead he'd venture another look down into the hole, just to prove to himself that . . .

Goddammit, Sam, you get over here right this minute.

Sam obeyed, certain he was hallucinating. But the force of the command, the implied but very strong *or else* he heard in it nearly levitated him to the edge of the hole.

He leaned over, peered in, and—

No. Can't be. But there in the wet depths *under* the filthy bilge water floated his father's face: long lantern jaw, cleft chin, and full mouth. And the eyes . . .

Oh, those were his father's eyes, all right, only now they were pure white, as if soaked for a long time in salt water. Eyes like a couple of pearl onions staring at him.

Sam bent down into the hole, trying to see better, to find any sanity-saving scrap of evidence at all to tell him that this was an optical illusion or hallucination of some kind, and not his dead father barking orders at him from inside the hull of a sinking sailboat.

"Dad?" he whispered. The face smiled. . . .

And then a lot of things happened at once: the scream of the overloaded winch motor, a bang like a gunshot, Richard's shout of dismay. An instant later something smashed fast through the wall of the sailboat's cabin, just missing Sam's bent head as it flew by with a hot, deadly-sounding *zzt!*

It smashed out again through the aft porthole, ripping away a chunk of the teak trim as it exited. Seconds later Richard scrambled aboard, nearly weeping.

"Jesus, oh, Jesus. Sam, are you okay? Are you—"

Sam straightened. He could feel *Courtesan* sliding down off the trailer she'd been half perched on, back into the water. But not floating; with all those holes bashed into her, she couldn't. Instead, she was settling fast, in a swift, decisively straight-down fashion that would put her keel on the bottom in—

Less than a minute. He grabbed Richard's slick, wet-suit-covered arm, dragged him along behind him as he scrambled out the hatchway opening. "Come on, we've got to—"

Because she wasn't going to sit keel-down, he could feel it in the way she wallowed beneath him. She was sly, this vessel, so she would try to trick them into thinking she was stable, but at the last moment she would . . .

"Come *on!*" Already the deck slanted a good thirty degrees to port. "Go, go, go . . ."

The mast dipped to forty-five degrees. Sam shoved Richard up over the rail, forcing him to clamber onto the dock. Right behind him, Sam put a foot on the rail, too, meaning to follow. But at that moment, *Courtesan* gave a mighty shudder, unbalancing him.

Oh, hell, he thought very clearly as his foot slipped from the wet rail. Then both his feet were in the air; past them, he could see a sea-gull, just one, afloat in the cold, blue sky.

Then the back of his head hit the deck very hard, and he saw no more.

It took a couple of hours to get the lumber sorted out, it being a rule that lumber-delivery guys always stack boards in the opposite order from the one in which they will be needed.

"I should go soon," Ellie said when we'd finished piling the boards for the railings, the ones for the steps, and at last the narrower planks that the floor would be made of, already cut to the lengths I'd speci-fied. "But . . ."

I took a wild guess. "But let's drain the culvert first?"

She nodded. "Otherwise, if we get more rain . . ."

"Ellie, the storm's gone by." Even as I said it, though, I could feel the air cooling, wisps of clouds over the sun hinting at more rain to come. And the water in the pond *was* very high. . . .

"But what if something happened," Ellie persisted, "and you tried calling someone on your cellphone for help, only no one could get here to rescue you? Or—"

By "something," I knew she must mean an accident with the chain saw. Out here with no electricity—the solar panels didn't provide enough juice to run power tools—it was a necessity, and she was nervous about my arm maybe getting cut off, and then no one being able to get out here over the flooded-out road to help me apply a tourniquet.

"Look," Ellie wheedled, "let's just drive out to the culvert with a couple of crowbars. Maybe a little encouragement is all it needs."

In my experience, a beaver-dammed culvert generally needs more than sweet talk, even if it's teamed with crowbars. An atom bomb might do the trick. Or maybe a missile strike. But Ellie was going to be disappointed if we didn't at least try, and she had put that lovely bath bag together for me.

So after a little more grumbling, I gave in. Minutes later, following another brief, bumpy ride, the two of us were hopping out of the truck onto the dirt road bisecting the pond, still way too full—nearly over-flowing, in fact—on one side, and muck-empty on the other.

"Oh," Ellie breathed, looking around happily, and I had to agree. It was a really glorious autumn afternoon, the kind Mother Nature doles out every once in a while between her more usual offerings of blizzards and typhoons.

Flame-red leaves fluttered like danger flags on the azure sky. Russet-hued cattails thrust up from grassy thickets, platelike green lily pads overlapped on the water's surface, and hawks sailed with wings out-spread, spying out the whisker-twitchings of rabbits they could swoop down on and devour.

The birds reminded me that despite its beauty, this remote wilder-ness really was a kill-or-be-killed kind of place, however cozy I might manage to make it inside the cottage. An unprepared or merely un-lucky person could perish; just a week earlier, one hunter apparently had, walking into the woods before dawn with a gun on his shoulder and not walking out again. His body had still not been found. And I would be all alone here, so the road could indeed be a safety issue just as Ellie had suggested.

But I still didn't think the culvert-clearing project was urgent. I wanted to start working on the deck, not on a job that hadn't even been on my to-do list a few hours ago.

"Just let me take a poke at it, though," said Ellie, seeing my ex-

pression. Balancing easily, she stepped out along the metal culvert
pipe's length, nearer to its plugged-up opening. Small ripples slopped
right up over the corrugated pipe's top. "If it doesn't start breaking up
right away, I promise I'll . . ."

"Ellie," I said cautioningly, because I'd heard enough tales of kids
who'd ventured too near a flooded culvert, got sucked in, and
drowned.

She hopped onto a smooth, flat rock and perched there while poking repeatedly at the culvert's blocked end with one of the crowbars
we'd brought. Every so often she pulled away a solid mass of grass
and mud with the tool's curved end, and in response a blurp of water
burst from the other end where I was stationed.

Then suddenly the blurps connected into a thin trickle that turned
to a steady gushing. And even with that deck on my mind, I couldn't
very well stop her when she was making good progress.

The gush became a torrent. "All right!" Ellie shouted, and started
to give a fist pump. But then she froze, her eyes on the water flowing
from the far side of the pond, *toward* the culvert.

A *lot* of water. Something had given way upstream, the pond was
suddenly rising very fast, and what had been a rivulet atop the road
became a flood. Ellie scrambled back to stand beside me.

"Jake? Do you see what . . . Oh, my God. Is that . . . ?"

"Yes," I said. The road was already awash, a thick torrent of pond
water carrying away great swaths of gravel and even some sizable
stones.

But the flood itself wasn't what had captured my attention so completely. Or hers, either. She stared, her look changing from startled
disbelief to frank horror as she aimed a shaking finger. "Jake, I think
that's a . . ."

Words failed her. But I didn't need anyone to tell me what was
floating swiftly toward us, shifting and turning as the fast current rushing toward the newly unblocked culvert sped it along.

It was a body.

CHAPTER 5

*Unstick a balky metal window
screen with a few squirts of
powdered graphite.*
—Tiptree's Tips

By the time Eastport police chief Bob Arnold arrived at the culvert, it was nearly four o'clock and the pale autumn sunshine was deepening to the color of old sherry. He'd called the Calais cops, too, because the land around the flooded pond lay in that town's jurisdiction, not Eastport's.

So while Ellie and I stood watching, two unhappy-looking Calais officers made their way along the beaver pond's muddy bank to where the corpse lay. Between us and them, a gully a foot deep and a couple of feet across now cut diagonally across the road, with water still running through it.

Bob stood on the far side of the flood-dug trench, where his squad car was parked. "Looks pretty soft," he said, meaning the soaked roadbed. "You could probably still drive across, but . . ."

But if not, then my truck was stuck on *this* side of the gully, over here with me. "Yeah," I said doubtfully. "Maybe."

Pink and plump in his blue uniform, black shoes, and a black leather duty belt loaded with Mace, handcuffs, a whistle, his nightstick, and his service weapon, Bob had thinning blond hair and a pink rosebud mouth that did not look as if it belonged on a police officer. Any crooks who were fooled by his appearance, however, soon found out that looks weren't everything.

"But it's probably a better idea for you both to just jump across and ride back to Eastport in my car," he finished.

I looked up past the pond's far edge to where the stream that fed it vanished among the reeds. "Why'd it stop?" I wondered aloud.

Because it shouldn't have; if the high-water condition of the lake was any indication—and it was—there were tens of thousands of gallons of water still up there, in a stream that was also near to overflowing its banks. So why wasn't the flood still raging?

One of the Calais cops heard me as he slogged up out of the marsh; he'd been back there to see if he could find where the body had been, before it washed out.

"Big log dammed it off," he reported. "Must've floated down from upstream somewhere; now it's stuck hard across the stream."

Bob looked sternly at me. "Hear that? You two should come out with me. 'Cause if you decide later that you want to . . ."

I got it. A big log lying haphazardly across a stream is not a reliable flood prevention device, he meant. If it floated free, that water could be roaring across the road again in a heartbeat. And if it happened to do so while we were driving *on* the road . . .

"Six inches," Bob reminded me very seriously. "That's all it takes to float your tires sideways. Less, if the road dissolves, and this road is no great shakes in the solidness department."

He pointed at the lower section of pond, on the far side of the road where the culvert drained. An empty muck hole hours ago, now it was brimful, the water in it at least eight feet deep.

"You do *not* want to end up in there," Bob said. "I mean it, Jake; are you hearing me?"

"I hear you." The water down there roiled wildly on its way to some larger stream, deep in the woods. Foaming and churning, it made thick, loud sucking noises as if smacking its lips at the thought of swallowing someone, pulling them down into its cold, strangling clutches and drowning them mercilessly.

"Don't worry," I added to Bob, because he was right: we did *not* want to end up in it.

The Calais cops turned the body over, at which point any idea that there might be life left in it vanished. Floating face-down, it had been merely a bundle of waterlogged clothing.

Face-up, though, was another matter entirely. "Should they be moving him that way?" Ellie wanted to know.

Ignoring her, the two Calais officers went through the dead man's pockets, coming up with a wet wallet. "I mean, shouldn't we wait for the . . ."

One of the cops looked up. "Coyotes're out here. Bobcats, too." He gestured at the dead man, whose deeply gashed forehead made his face a meaty horror.

"You want to tell his loved ones there's no body for them to bury 'cause we let the wild things gobble it up?"

He had a point. You never saw dead animals out here, or the parts of shot deer left by hunters who dressed out the carcasses in the field, either.

Just scattered bones. Besides, this wasn't a crime scene as far as I could see, only an unattended death. So they'd haul the body in, do the autopsy later in Augusta.

The cop held up a driver's license. "Harold Brautigan," he read. "New York, New York."

After examining the money in it—a ten and a few singles—he slapped the wallet shut wetly and looked at Bob.

"Tourist. Out here on a hike, looks like. But man, look at those shoes."

The dead man wore leather sandals over black socks, which in my opinion would've been a poor choice for any location. But they were especially inappropriate for the woods.

"Slipped and fell, hit his head on a rock, tumbled into the water," Bob theorized aloud.

The guy's face looked worse than that. But I guessed it was the likeliest explanation, especially if you added in the effects of bird or animal activity, after the guy drowned.

The Calais cops dragged the body up the slippery bank and rolled it into a tarp. They'd driven here in a pickup truck with City of Calais logos on the doors; I winced as they hoisted the wrapped corpse into the truck bed and let it drop with a thump.

Soon after that, both Calais officers drove off with Harold Brautigan's body in the back of their vehicle; on that road full of potholes, it was going to be an awfully bumpy ride. But then, he wouldn't care. Bob got ready to go, too.

"You sure you both don't want to come back to town with me?" he offered again. "Or I could ride you back to where Ellie's car is parked?"

"Nah," I said. "I'm staying." But then to my surprise, Ellie refused to be rescued, also.

"I'll stay the night, too, I guess," she said. "George and Lee"—her husband and daughter, she meant—"are visiting my aunt in Damariscotta. They won't be home until tomorrow, anyway."

The Calais cops had said they would send a town truck full of gravel, probably tomorrow morning. By afternoon the dirt road would be repaired, so we could get out on our own.

"Suit yourselves," Bob agreed, not looking as if he liked it. But he could see we meant to stay, so a little while later he also took off in the squad car.

Clearly, he didn't think anything was strange about the corpse we'd found; other, I mean, than that we'd found one at all. But driving back to the cabin, Ellie said what we both were thinking.

"Not much money in that wallet." For a tourist, she meant.

I pulled up by the cottage and parked. A bright pink sunset was spreading across the pine-notched horizon on the far side of the lake. "Maybe he used credit cards."

We got out. The air smelled like evergreens and cold water.

"And that head wound," Ellie added, ignoring my remark.

Face, too, actually. It was a very extensive injury. We went inside, where deep bluish shadows were already filling the room. The fire in the stove had nearly gone out, and the chill in the air was palpable.

"Do you think a rock could really open a gash that big?" she asked. "And beat up the rest of his face so badly, besides?"

"Well. He could've been in the water awhile, I guess. That might make a wound look a lot worse. Predators would, too."

Like Cheezil, for instance. We thought the weasel was cute, but to a prey animal, he wasn't, and I doubted he'd turn up his nose at a piece of fresh meat just because it was human, either.

"I guess with the nighttime temperatures so cold lately, he might've stayed in decent shape otherwise for a while, especially if he'd been in a shady spot," said Ellie. "Then when the water started moving so fast, the current washed him out at us."

"Could be. Guy's from New York, doesn't know how challenging the environment is here." I looked out at the granite boulders studding the area around the clearing. "So he takes a fall, lands on his face. I mean, come on. Sandals?"

No wonder he'd turned up dead. Kneeling to feed the stove embers a handful of kindling, Ellie nodded. "You're right, maybe I shouldn't look for any worse trouble than he really had."

The last of the light outside was fading fast now that the sun had set, the nearly bare tree branches black scrawls against the deepening sky. Soon it was going to be dark enough to turn on our solar lamps, whose glow I always regarded with the glee of a child witnessing magic tricks: look, Ma, no electric bill!

But the thought of the coming darkness still wasn't welcome. "Maybe we should've brought along one of the dogs," I said as I gazed out at the gathering night. "Or even both of them."

Suddenly I was lonely for home and, although I didn't like admitting it, feeling anxious as well.

But Ellie shook her head. "We'd just have to take care of them, on top of all the other things we need to do."

Hearing that "we" made me feel better. Ellie was a brick, never whiny or moody, always ready to tackle a project. Also, she was a fine cabin cook, able to turn plain camp fare into meals tempting to the pickiest eater.

She pulled her cellphone from her satchel and plopped onto the daybed, looking as comfy as if she were surrounded by luxury instead of stuck at a rustic lake house where the only hot water available came from a kettle on the stove.

"Hey. Thanks for staying," I told her, touched. "I really—"

She waved me off. "Don't worry about it. I'll just call home and leave a message for George on the machine."

It was one of the reasons why the cottage wasn't really a dangerous place, despite its isolation; good cellphone reception here meant that even if someone did have an accident or any other kind of trouble, help was just a dial tone away.

"You go on out and finish arranging the lumber to suit you," Ellie added. "I'll get things going inside, tend the fire, and get something to eat started and so on."

It was a more-than-acceptable division of labor, especially since I'd been planning baked beans on toast for dinner; with her in charge, it was more likely to be something involving homemade biscuits. Anticipating these, I went out into the chilly evening, where the sun sent a few last deep red streamers across the lake and a loon's laugh rang eerily in the stillness.

On the lake side of the cottage, I began arranging the deck flooring into two piles, long ones and short ones; cut that way, they could be laid out in a more attractive pattern than if they were all the same length. Above, the back door that used to lead out to the old deck now opened onto thin air, four feet off the ground, but soon—or so I told myself encouragingly—we'd be able to set chairs out there again.

Half an hour later I'd finished my prep work, and stars had begun prickling the sky. Inside, a warm fire puttered cheerily in the stove and lamplight the color of honey picked out the red curtains, sewn long ago out of remnants from a nearby woolen mill. Also, the place smelled delicious; whatever Ellie had found to cook on the kitchenette's gas stove, it wasn't beans on toast.

"So who do you suppose that poor guy was?" Ellie wondered aloud as we ate dinner a little later. From half a roast chicken out of the cooler, she'd made chicken à la king; with it we were having a bottle of good Cabernet, not what a wine expert might choose to accompany a chicken dish but delicious nonetheless.

I looked around at the fire glowing behind the woodstove's window, and the solar electric lamp diligently shining out light collected from the sun. Puffs of steam huffing companionably from the kettle's spout promised plenty of hot water for doing dishes, and later for washing up before bed.

Victor, the thought came suddenly to me, *would've liked all this. Especially the fancy wine.*

Ellie raised her glass in a toast. "To absent friends," she said with a smile, as if she'd caught my thought, and I smiled, too.

She was stretching it, but what the heck; he was absent so her toast was at least half true.

And maybe more than half, I admitted grudgingly to myself; he'd been gone for a long time. What I did know for sure, though, was that right now Ellie and I were here: warm, safe, and happy.

Or at least that's how I imagine we must've looked to Dewey Hooper, who I later learned was at that very moment standing just outside the cottage, in the darkness of the clearing, staring in at us through one of the windows.

. . .

Back in prison they'd told Dewey Hooper to reflect on how he'd gotten there, and what he might do to avoid ever being in that situation again. They'd advised him to think about his good traits and his less good ones, to identify his strengths and weaknesses.

But Dewey had already known what they were. Patience, that was the first of his strong points, and the next was the ability to plan out a course of action and stick to it, no matter what got in his way.

Such as, for instance, the plan that had gotten him out of prison a good thirteen years earlier than his scheduled release. Now, three days after his escape from the medium-security facility in Lakesmith, Maine, he stood outside a cabin in the remote rural area very near where he'd been born, and where (with a few short breaks for sentences in juvenile facilities) he'd spent his life.

So: Patience. Planning skills. More than enough wilderness know-how to allow him to survive out here in the woods for a long time, and—well, even Dewey knew he wasn't very smart, or anyway not book smart. But he was cunning and adaptable, and able to zig instead of zag on an instant's notice.

And that, he thought, was a much more useful talent to have than a knack for, say, arithmetic, or the ability to make sense of a newspaper article. He was loyal, too, when he got a chance to be, which wasn't very often; most people didn't deserve it, he'd found, but when they did, there was no truer pal than Dewey. Hey, just look at what he'd done for poor old Bentley Hodell.

As for his negatives, he saw no point in dwelling on them. "Think positive" was his motto, although if pressed he might have conceded that his temper had bollixed him up occasionally. Since his escape, he'd noticed also that he was having trouble making decisions; out of practice, he supposed, after so long pretending to go along with other people making them for him. Also, a lot of folks might say he was *too* superstitious.

But he didn't agree. To him, habits like avoiding black cats and not walking under ladders were only the beginning. Under the common run of so-called old wives' tales lay another whole realm of reality entirely, he knew: signs and portents, omens and premonitions, sixth-sense perceptions he couldn't describe but that he trusted completely.

So that as he peeked through a cottage window and saw the women inside—and especially *that* one, the sight of her like a lightning bolt to his brain—he knew he'd been drawn here for a reason. The window was open a crack, whiffs of woodsmoke and the delicious aroma of chicken stew escaping through it. The smells made his stomach growl hungrily, but it wasn't the food that held his attention.

It was her. Not Jake Tiptree, whose big mouth had helped put him in prison: slim, dark-haired, wearing jeans and a dark green sweatshirt . . . the mere fact that she'd testified against him at his trial was more than enough reason to hate her with a passion, and he did.

Oh, he definitely did. But it was her companion he couldn't tear his gaze from now. Tall and slender, she had red hair pulled back into an elastic from which a few softly curling tendrils escaped, framing her fine-boned features. Her brows were wing shaped, her lips pale pink and curved in a smile.

She looked like an angel . . . or a ghost, he thought with a faint shudder. It was what she must be, even though the Tiptree woman called her Ellie—

But it wasn't her name. Calling her that was just some kind of trick, meant to fool him. *That face* . . . lightly freckled, with perfect features and large, light colored eyes. Beautiful, and so *familiar*—

It was her. It was his dead wife, Marianne. Impossible, but there she was. Glaring up at him the last time he'd seen her, she'd spat at him, then sworn with her last breath that he would pay, that she would come back to *make* him pay. . . .

Which she had, just the sound of her name driving him crazy the whole time he'd been in prison, whispering in his head . . . and now here she was. Practically writhing in a spasm of fury mingled with panicky sixth-sense flappings of superstitious fright, he moved closer to the window. *Her* . . .

The daughter of a fisherman and a well-known midwife—he skinny and silent, she massively motherish—Marianne had always been the witchy type, even as a young girl a brewer of odd teas and maker of weird, pungent potions.

It was part of what had attracted Dewey to her in the first place. Marianne was always picking and drying the leaves of odd plants, bringing home mushrooms she'd found out in the woods and mashing them up with pinches of this and that. After her parents died, she'd lived alone for a while, marrying Dewey only after he'd courted her for a whole winter with smoked salmon, venison haunches, and firewood.

And the result had been worth it: a warm house, a soft bed. One way and another, she'd been the prize in the box of Cracker Jacks, at first. But then the trouble began. Why did he have to drink, why couldn't he hunt in season like other men instead of poaching . . . why, why, why?

Some people had said Marianne could tell what ailed you by the pulse in your throat, or fix a barren woman so she could have children. They said she could predict your future from the way a few tea leaves lay drowned at the bottom of your cup.

A grim smile twisted his lips at that last thought. Hell, she couldn't really have been too great in the fortune-telling department, or she'd have seen ahead to her own choked throat, wouldn't she?

But his smirk fled when she looked up suddenly toward him. For no reason that he could tell, she strode to the window and yanked the shade down, then went around to all the other cottage windows and covered them, too.

Shutting him out. Just like always. She'd thought she was so good, too good for the likes of him once she got to know him. But he'd taught her a lesson, showed her who had the upper hand. . . .

Both hands, actually. Around her throat, choking the life out of her while she fought and sputtered. Cursing him all the while, even when she no longer had breath enough to make a sound.

In the end, they'd gotten him for her death. His attack had left marks, the result of his temper getting the better of him. But only for manslaughter; no one could prove he'd been planning it, that he'd decided enough was enough.

No one but her, and she wasn't ever going to be able to tell, was she? Not after his thumbs had been pressed so far into her throat, he'd felt small bones in there cracking. No one . . .

Not until now. Slowly he backed away from the cabin, his feet finding the small stones of the clearing and moving lightly on them to avoid making a sound. Suddenly the cabin door opened and he froze, certain that he had been detected.

But then, framed in the glow of the open doorway, the dark-haired one named Jake only flung water from a pan at the bushes and went back inside again, closing the door behind her.

Dewey let his breath out. Being imprisoned had taught him the value of his patience; he'd planned his way out, going over every step again and again, taking a couple of years to make sure he'd thought of every eventuality, plugged up any potential hole in his scheme.

Thinking of it all again, pushing the hex she'd put on him determinedly from his mind, he crept away from the cottage. Back in prison, he'd had to gain trust, be a good boy so he could get a spot in the prison's work program, in which inmates whose release was at least theoretically possible were encouraged to learn new, useful skills like cooking, laundry, or landscaping.

Already planning, he'd told the counselor he wanted to be a health-care worker, so in their wisdom they'd made him a janitor in the infirmary. There, silently pushing a broom, emptying wastebins, and wiping out sinks, he'd learned to control the fiery urgings of that temper of his. He'd become—on the outside—the kind of inmate the authorities wanted to see: the kind that everything alive had been systematically reamed out of, leaving only a husk who would follow rules and regulations to the letter.

That was the first step; then there'd been a long period of waiting for an inmate to die naturally, which right there was a rare event. Usually if a guy got so sick that he might kick the bucket, they sent him out to a hospital for a tune-up, not out of concern for the guy but to avoid trouble from lawsuit-happy relatives, weeping crocodile tears while secretly relieved to be rid of the bum. And if they could squeeze a big payday out of a negligence claim, so much the better.

But at last Sonny Sawtelle had clutched both paws to his barrel chest one morning while slopping gray oatmeal onto orange plastic breakfast trays in the cafeteria, and bingo, Dewey had his exit pass. Still, for all his planning, there wound up being a twist he hadn't predicted.

Sneaking down the dirt road away from the cabin in the woods where Marianne's ghost—or whatever it was—now sheltered, he recalled the next part of his escape with a scowl. Faking up a body in his own bed hadn't been any real trouble; prison guards were as stupid and lazy as anyone alive, and after a while of a guy's good behavior they let things slide. If an inmate always showed up for roll call in the morning whether they'd done an overnight bed check or not, the guards got complacent, and their routines got even sloppier than they ordinarily were.

So on the night when a guy wasn't there at all, they didn't notice. Not that he'd taken *that* for granted, though, either. On the night in question, he'd made sure that the pod staff thought he was supposed to be at work in the infirmary, and the infirmary guards thought he was supposed to be in his bed. That gained him a block of time when no one expected to see him. . . .

Without warning, Marianne's face loomed up before him; with a yelp he backpedaled in the darkness, then realized it wasn't real and stormed forward angrily again. *That face . . .*

It was the face of a woman who couldn't keep her yap shut, who'd gone on choking out threats and curses at him even as her face turned blue and her eyes rolled up in her head. *I'll be back for you,* she'd gagged at him, and Dewey had laughed.

Only now it was starting to look to him as if maybe she really would. As if she *had;* after all, he thought nervously as he recalled her threat, what else could explain what he'd seen?

There was just no getting around it, he realized. She was here, and if her big mouth had been trouble before, that was nothing compared to what it might turn into now, because the manslaughter he'd been convicted of was bad enough.

But if she opened her mouth to tell what'd really happened, well, that could be a whole lot more trouble. First-degree-murder trouble, because she could reveal—in fact, she was the *only* one who could—that he'd been planning it before he did it.

Threatening her, describing it to her, how he'd do it, what he'd do and why. And she hadn't dared leave him, either, since by then she'd figured out a few things.

About her parents' deaths, for instance: both accidental and un-witnessed, one right after the other. And that wild animals, in season or out, weren't the only things Dewey knew how to track.

That he could track *her* . . . Yeah, he'd scared her, all right. Shut that mouth of hers . . . just not quite enough, apparently. Not *perma-nently* enough. So now . . . now he'd have to finish the job.

When he figured he was far enough from the cottage to risk it, he snapped on the penlight he'd filched from one of the cars he'd stolen just after his escape. The woods appeared around him, spooky and silent, like ghosts of trees in a haunted forest.

No doubt she was pretty mad. No doubt she would do what she could to hurt him, just as she'd promised.

No doubt she'd tell. And although he didn't intend to get caught—he planned to stay in the woods for a while, then sneak across the bor-der to Canada—if he did get sent back to prison, she could make sure he stayed there for the rest of his life.

Because dead or alive, he knew people would believe her. You couldn't see that face and *not* believe. . . .

Then it hit him. Of course; the answer was simple. He only wondered why he hadn't thought of it sooner; man, being in jail had messed him up, head-wise. But his frown changed to a smile as he sauntered a hundred more yards down the dirt road, nearly to the place where the unfortunate hiker from the city had ended up.

Dewey had dropped out of the dead tree like a bag of rocks, piggy-backing the guy before he knew what hit him, the shock on the guy's face barely getting time to change into something else before his ex-pression faded entirely. There'd been food in his pack and money in his wallet, though Dewey hadn't taken it all in case someone might think an empty wallet looked suspicious.

After that he'd clothed poor old Bentley Hodell decently and arranged both bodies by the edge of the nearby stream that ran to the beaver pond; that way, both land- and water-dwelling animals could get at them.

Flesh eaten, bones gnawed and scattered . . . in a short while it would be almost as if neither of them had been here at all.

Or so Dewey had thought. Instead, those two meddling women had unblocked the culvert. He hadn't dared stick his head up to see them doing it, but he'd heard them; worse yet, before Dewey could scramble back to undo the body arrangement he'd worked so hard on, the sudden draining away of so much water had collapsed the stream's soft bank. After that, an upstream blockage of sticks and leaves washed in by the recent heavy rains had given way, and the next thing Dewey knew . . .

Damn, Dewey thought, fingering the rabbit's foot he'd found in Bentley's pants pocket and shrugging Bentley's warm jacket up around his shoulders. Squinting in the penlight's thin glow, he searched around by the side of the dirt road for the place he'd seen earlier . . . *there.*

Then, stepping carefully in the gloom, he sank into a bed of leaves and pine needles, where he settled down in relative comfort. This was a lot better than getting into that damned body bag, back at the prison; closing his eyes, he let his mind drift.

Slipping out through the loading dock and into the ambulance had taken a mere thirty seconds. It was the only time he'd been worried at all about getting caught, but just as he expected, the guard and the ambulance guy sneaked out into the driveway for a smoke instead of sticking to the rule: no door or gate unlocked without a guard standing ready by it.

But then, jeeze, what a fright he'd had. Because the thing he hadn't thought of while he was planning was that there was no room in the coffin for him and the dead guy together, because there was no coffin. Instead it was a body bag they'd shoved the guy into, and Sonny Sawtelle was a big guy, not an inch left to spare. So Dewey had needed to improvise on the spot:

While the guys were still smoking and yakking at the far end of the row of Dumpsters, he'd lugged the dead body to the nearest of the big metal bins and rolled it in. A soft thud was the only sound as the body landed in heaps of food waste, paper from wastebaskets, and who knew what else.

In the next moment, Dewey trotted back to the ambulance, hopped in, and zipped himself into the bag. After that and a ride in the ambulance—that's what they used at the prison, not a hearse—getting out of the hospital morgue had been a snap; who worries about an escaping corpse?

One car stolen out of the hospital's parking lot, a panel truck from Portland, finally a mommy van with the keys hanging in it outside a convenience store in Scarborough and bingo, he'd laid a trail of breadcrumbs for them to follow.

All the vehicles had some money in them: change, a few stray dollar bills. Food, too, and to his delight the mommy van had contained a nearly full fifth of vodka plus the orange juice to go with it.

Finally, after cutting his hair and shaving—the panel truck had been loaded with health-and-beauty products bound, he supposed, for supermarkets and drugstores—he'd poured the vodka into the orange juice and brought it along with him, on the bus back up here to his familiar stomping grounds in downeast Maine.

Easy-peasy. And taking care of the Marianne problem was going to be equally trouble-free, he reassured himself as he settled to sleep. The only hard part would be making it look like an accident, so no one would realize he'd been here at all.

But a night's rest and a little more thought, he felt sure, would take care of that. Breathing in the cool night air—*free* air, he realized, luxuriating in the smell of damp leaves, pine sap, and the dank mineral fragrance of the nearby lake—he gazed up at the sky through an inky-black lacework of bare branches.

He would come up with a plan, a simple plan that would work flawlessly, the way he'd done getting out of prison. And then—

Without warning, Marianne rose before him once more, against his closed eyelids: tall and slender, her wavy red hair softly glowing in the lamplight, warm and alive.

Alive, alive, oh . . . Dewey shuddered, his memories of Sonny's corpse all mingled up dreadfully with this phantasm, this . . .

This impossibly living *thing* she'd become. And however she'd managed it, there was only one thing to do about it.

He'd just have to kill her again.

"Hey! Hey, buddy, are you all right?"

Sam Tiptree blinked startledly as fingers snapped in front of his face. "Huh? Oh, yeah . . ."

Sitting at a table in the Rusty Rudder café in Eastport, he shook his head to clear away the fog of daydreaming that had overcome him. Night-dreaming, rather; evening came early here in autumn, and although it was only 6 p.m., outside the restaurant's big plate-glass front window, it was dark.

"Yeah, I'm fine," he told the pair sitting with him: Richard Stedman, owner of the ill-fated *Courtesan,* and his beautiful sister, Carol, had insisted on bringing him here to express their gratitude for his help—and their contrition over nearly getting him killed—by buying him dinner. They'd both gone back to their motel rooms to change clothes while he finished up at work.

So now Richard wore a loosened silk tie with a collared shirt and blue blazer, his sister an elegant long tunic-type thing over leggings and metallic sandals, and even in decent chinos and the clean sweatshirt he'd pulled on, Sam felt seriously underdressed. Under-everything, in fact, with these two elegantly turned-out young people he'd somehow fallen in with sitting across from him.

"What you need," Richard pronounced, "is a drink."

"Uh," Sam began, but before he could go on, Richard had done whatever it was that made waiters appear at his side as if by magic, ordered a double gin-and-lemon—"It'll fix you right up," Richard declared as Sam went on protesting—and whisked his hands in a "done and dusted" gesture as the waiter scurried off.

From across the table, Carol smiled and reached over to touch Sam's wrist briefly, a touch that lingered warmly on his skin. "Poor Sam. Take it a little easy on him, Richard, he's not used to us."

Her eyes twinkled confidentially at Sam in a way that made him think that maybe he could simply tell them, just blurt it out the way he always did: "I don't drink."

But somehow the moment passed. He looked around at the familiar dining room, glimmering with candlelight elegantly reflected in silver and stemware. Rarely anymore was he envious of people who could drink alcohol.

But he was now. "So, Sam, what's fun around here?" Richard asked.

Sam felt Carol's eyes on him as he fumbled for a reply. A minute ago Richard had been holding forth on the latest actions of the Federal Reserve, while Carol had mentioned the book she was reading, an eight-hundred-page novel that was all the rage, apparently.

Sam felt thick and stupid by comparison. He got up. "Uh, I'll be right back." Crossing the dining room, he continued past the guitarists playing jazz tunes near the hostess station, and on into the bar.

Instantly a feeling of déjà vu came over him. "Hey, Tony," he said to the bartender, "leave the booze out of mine, will you? And be quiet about it?"

He put a five on the bar. But Tony, an old buddy of Sam's from high school, shoved the bill back toward him, not missing a beat as he mixed a trayful of martinis.

"No prob, guy, I've already gotcha covered."

Relieved, Sam stopped in the men's room, washed his hands, and eyed himself in the mirror over the sink. He looked haunted, as hollow-eyed as if he'd been out on a bender last night instead of home in his own bed.

Nah. Never happened, he told the guy in the mirror. But the guy in the mirror knew better: *Oh, yes, it did. You don't want to believe it. But it most definitely did.* He returned to the table just as the waiter set down his virgin gin-and-lemon.

"You okay, Sam?" Richard asked again, and Carol tipped her head in concern. She'd taken her glossy, dark hair out of its elastic for the evening, and now it moved on her shoulders in a smooth, near-iridescent wave.

"Yeah, fine," Sam said, taking a sip of his drink. But he wasn't. Six hours earlier, after he had seen whatever it was he'd seen down in that bilge—

You know what it was. Or rather, who *it was.*

—he'd woken, flat on his back on the dock. Peering down at him had been five worried faces: the three Nathans, their big ugly mugs pale with concern, and behind them Richard and Carol. Richard had been in the act of calling for help on his cellphone.

But when Sam sat up, then got to his feet shakily, Richard had put the phone away. Now Carol smiled at him, touching his hand again with her cool, neatly manicured fingertips.

"It was all I could do not to kiss you when I found out you were okay," she said sweetly.

Sam felt a blush climbing his neck. "Uh, yeah," he muttered stupidly, swallowing more lemonade to cover his confusion.

On the dock, she'd let him alone while he checked himself all over, finding no serious injury other than the bump on his head. The

Nathans had backed off, too, so Sam could walk around getting his legs back under him. At the same time, he'd eyed the trailer with the winch mounted on it and figured out what must have happened.

"Guess my idea wasn't so great after all," Richard said now a little shamefacedly, sipping his martini. "I thought bashing those holes in her stern would lighten her up enough, but . . ."

"Yeah." Sam spread his hands in a "who knew?" gesture. The hauling equipment had simply been unequal to the massiveness of the task: the winch line, overloaded by the weight of the boat with a lot of water still in it, had snapped.

"Lucky it didn't take my head off," Sam added. A piece of the winch cable with a heavy steel clip attached to it had flown like a wrecking ball. Only the fact that he'd been crouched down, peering into the flooded bilge, had saved him.

"Live and learn," he added. *But I should've checked,* he thought again as the food came: steak for Richard, baked haddock for Sam, and for Carol a plate-sized lobster pizza loaded with claw meat, which she immediately began devouring, the pleasure of the good food evident on her cherries-and-cream complexion.

I should've checked all the equipment. It was, after all, his job. "Hey, Richard, I just want to apologize again for—"

But even though *Courtesan* had sunk like a rock and was now lying on her side underwater awaiting a crane big enough to lift her, Richard wasn't having any of it.

He drained the rest of his martini. The Rusty Rudder had great martini glasses, large and thin stemmed. Sam took another gulp of his lemon drink.

"Look, man, I was the one who scuttled her, okay? It was my bad, not yours," Richard assured Sam as Carol leaned forward in earnest agreement.

"You did everything you could. I mean, gosh, you nearly got killed." Outside, evening fog turned the dark street to a smeary palette of headlights and neon-sign colors. In here, though, it was bright and warm, good smells of food and candles sweetening the air; Sam didn't know why he felt so chilled.

Maybe he was coming down with something. Or maybe he'd hit his head harder than he'd thought when he fell. Suddenly the voices from the other tables seemed too loud, women screeching and the men laughing in great, swinish-sounding *haw-haw-haw*s.

Richard drank again, beads of moisture sliding down the side of his refilled glass—and how had *that* happened?—as his lips melted the frost. Sam got unsteadily to his feet. "I don't . . ."

Feel so good. But why? He'd watched other people drink lots of times before, and he'd been sober for so long it didn't bother him. It was a kind of freedom, one he luxuriated in.

Until tonight. Because if ever there was a time when this virgin lemonade was absolutely not enough, it was . . .

Dimly, he was aware that Richard and Carol were looking up at him in dismay. The room turned slowly around him, then faster.

"I need to . . ."

Sam. Suddenly what he'd been trying not to remember in any detail slammed into him: that dead face with its bleached white eyes and howling mouth, swirling up at him like smoke up through a chimney out of the bilge of the good ship *Courtesan,* now sunk. As the memory assaulted him he staggered, nearly fell, catching himself with a hand flattened on the table.

He glimpsed the owner of the Rudder, wearing a striped apron and chef's hat, frowning from behind the grill, scrutinizing him. But he was too busy trying to maintain his equilibrium to correct the impression he must be giving.

Sam. Looking down into the flooded bilge, unable to believe his eyes . . . it had been his father's face in the sloshing filth down there, his father's voice coming up out of the hole.

"I'm sorry," he whispered, feeling a cold sweat break out on his forehead. He tried a laugh, didn't manage it very well. His companions, anyway, weren't the least bit fooled.

Richard pulled a credit card from his wallet, signaled to the waiter.

"I think you might've hit your head harder than we knew," he said. "I think you need to go to the hospital, now."

"No!" They drew back, shocked at his vehemence. "I mean, no, thank you," he amended faintly, still seeing the drowned, white, oh-so-*familiar* face in the black water.

He forced a smile. "I need some air. You two stay and eat."

"Nonsense." Carol crumpled her napkin and flung it onto the table. "You're not going anywhere alone. If you want air, you can get it by taking me for a walk."

The waiter returned with the credit card slip, which Richard signed without looking at. "Better go along with her, buddy. She has a habit of getting nasty when she doesn't get her way."

But he grinned when he said it, and Carol was smiling so charmingly and persuasively that Sam couldn't argue with her.

"And anyway," she said, taking Sam's arm and squeezing it in a sweet, confidential way that utterly finished him off, "I've already eaten half of that pizza. I'm *such* a little food hound."

Feeling her slim form against him, Sam didn't think it could be true. Maybe the heat and energy she radiated used up calories, he thought distractedly as he let her usher him into the rainy night.

Why the hell was my dead father yelling up out of a hole at me? he wondered. *Did he want me to duck, the way I did, or stay and get my head taken off by that flying metal cable? And was I really about to steal a swallow of Richard's martini just now?*

He didn't know which of those questions he might dislike the answer to more, the one that suggested he'd better start going to a lot more AA meetings, or the one that suggested he was losing his marbles and should find himself a psychiatrist, toot sweet.

What you'd really better do, buddy, is go and check on your mother, up at that cottage.

And where had *that* idea come from? His mother had said she wanted to be alone at the cottage, and she was fine there.

Of course she was . . . wasn't she?

CHAPTER 6

You can add ceiling trim to any room easily with pre-cut molding pieces, finishing nails, and paint.
—Tiptree's Tips

Long before dawn the next morning, the chuckling percolator sent coffee smells wafting under my nose, luring me from my nest of blankets. Ellie crouched by the woodstove, feeding thin-split lengths of maple into its glowing maw.

"Rise and shine," she said, noticing that my eyes were open. "Big day ahead; I guessed you'd want to get right to it."

"Ugh. You're awfully chipper." But she was right. Sunrise comes first to downeast Maine, but so does sunset, and in autumn the daylight ends shortly after 5 p.m. So if I wanted to get much done, I needed to hop to it.

Also, there was still that newspaper column I'd promised to write. Thus far, I'd managed to suppress the whole idea of it, but that wouldn't last unless I had something occupying me.

Thinking this, I put my feet on the cold floor, then yanked them back up under the blankets reflexively. But before a yelp made it out of my mouth, Ellie was there with my slippers in one hand and a steaming coffee mug in the other.

"After we eat our breakfast, it'll be light enough to start," she said cheerfully.

I swallowed some more coffee. "Have you ever thought about getting your thyroid checked?"

She just laughed, meanwhile stirring pancake batter, wiping off all the gas lights' glass shades, sweeping up bark bits from in front of the woodstove, and pouring out two glasses of orange juice, all without even breaking a sweat.

Ellie believed that just because you were out in the woods with no proper electricity, no running water, and a woodstove that by the time it got the cabin warmed up, we'd have been outdoors working for a couple of hours—well, none of that was any excuse not to enjoy the little things in life.

Like, for instance, real cream for coffee, and orange juice freshly squeezed out of real oranges. "I brought a bag of them," she explained while I pulled on as many clothes as I could, as fast as I could.

She turned the radio on to Maine Public Broadcasting, which was running a local newscast; it was too early even for "Morning Edition."

"*. . . authorities say Hooper, who is believed to have stolen a series of vehicles during his escape, could by now have gotten as far south as New York City. . . .*"

"Good," said Ellie. "Let them have him." She dished out the pancakes, having of course set out real butter and a pitcher of real maple syrup to douse them in. Breakfast isn't ordinarily my favorite meal, but this morning I ate like a starving person.

Cottage life will do that to you, I'd found. Outside, the sky turned from black to marine blue. Branches, some with leaves clinging to them, materialized against it. Ellie had heated water, so we did the dishes, rinsing them with the steaming kettle from the gas stove, and then we went out into an early morning so coldly clear, it shocked me instantly the rest of the way awake.

"All right, now," I said, privately not as sure as I wanted to appear that I could do this at all. Our first task of the day was to dig the foundation hole for the stair rail's bottom post, but before that I had to locate the hole, measuring straight out from the deck to a spot just left of where the bottom step would end up.

And this, using only a tape measure, string, and a T square to find the right angle—needed to make the stairs run straight out from the deck instead of some other cockeyed direction—was a tricky task. An hour later, though, after only a few backtrackings and remeasurings, we'd X-marked the spot with a squirt of spray paint.

Next came digging, which in downeast Maine is best done with (a) a backhoe, or (b) nitroglycerin. But all we had were two shovels and a pry bar, so by the time we'd finished excavating a hole deep enough to sink the post in, I felt ready to be buried in it myself.

Fortunately, Wade and I had already poured a concrete block, setting a metal bracket into it before the concrete hardened; all I had to do was sit the post down into the bracket, then drive a few nails through the bracket's holes and into the post.

"Okay!" said Ellie when we were finished. "Now let's go to the gravel pit."

Because of course once the post was on the block and the block was in the hole, the hole had to be filled again. And it had to be with something heavy, so the block with the post fastened to it wouldn't shift. Which meant gravel: dug, hauled, and shoveled into the hole atop the block . . .

I laid down the pry bar that we'd used to lever boulders out while we were digging. What I wanted to do was smack myself in the head with it a few times, since if I knocked myself out maybe my back would stop hurting.

But Ellie was here to help now, which was why we were doing all this heavy work before I tackled the decking or the step building. "Tell you what," I bargained. "How about first we take a look at that culvert again? See if the road crew's there yet."

If they were, Ellie would be going home after lunch, a good-news/bad-news situation for me. I'd certainly gotten a lot more done with her here than I would have without her; on the other hand, if she stayed much longer they'd be laying out my dead-of-exhaustion corpse on that new deck.

Ellie rode silently as we trundled along in the truck. "You all right?" I said at last. There was always the possibility that she was tired, too, I supposed. But it wasn't likely.

"I'm fine," she said and sighed. "It's just . . . well. It's still that thing about Dewey Hooper," she admitted.

We were nearly to the culvert; I pulled the truck over and we got out. The day had dawned clear, but now dark thunderheads were mounding stealthily again and a sneaky breeze rustled the cattails around the beaver pond.

"I wish I'd . . . I don't know," she began again. "I didn't know Marianne. There was nothing I could've done about her. Or that you could've, either," she added, seeing my face.

"Maybe not," I admitted. Marianne had been very stubborn. "But I know what you mean. It feels like I should have, somehow."

Ahead, the dirt road ran fairly undamaged over the culvert, except for the one deep crosswise channel the flood had cut. Tire tracks on the far side of the channel showed where Bob Arnold and the Calais cops had parked to retrieve the body we'd found.

The road surface itself was still soft and wet, and the guys whose job it was to repair it had not yet arrived. The pond itself was nearly full again, the culvert as crammed with branches and clots of mud as if it had never been opened.

"The beaver must've worked overtime," I said, hunkering down to peer into the culvert pipe. Across the road, Ellie looked into the other side.

"Not even a trickle," she reported, glancing uneasily at the sky where more clouds gathered. "And if it rains hard again . . .

"Then the pond will flood again, and the road will wash out even more this time, gravel or no gravel. Ellie, look at this."

She came over to crouch beside me.

"See all the grass clumps stuffed in there, like chunks of turf?"

"So? Beavers use their claws to dig up . . . oh." She looked at me. "But those aren't exactly like claw marks, are they? More like—"

"A blade," I agreed. "Like the roots were dug with a garden spade or . . ."

A big knife, I didn't say as we looked at each other. But it was what those marks suggested.

We got up simultaneously. Not twenty-four hours earlier, a dead body had been lying a few feet from where we stood. A chill that had nothing to do with the breeze went through me.

"Ellie, you don't suppose . . ."

"That the hiker got killed by somebody, and that somebody is still around here stuffing mud and sticks into the culvert, maybe as part of a plan to try killing us, too? Murder by beaver pond, for no reason?"

She knew me and my sometimes convoluted thought processes too well. When I didn't answer, she tipped her head skeptically, hands on hips. "You know, I think I'll just stick with the he-fell-and-hit-his-head theory, okay?"

Right again. And the thing was, she *was* absolutely right: it was a ridiculous notion. For one thing, it was a pretty dumb way to try killing somebody (even if you did have a motive, which as far as I knew no one had one of those vis-à-vis us). You'd have to make sure your victim was here by the pond when it flooded and couldn't just run away, and—oh, all sorts of sensible reasons.

Also, it's not as if I were a nature expert, able to identify beaver claw marks at ten paces. Probably the industrious little animals had filled the culvert again, and the straight cut-marks were made by the edges of their strong, flat tails, or something; they were well known to be fast builders.

Besides, Ellie was halfway to killing me herself; all she had to do was work me a little harder. Speaking of which:

"So, while we wait for the road crew, how about we hit that gravel pit? I tossed two shovels in back," she added helpfully.

Great, so I couldn't have the position I so dearly aspired to, that of nonworking supervisor. Five minutes later we were bouncing downhill in the pickup, following a dirt track into a huge, roughly circular depression in the earth, about three hundred yards wide and twenty or so feet deep. Its floor was of sand, rocks the size of my fist, and pea gravel: lots and lots of gorgeous, multihued natural pea gravel.

Which is, of course, pea-sized. Eons ago glaciers ground it down; then the glaciers melted to streams, depositing the gravel where water flowed. Where the dirt road ended, we stopped, jumped out, and got the shovels out of the truck bed.

I'd put a half-dozen big plastic buckets in the truck, for transporting the pea gravel, and some of the large black plastic basins that I used for mixing concrete, as well; there's no such thing as too much gravel, and if I had any left I could spread it around the clearing or on the path down to the dock. Lowering the truck's tailgate, we got to work digging shovelfuls from the wall of the pit, then hefting them up into the buckets and basins.

It was about ten-thirty by now, and the sun still peeping between the gathering storm clouds was as high overhead as it got this time of year; even though it was autumn-cool back up on the road, we began sweating almost at once.

"Oof," said Ellie, stepping back quickly as her shovel set off a mini-landslide in the pit's high wall. Above hung the half-exposed root ball of an enormous dead pine tree, its trunk rotted out so I could look up and see the sky through it.

"Be careful." Another loose bunch of stones and soil rattled down. "I don't want to have to dig *you* out," I cautioned.

But she wasn't listening, her eyes widening in alarm as she dropped her shovel and dove at me, hitting me waist-high. As her momentum knocked me backwards I had just enough time to see that pine tree's root ball barreling downhill at me, carrying with it an enormous avalanche of boulders and gravel.

My head hit the truck's rear tire. My shovel went flying, an edge of its sharp blade just barely not taking my ear off. The roar was amazing, like a jet plane revving its engines a few feet away, and so *fast;* ten seconds later, it was over.

"Ugh." I was on my back, Ellie half on top of me. Pushing up on my elbows, I saw she was unhurt; checking my extremities and noticing that they moved, I figured so was I.

And then I saw the wall of the gravel pit. Or rather, where it had been. Now a house-sized mound of sand, gravel, and stones was heaped atop the fallen tree where the wall had come down.

A dead, crooked branch stuck up out of the heap like a giant skeletal finger; my stomach lurched at the thought of how close we'd come to being impaled by it. *Buried* and impaled . . .

Ellie got up, brushing sand from her clothes. "Whew," she said, which I thought was an understatement.

"Um, yeah," I agreed, not wanting to sound like a wimp.

But when I clambered to my feet, my legs felt as if my bones were dissolving, wobbly and loose. Around us, the gravel pit was as silent as the tomb it had so nearly become.

There'd been no warning. We must've loosened the gravel with our digging until at some point the weight above exceeded support from below. It was a known hazard in gravel pits, but until now I had never realized just *how* hazardous.

"How'd you know that was coming?" I managed, crossing the stony expanse of the pit floor for the shovel, which my outflung arm had hurled twenty feet.

Ellie stood by the truck, looking up past the dead pine tree that the avalanche of gravel had brought down and nearly covered. "I didn't. I heard something and when I looked"—She made a downward-sweeping motion with her arms—"it was already on its way." Picking up her own shovel, she turned to the fresh gravel, now conveniently near the bed of the pickup truck.

"At least now we don't have to carry it so far to get it into the buckets," she said, and began digging again.

Right, and if it had buried us both completely, I thought, at least no one would have to dig our graves. But it hadn't, and half an hour later we'd loaded enough.

As we drove back to the cottage, the wilderness was full of sounds: crickets chirping, woodpeckers rat-a-tatting, the rush of a rising breeze chattering in the dry leaves and clicking brittle branches together. Glancing back at the culvert, I noticed that in the little time since we'd seen it last, the pond had already risen back nearly to the level that it was before the flood.

"You're *sure?*" Wade Sorenson put both big hands flat on Bob Arnold's old gray metal office desk and leaned over it intently.

Not for the first time, Bob felt glad that Wade was one of the good guys. "Well, let's see, now," he replied. "Guy goes into the woods with no more idea what he's doing than I would have if I stepped out onto the moon."

Wade looked skeptical, but he kept listening. "Wrong gear, wrong clothes, wrong time of year," Bob went on. "No cellphone on him, either, no way to call help if he gets in trouble. Next thing you know, he turns up deceased. That surprise you a whole lot, does it?" he asked.

Reluctantly, Wade shook his head. "No," he admitted. "City people don't realize how it is, way back in there. Dead when he hit the water, the M.E. says?"

For the past twenty hours, Wade had been out on a tugboat helping bring in a freighter. So he'd just learned about the body Jake and Ellie had found, and of course he didn't like it.

To put it mildly. "Yup," Bob said, glad he could answer with certainty. Because they didn't know where the death site was, an autopsy had been done right away, just to make sure an accident really was all they were dealing with.

"Victim had a heart attack, it turns out. Must've been by the water when it hit him, he fell forward onto a rock, smashed his face up, and *splash*—so sayeth the autopsy report, anyway, and I think I'll just go ahead and believe it, if that's okay."

That, at least, seemed to pacify Wade, whose problem Bob understood. If Wade rushed on up to the cottage to check on his wife, Jake, she might feel that he was patronizing her, as if he thought she couldn't take care of herself.

But if he didn't go, he'd keep on feeling that he should've. "Give her a call, you want to know for sure everything's okay," Bob advised just as his own phone rang.

"Yeah," he answered it, recognizing the caller ID number. As he listened, he looked out through the big glass front door of the old Frontier Bank, on Water Street in downtown Eastport.

"So you got stiffed, huh? Yeah, I can come in and take a report." In a few days the police station would be moving to its new quarters, two blocks away in the refurbished A&P building. There he would have clean white walls, tiled floors, upgraded lights and heating, and an honest-to-God holding cell.

He supposed he ought to be happy about it. "But why don't I take a walk around town, first," he said into the phone, "and make sure your pair of deadbeats aren't still around? Maybe they haven't quite gotten out of town yet."

He listened briefly. "Good, then, I'll be by in about half an hour." But his caller wasn't done.

"Huh," Bob said again when the last bit of information the Rusty Rudder's owner had to say to him had been communicated.

The last, least-welcome bit. "Uh, listen," he said when he had heard it. "Wade's here, you want me to put you on speaker?"

He hated the speakerphone. Talking, it was like shouting into a cave, and listening was worse. But it had its uses, and now was one of them; at least he wasn't having to give the bad news.

"Wade?" said the restaurant owner, his voice thinly echoey, then went on apologetically. "Listen, you know I'm not one to say much about my customers."

"Right," Wade and Bob replied together. The Rusty Rudder owner never said word one about what his customers did, said, or consumed while they were in his establishment.

Or about them any other time, either, for that matter, and everyone knew it. "But Sam asked me to," he continued. "Couple years ago now, Sam came in and *asked* me. He made me promise him this, you understand?"

"Promise what, pal?" Wade asked patiently. Even on the tinny speakerphone, he and Bob could both hear the tension in the pub owner's voice.

"About drinking," came the reply. At this, Wade's blue eyes opened wider in surprise and his square jaw tucked down abruptly, as if he were reflexively rejecting what he'd just heard.

"He asked me, if I ever saw him drinking in here, to go to one of his family members. Right away, he said. So now I am."

"Well, now," Wade temporized, a clash of emotions clearly visible on his rough-hewn face. "That's fine, I mean, I'm glad he said that, and that you kept your promise, too. But are you sure he wasn't just sitting with people who were . . . ?"

"No. And that's the other thing," came the answer. "I just told Bob I had a couple of visitors in here with a stolen credit card last night. I didn't tell him, but I'm telling you, that's the pair that Sam was with."

The restaurant owner took a breath. "Drinks, dinner, the whole shebang, and now I got a guy in here, he says that card is his. Says he thinks he left it at the boatyard yesterday, credit card company called him late last night to say it was used, and was he the one who used it? Which he wasn't."

Worse and worse; Bob looked at Wade and shook his head wonderingly as the food-and-drinks man kept talking.

"See, when the card got used, the owner hadn't realized that it was lost yet, so he hadn't—"

"Reported it yet," Bob finished. "Yeah, I get it. But calm down, okay? Everything's all right, we'll straighten it out."

He hung up. It wasn't all right; in fact, it was pretty goddamned far from anything that was even anywhere near all right.

"Look, Wade, just leaving Sam aside for a moment . . ."

Wade glanced up. "What?" he snapped, but then his expression softened; he knew none of it was Bob's fault.

"Look, as far as Jake and Ellie being at the cottage goes, I know what you're really worried about, okay?" Might as well at least get that off the agenda, Bob thought.

"But Dewey Hooper's just a lowlife wife abuser who went too far, not some criminal mastermind. Also, turns out he was kind of nuts on the topic of the woman he killed, according to the prison guys the state police investigators are talking to. Obsessed with her, they say, and she's buried in New Hampshire where her sister lives now."

Bob took a breath. "They think he might be headed for her grave, down around Nashua. And besides, if he were around here, by now someone would've seen him and recognized him."

He got up, picked the telephone handset back up out of its base, and with the ease of long practice punched in the keystrokes that set it to forward calls to his cellphone. Then out of habit he checked to make sure the wires leading to his computer modem and fax machine were all plugged in securely.

Once he moved to his new office, he could say goodbye to the tangle of wires. In its place he would have high-speed broadband, and a new, much more powerful computer that could send or receive big files—crime-scene photographs, surveillance videos, and so on—without the machine crashing and having to be restarted just as the data transfer had nearly completed.

All of which was fine, he supposed, and he was grateful for the grant that had gotten it all for the city, and thus for him, because that was where the city council had decided to spend it. He'd taken it as a compliment, appreciating what he regarded as a vote of confidence.

But personally, he wasn't looking forward to the move a bit. He'd gotten used to this place, with the heavy brocade floral curtains at the high, arched windows, the marble counters, and the old carpet on the floor. Plus the vault came in handy for storing valuables, weapons, and contraband.

"Yeah, I guess Hooper wouldn't come back here," Wade said. "What I don't get, though, is how he avoided the cameras in the prison in the first place. I mean, being as we agree he's not the genius type."

Bob looked up from untangling one of the phone wires. "So you knew him?"

Wade shrugged. "Not really. Ran into him once or twice, and that was enough. Unusual type of guy, not that there's anything wrong with that."

"Right," Bob agreed. "Hell, half our upstanding citizens are unusual." He put a wry twist on the word. Way the hell out here in what the rest of the world thought was the boondocks, *unusual* was pretty much a requirement.

"He didn't strike me as a real smart fellow, though," Wade went on, still frowning over what he'd heard on the phone. "Smart enough to fool people whose jobs're not to *get* fooled, I mean."

State prisons ran surveillance cameras 24/7, and there was no way to disable one or otherwise thwart it without the attempt getting noticed by the officers watching the monitors' display. They glanced away once in a while, sure, human nature being what it was. But you still couldn't count on them doing it just when *you* were doing whatever it was you didn't want observed.

Like, for instance, escaping. "Right," said Bob. "No genius, and not very stable, either, according to the guys at the prison who ought to know. They were surprised he had the wherewithal to make a plan like he must've had, and keep it together."

"Yeah? Unpredictable, was he?" Wade asked distractedly. As he spoke he gazed out the bank building's front window to where a tugboat was pulling in at the fish pier, down the block and over on the other side of Water Street, in the harbor.

Sam wasn't there. "Nope," said Bob. "The opposite. And that, see, is what turned out to be his special talent."

Bob gazed around the old bank interior. "My understanding is that Hooper spent seven long years being a good little inmate who never gave anyone any grief."

Huge old double-hung sashes, each four feet high, sent thin, slanting October sunshine into the high-ceilinged room. Bob liked those windows, and particularly liked the bank's high, marble-topped counter that he could stand behind or emerge from behind, depending on whether the person who'd come in to talk to him was a serious visitor or just a run-of-the-mill pain in the butt.

"And the night he skedaddled," Bob went on, "he did all the things he ordinarily did, and no other things."

Except for slipping through the open bay door and into a waiting ambulance, of course. "He walked out into the fenced yard, and then he didn't show up again, but the guys viewing the monitors were so used to seeing his routine—emptying the trash in the Dumpster, for instance—that he'd become invisible, kind of."

Bob sighed heavily. "So they didn't notice when he really wasn't there, either, and it just happened to be that time, the *only* time when it really mattered, that the trash he was dumping was a dead body."

Bob took a breath. "Which he replaced in the ambulance with his *own* body, for long enough to get outside the fence."

Whereupon he had either jumped from the moving vehicle or somehow gotten out of the hospital morgue, and by the time anyone figured it out, Dewey Hooper was gone like a wisp of fog.

"Not that he was normal," Bob added. "Guards who knew him say all you had to do was look at his face an' you'd know he was going to blow up sooner or later. Guys get an expression, they say, doesn't look like any other facial expression, when they're getting ready to lose it. Medical staff, social workers . . ."

Sure, now they all said so, now when it was too late. But Bob didn't guess anyone would've listened to any of them before, anyway, institutional hierarchies being what they were.

"I guess that look was one more thing they got used to about Hooper," he said. "Which maybe was the idea in the first place."

Wade nodded, charitably not remarking on what a balls-up mess the whole situation had been. But then, he wouldn't; Wade wasn't the type to state the obvious.

Bob didn't quite know what Wade might do, though, with the information he'd just gotten from the Rusty Rudder's proprietor. Hell, he wasn't sure what to do with it himself.

He turned to Wade. "I remember Dewey. Arrested him many a time, drunk and disorderly and so on. He had the same look then. Our Mr. Hooper is the kind of guy gives the other 99.9 percent of unusual people a bad name. Hell, I knew it long before he did away with his wife."

Maybe not anything a psychiatrist could diagnose, but just the same . . . Bob felt uneasy simply remembering Hooper. "Come on, take a walk with me," he told Wade, getting up.

His old office chair let out a horrendous creak; in the new place, he would have all new office furniture, tables and file cabinets and bookcases that were on their way right now from the Office Depot in Bangor. Place was going to have restrooms, brand-new ones, and a locker room with a shower, even.

But he was going to miss that old chair. He'd take it with him, but he knew it wouldn't look right in the new place. That it wouldn't fit in; he wondered yet again if he would.

Outside, the sky was still blue but a new crop of huge, dark storm clouds lowered to the east; the weather of two days earlier was backing around for another whack at the coast. He crossed the street with Wade, between a pickup whose fenders were patched with silver duct tape and a Toyota whose inspection sticker was three months out of date; Bob made a mental note of the Toyota.

"The thing is," Wade said, "I bet Jake a hundred bucks that she couldn't finish the deck we've been building up there at the cottage. Now, if I go up there myself, if she's having trouble with it she might feel like I'm rubbing it in, and if she's not, she'll wish I'd waited so she could surprise me with how well she did it."

"And if you tell her what you just heard about Sam, she'll be upset, but if you don't tell her . . ."

"Yeah. That, too," Wade agreed. "Man, and this started out to be a good day, you know?" he added as they walked on.

Past the granite riprap that formed a wall along one side of the walkway running along the edge of the harbor, the tugboat *Ahoskie* bobbed gently at the fish pier, her crisp, new blue-and-white paint job making her resemble a child's bathtub toy.

"Yeah, well," Bob said. "That's women for you. Damned if you do or if you don't."

Which wasn't really what either of them thought, just shorthand for how dumb a guy could get to feeling sometimes, not knowing what to do. Bob tried to remember when he hadn't felt that way about something or another, and couldn't.

On their right, Passamaquoddy Bay spread blue and calm. Too calm, Bob thought, its surface glassy-flat. He made another mental note, this time to put a deputy in a squad car on the end of the cause-way later if the weather really did blow up again.

Between nabbing speeders and reassuring everyone else of a police presence, a cop visible in a storm was smart, safety-wise and politically. After all, having the city council on his side now didn't mean he wouldn't do or say something unpopular later.

In fact he almost certainly would. At the end of the walkway stood the small, white wood-frame *Quoddy Tides* building, where the eastern-most newspaper in the U.S. was published, and next to it a terraced perennial garden rising up to sidewalk level. The garden was a com-munity project, miraculously unmolested by local youngsters; *so far,* Bob thought with a realism born of long-term experience. All it took was one dumb thug, but so far, so good.

Past the garden they turned left, onto Water Street between the granite-block post office building and a long row of red-brick, two-story commercial buildings with fancy galleries and art shops on the first floors, apartments above.

The shops were all closed, now that the tourist season was mostly over, and the apartments soon would be. With a view of the water out the back windows and lots of exposed brick inside, they were charming in summer. But in the winter with the wind blowing, you might as well try heating a lobster trap.

Bob glanced at each one of the doors to make sure none of the locks had new pry marks on them, then stopped, scanning the length of the street. Eastport in the off-season was another kind of place entirely: less noise, less activity.

Less of everything, including money, and when budgets got tight the copper pipes had a way of disappearing out of vacant buildings. So all winter he'd be checking those doors regularly.

"Listen, Wade," he began, taking an inventory of the street. But no unfamiliar faces or strange cars were in sight; so much for nabbing the credit card crooks before they left town.

Wade looked out across the water, the muscles in his jaw twitching as a series of emotions chased one another across his face. Sam Tiptree's triumph over his own demons had nearly killed him. But he'd beaten them, or at any rate wrestled them to a draw.

Until now. "It's a symptom," Bob said. "Of the disease. Not a disaster." A relapse, he meant, of the kind Sam had apparently had.

"He'll be okay," Bob went on. "You all will be." Being a small-town cop was the only job he'd ever wanted, but sometimes it was the pits.

Wade squared his shoulders. "Yeah. All right. Guess I'll be on my way, then. Better track the kid down now, before his mom comes home and hears about this."

Clearly the phone call to Jake, much less a visit, had been put on hold. Wade would want to find Sam, find out what was going on and what he could do to fix it, before he broke the bad news.

They turned back down Water Street. "I'll keep an eye peeled for him, call you if I see him," Bob said as they parted.

Wade nodded, still looking distracted. Funny, Bob thought, how a couple of hours—less, in this case—could make all the difference. A little while ago Wade had been debating taking a ride up to the cottage, wanting to ease his mind about a wife-killing prison escapee who by all reports was actually about three hundred miles away.

But now if he didn't find Sam and get a handle on the kid's newly relapsed drinking habit—

Well, if that happened, the only murder Wade would have to deal with was the bloody murder his wife, Jake Tiptree, would start screaming when she heard about her son Sam's first alcoholic slip in a couple of years, last night with his new pals in the Rusty Rudder.

If at first you don't succeed . . .

Perched on a marshy hummock at the edge of the beaver pond, about fifty yards upstream from the culvert, Dewey Hooper wiggled the big log blocking the stream's flow.

He wasn't angry that his gravel-pit plan had failed. It was really no big surprise that his first attempt at killing the two women hadn't worked out quite right.

. . . *try again.* No doubt some witchy premonition of Marianne's had let them escape, and this only confirmed his opinion: that she was dangerous, and had to be put down permanently as soon as possible. Besides, the avalanche in the gravel pit had been a hell of a lot of fun to create.

This project he had embarked upon now was pretty enjoyable, too, actually. He wiggled the log again, finding it lodged very solidly there where it had floated and stuck. With its roots all still attached and wedged crosswise against the water's flow, it made an excellent dam.

But he could move it. If he wanted to, he could pull it out entirely. If he wanted a sudden flood, for example, just when the two women were driving over the culvert on a trip whose urgency he would also have to engineer . . .

But he could do that part easily. Six inches . . . he'd heard Bob

Arnold say that much flowing water was all it would take. After that, once their truck tires hit the drop-off by the edge of the road, the vehicle would roll over via its own momentum, into the drainage pond.

There was of course the small matter of the truck that was supposed to be coming, town guys set to repair the road. But Dewey had already taken care of that first thing this morning, by sneaking back to one of the houses he'd stolen clothes from.

Choosing one whose residents were at work all day—not a problem for a guy who'd been pulling burglaries since he was eleven—he'd used their phone to call the town offices. Claiming to be a local landowner, he'd said he'd repaired the flooded road himself, with gravel from the nearby gravel pit.

No need for any attention from the city crew, he'd said; no doubt the guys'd be glad to cross that backbreaking job off their list, and the clerk he'd talked to had agreed.

The one thing that bothered Dewey was that his voice had been shaking so bad when he made the call, he'd feared the clerk would know something was up. Nerves . . . hour by hour, it seemed, he was getting wonkier in the head, almost as if he missed his cell, the smooth featurelessness of it, and the safety of the prison's locked doors and enclosing walls. But that—Dewey shook himself angrily like a dog, to rid himself of it—that was crazy talk.

He would get over it. He wiggled the log again, careful not to dislodge it. Once removed, it would release lots of water, fast. Like a tidal wave over the road . . .

Around him the marsh was still, the surface of the pond he knelt by as smooth as if it were frozen solid. Overhead, clouds went on thickening, but he didn't care; after years in prison, it all felt like heaven to him. The whole thing was going to look like just some tragic, random act of nature, the kind of bad accident that happened sometimes out here in the woods.

The pond's surface began clouding intermittently with bursts of cold mist. No matter; soon he'd be warm and dry, and free of Marianne once more, too: her and the big-mouthed pal she had with her, that tattletale Jake Tiptree.

And after that, neither one of them would be running their mouths ever again. He got to his feet, stretched the kinks out of his back, and picked his way easily from one marshy mound to the next until he got to the dirt road.

Then, in the gathering dusk, he set off for the cottage the women were staying at, and for the last part of his preparations. In the near darkness he found where he'd hidden Bentley Hodell's shotgun, which had turned out to be in good condition despite the drenching it had suffered. Bentley had ammo, too, plenty of it.

And now so did Dewey. Ahead, the pale dirt of the road between the trees divided: one winding uphill, the other a narrow curving track through low huckleberry bushes. With the shotgun over his shoulder and the shells in his pockets, he chose the low path, alert for sounds and careful not to make any himself.

This next part could be tricky. Easing along in silence, not even breathing heavily, he came upon their pickup truck backed in among the huge white pines that surrounded the cabin. From the windows came a warm yellow glow, and a fire in the woodstove scented the air sharply, as it had the night before.

He sidled up alongside the truck until he reached its door. So far, so good. Both women were indoors; the dark-haired one doing something over the kitchen stove, Marianne sitting at the table, clearly visible through the window.

At the sight of her, his hard-won calm fled and an icy fury seized him. There she was, mocking him by her presence, every breath she took an insolent slap in Dewey's face.

She couldn't be alive. She *couldn't*. He'd killed her. And yet there she sat: a travesty, an abomination. And a *dangerous* one, because who else could testify better to the circumstances of her death than the victim herself?

So even though he knew what he was seeing couldn't be true, he just couldn't take the chance. She'd told him she'd come back, and she had; that was what he had to base his plans on.

Because Marianne was beautiful, and maddening, and oh, so dead; he'd felt that with his own hands. But she'd been *witchy:* the kind of woman who might really manage to return, if anyone could. And that . . . that could mean absolute disaster for him.

For one thing, if he could see her, then maybe so could the cops. She could go to them, start talking. Start *telling* . . .

He knew he couldn't be tried again for killing her. But he also knew enough about other people to feel certain that they would find some way of punishing him, even if the law couldn't.

By, for instance, trying him for the whole host of crimes he had committed while escaping, then sentencing him as harshly as possible for those. Everyone would be against him; Marianne would make sure of that, too. After all, she'd already gotten the hated Tiptree woman on her side, hadn't she?

Even though she was dead. Shuddering, Dewey didn't even want to think about what nasty magic she must've done to make herself look normal and alive. Because what she *really* looked like . . .

Well, after seven long years buried in her grave down there in New Hampshire, what Marianne must really look like by now couldn't be good.

Banishing the thought, he rummaged their toolshed swiftly, then worked the handle on the driver's-side door of the truck. Careful, careful . . . because the dome light in the truck was going to be a problem, and he had to deal with it now, while there was still some faint background illumination from the evening sky to dilute its glow. Otherwise if one of them happened to look out a window when he opened the truck door, the jig would be up. So:

Pull the handle until the latch clicked. Aim the shotgun at the dome light. Smash the dome light with the barrel's end. . . .

But when he opened the door, a dashboard light winked on. A chime began dinging; cursing silently, he lurched up into the cab to snatch the key out of the ignition, missing it on the first grab but grabbing it on the next.

Wrong, this was all going badly. . . . The dome light glowed, the end of the shotgun's barrel scraping but not breaking it; in a panic, lunging up, he shoved his bare fist into the light's plastic covering as hard as he could, shattering it.

Darkness. Silence. But the door of the cottage was already opening; no time to run. Gasping, he flung himself to the floor of the cab, yanked a blanket down over himself.

And waited. ". . . heard something?" one of them said.

Barely breathing, he listened as the women circled the truck and stopped on the driver's side. *Don't open the door,* he thought at them, aiming the shotgun from under the steering wheel.

Loading the weapon had been smart, in case of emergency. But what he wanted was for people to come later upon the scene of a tragic accident, not a double shotgun killing.

Not if he could help it. The driver's-side door opened a fraction; his trigger finger tightened. But at that moment from inside the cottage came a teakettle's exuberant whistle.

The truck's door opened a little more. The last light of the evening blued the gun's barrel. Then the door slammed shut again and he let his breath out, relaxing his grip on the weapon.

The women went back inside, closing the cottage door behind them. Slowly he pushed himself up off the floor of the vehicle, relieved; they hadn't noticed the broken dome light.

They wouldn't notice what he was about to do next, either, first to the driver's side, then on the other side; not until it was too late. A boom of distant thunder from somewhere to the east rolled through the night; a breeze rustled the pine boughs overhead and subsided for now.

By the time he'd completed his task with the small hacksaw he'd stolen from their shed and was slipping away unseen, the first cold spatters of rain were falling and thunder rumbled in long, rolling booms, approaching from the northeast.

Dewey's heart pounded. Without at all wanting to, he thought of his bed back at Lakesmith, the coughs and snorts of the other men in their cells all around him, the dull, featureless, utter predictability of the prison.

Warm, dry, safe. While out here in the free world . . .

Out here, it was going to be a bad night.

"I don't care," Bella Diamond insisted. "We should go up and check on them. Ellie should've been home hours ago."

It was past seven-thirty, pitch dark outside with another big storm brewing. Ellie wasn't answering the phone at her house, and Sam and Wade hadn't come home for dinner, either, all these being circumstances that put Bella's nerves on edge even more than they were already.

"Why should Ellie be home?" Bella's husband, Jacob Tiptree, inquired with his usual infuriating reasonableness. "No one else is home. George and the little girl won't be back till tomorrow."

He looked up from the pipe bowl he was carving from a beech burl, in the rocker by one of the kitchen's big, bare windows. A bolt of lightning split the night outside. "Maybe," he added with a touch of asperity, "all she wants is a little peace."

"Hmph," said Bella, bracing herself for a crack of thunder, and when it was over turned back to the stove, stirring the batch of spiced grape jam she'd begun making to try taking her mind off everything. But even the exotic smell of cinnamon and cloves mingling with the pungent grape aroma did nothing to ease her mind now.

Bella . . . The voice echoed in her head, and she couldn't stop seeing that face in the mirror upstairs, either, melting like a wax mask held over a fire, and so *familiar* . . .

Jacob was a long, lean man whose face, sweet and wrinkled as a winter apple, belied the hardness of the life he had led until coming to Eastport. Years ago he'd been a fugitive on account of some things he'd done, and some he hadn't; life on the run had kept him away from his daughter, Jake, and his grandson, Sam, for more than three decades. Then, just a few years ago, he'd found Jake once more, settled his law troubles, and married Bella.

So he had a family again, and now it was clear that all he wanted was a quiet existence, the daily doings of the extended household, and his whittling tools.

While she, Bella had to admit as she added sugar to the pot, was always spoiling for a fight. She pulled on an oven mitt to protect her arm from hot jelly splatters, and began stirring again.

"Why don't you just call them?" Jacob asked, removing more wood shavings from the burl he was carving. "Jake's got a cell."

The surface of the jelly moved sluggishly with the heat coming up through it. "Because she'll either not answer"—Jake had a habit of turning off her phone; Bella suspected it was to ward off calls like the one she was contemplating—"or she *will* answer, and she'll claim that she's fine whether she is or not. You *know* how she can be."

Stiff-necked, independent, stubborn . . . The old man frowned over a particularly tricky bit of his carving, not looking up. "Ayuh," he said.

The jelly came up all at once into a rolling boil; she set the stove timer and kept stirring, glancing out the window again as rain slashed the glass. "And where *are* Sam and Wade, anyway?" she fretted.

Jacob sat straight. "Listen, old girl, you've got yourself all worked up over nothing. Unless"—he peered closely at her—"there's more you're not telling me?"

Oh, but he was a wise one. Ordinarily, his perceptiveness might have comforted her, but now at his inquiry she felt herself closing up inside, tight as a clam. Women seeing ghosts, talking to them—and even worse, getting answers—might be fine in the stories on the television, the scary movies that Sam, especially, liked to see. But just try it in real life and the next thing you knew, Bella felt unhappily sure, your family would be setting up an appointment with the doctor for you, whether you wanted to go or not.

Bella had already talked to one doctor today. The trouble was that while she was talking to him, she could see through him.

Jacob put his tools down and set the burl with the half of a face carved into it—oh, why couldn't he carve something else for a change?—on the table beside him. He clasped his hands in his lap, sat back, and commenced rocking back and forth, back and forth, all the while mildly gazing at her.

Waiting. Not talking, not questioning or accusing. But he could, his expression and posture suggested, wait right there in the old wooden rocker until she told him what was bothering her. And he would, too, unless she spoke up about it this minute.

"All right," she gave in crossly when she had filled ten half-pint jelly jars with boiling-hot jelly, screwed the lids on, and turned them all up-side down on a clean linen dish cloth she'd spread for the purpose.

When the scalding jelly had been in contact with the insides of the jar lids for three minutes, killing any germs that might be there, she turned them right side up again. Soon each jar, wiped clean and set to cool on the fireplace mantel before being stored away in the butler's pantry, gleamed dark purple in the kitchen's lamplight like the old-fashioned jewel that it was.

And by that time, Bella was well into her story. She told him the whole thing, from the anxiety that had begun tormenting her weeks earlier to the final event that morning.

". . . thin air," she finished. Because that was how what she'd *seen* had gone *unseen* again: wispily, dissolving as if hinting it had never really been there at all. It was what she feared Jacob would believe, too.

But: "Well," he said slowly, then got up, plucking the keys to his old pickup truck from the hook by the door. "I don't suppose it would hurt to take a ride up there and check on them."

Outside, he took her arm. "We'll go just to ease your mind," he said, because he was much too levelheaded a man to believe in apparitions, warning or otherwise.

Of course he was. "All right," Bella said, reaching out for his strong arm again, holding even more tightly to it than usual as they went down the steps together into the rainy night.

Minutes later they were on the long, curving stretch of Route 190 that led to the causeway onto the mainland. Wind-whipped branches in the bare trees crowding in on either side of the pavement gleamed wetly in the headlights. Rain sluiced the windshield and the wipers fought to keep up.

Suddenly from between the trees a shape bounded, too fast for Bella to warn Jacob. She put her hands up reflexively, shrinking back from the animal already in the act of leaping.

Then came the crash.

"Oh, come on, Sam. It's not like anyone's going to know."

It was twenty-four hours since he'd had his woozy spell in the restaurant. Afterwards he and Carol Stedman had walked arm in arm all over town, under the streetlights and along the dark breakwater, drawing gradually closer until their shoulders at last snugged companionably together against the night's chill.

Companionably and a little more; only her brother's probable presence back at her motel room had kept Sam from pursuing a plan of perhaps going there with her himself.

And now, on the following evening, he *was* there and Carol's brother wasn't. Sitting cross-legged in the middle of the queen-sized bed at the Motel East, Carol held out her glass invitingly. But when he shook his head, her smile turned to a pout.

"I thought you were going to be more fun," she complained, draining the glass and reaching for the wine bottle on the bedside table, to pour herself another.

I thought so, too. But this whole thing had been a mistake, he saw now, maybe a big one.

"I don't understand," he said. What she'd just told him was stunning. "How'd you guys ever think you were going to get away with . . . ?"

Outside the motel room's big sliding glass doors leading to the deck, it was dark. He'd worked all day, driving to Bangor to pick up some parts a boatyard customer needed, then helping to install them.

After that, he'd come over here to pick her up; the plan was for the three of them to have dinner together once more at the Rusty Rudder, before the pair of siblings left town.

Richard was supposed to be here now, but he hadn't arrived yet. And while they waited, she'd unloaded this *information* on Sam, about them being con artists, her and Richard. Con artists, thieves . . . the list just went on.

Carol patted the bedspread. She was still very pretty, like a tennis star who modeled for a cosmetics company or something.

But now everything was different. He was so disappointed, he didn't know what to say. Scared, too, a little bit.

"Come on, get comfortable and have a glass of wine with me. It's not like it's whiskey or gin, for heaven's sake."

And when he still didn't move, "Boy, they've really got you brainwashed, haven't they?" She shook her head sadly, took a big swallow of the dark red, fruity liquid.

A drop leaked down her lip; she licked it away with the tip of her tongue. "That precious sobriety of yours must be pretty flimsy if one drink is all it takes to ruin it."

He'd had to tell her, of course. The night before, while they were out walking all over town until long after midnight, it seemed they'd discussed so many things, it had finally felt natural to confide to her that at one time he'd been pretty much the definition of a falling-down drunk.

A kiss or two later, it seemed, and they'd been at the motel, and it was only Sam's nervous feeling that Richard could show up again any minute to defend his sister's honor that had kept Sam from going in with her.

Now Carol glanced at him, so invitingly that he was sure it couldn't be a mistake, what he thought that smile promised. That dark, lustrous hair and sun-kissed skin, her red lips wet with the wine's grapey tartness . . .

"Sam." The clear-polished nail of her index finger engraved parallel lines on the motel bedspread. "Don't be mad at me."

"I'm not mad." He was, but he didn't feel like showing her that. "I'm just wondering what else you've lied to me about."

She looked coyly at him. "Well . . . how about that Richard's not coming? He's on his own tonight. Also, he's not my brother."

Confused, Sam sat on the edge of the bed. "But I thought—"

She leaned back against the pillows. "I know. It's just so much easier when we're traveling together, to let people think so. It gives them a story, one they can think they understand so they trust us more."

She touched his arm, idly letting her nail graze along it. "Until we know them. Until we know *we* can trust *them*."

The alarm bells going off in his head got a lot louder all of a sudden; still, he could barely hear them through the desire engulfing him. But when he turned his head, the mirror behind the room's dresser gave him his answer; who would know, indeed?

He managed a laugh, got up hastily before he could change his mind. "So you travel around ripping people off, basically. Is that it? Like Bonnie and Clyde, sort of?"

Her lips curved with the confidential sweetness that had so captured him the night before. "Uh-huh. And having adventures."

She sipped more wine, visibly savoring it, watching him.

But the moment had passed when he might have succumbed, and when she saw this, she put the glass down, slid off the bed.

At the mirror she picked up a hairbrush. "You were good at the boatyard yesterday," she said as she ran the brush through her hair. "Are you always so decisive?"

Apparently not, he thought. She'd put no hint of irony into the question, but he still felt the dig. Whatever invitation she had been extending was withdrawn, at least for now.

"Depends on the situation," he replied. "When things happen that fast, there's no time to think. I went on autopilot."

And nearly got my damn fool head knocked off, he thought but didn't add. Somehow he was beginning to believe that might be a frequent risk, hanging out with Richard and Carol.

"I still don't understand why you're telling me all this about yourself, though."

Through the sliding glass door, he could see the towering lights of a huge freighter sliding up the bay. At night, when all you could see were the lights and not the superstructure beneath them, these freighters' slowness was eerie and their size exaggerated by the optical illusion; it was as if the theme from *Close Encounters* ought to be playing.

"Why did you?" he repeated. "Tell me, I mean?"

The car they drove, he realized. The truck, too. All stolen. But not the boat; that, they'd almost surely had to pay cash for.

He wondered where they'd gotten the money. She laughed and leaned in toward the mirror to check her eye makeup.

"What can I say, we're criminals." Her reflection dared him to believe her. "We rob from the rich and give to the poor. The poor being us. And we wanted you to join us."

She batted her lashes comically at him, making fun of him and herself. "I did, anyway. Do."

"Come on." But he did believe her, and he couldn't help liking her self-mockery; she was good at it.

"So where's Richard now?"

She came over to him, barefoot and so pretty in her little red tank top and jean shorts. "Getting another car. He heard in the diner that the one we were driving might be trouble now."

"What, you mean the cops are looking for it? As in actively looking?" At this, the reality of what she'd been telling him washed over him with a shock, but she just nodded.

"It and us, actually." She cocked a hip, gazing pertly up at him. "So Richard ditched the car and he's getting a new one."

As she said this, another realization hit him: the credit card. They'd been talking about it that morning in the boatyard office just before he left for Bangor; a customer had called and said he thought his card had been stolen and used.

And Carol had been there in the office yesterday. "Sam," she said. Then, before he could do anything to stop her, she took his face in her two hands and kissed him, a rich, deep kiss that he did nothing to abbreviate.

"Oh," he said stupidly when it was over, feeling his heart thudding and his blood percolating.

Behind him the room's door burst open. A man stood in the doorway, which led straight outside. Sam could see cars going by, across the motel parking lot on Water Street. Suddenly he wanted to be out of there more than anything in the world.

But it was too late for that. The man in the doorway was Richard, Carol's brother or accomplice or whatever he was.

Richard didn't look happy. "We've had," he told Carol, "a change of plan."

And that thing in his hand, Sam saw with no real surprise at all . . .

That thing in his hand was a gun.

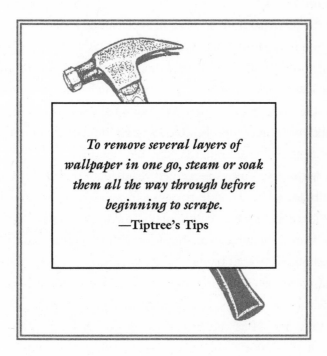

CHAPTER 7

*To remove several layers of
wallpaper in one go, steam or soak
them all the way through before
beginning to scrape.*
—Tiptree's Tips

Late on an autumn evening in a cottage in the Maine woods, the
floor is ice cold, while the stove is so hot that accidentally brushing up
against it raises blisters. And don't get me started again on the bathroom, located in another building entirely. Ours was large, airy,
freshly painted, and pine paneled, its door traditionally pierced by a
half-moon shape. With two windows and a stainless-steel washstand
like the one in an airplane restroom, it had a faucet that ran gravity-
fed cold water from a roof tank, or you could pour hot water from a
kettle into the sink.

In fact, except for the no-flush portion of the program, it was as nice as our bathroom at home: curtains on the windows, bright rag rugs on the floor. Decades-old *Reader's Digests* in the magazine rack harkened back to a time when "Humor in Uniform" wasn't yet an oxymoron.

But the place had one drawback: after sunset, a visit meant a brisk walk uphill in the dark via a path known for (a) its variety of tripping hazards, and (b) have I mentioned that it was cold and dark outside?

The walk back downhill, though, was enlivened by the cheery sight of the cabin itself, with yellow lamplight shining from its windows and the tang of woodsmoke hanging in the damp air. The starless sky suggested more rain to come, but right now we were between showers; a breeze sent pine-scented drops pattering down from the sodden branches as I made my way from the path to the clearing where the truck sat parked, and finally to the cottage door.

Ellie was at the table near the stove with her glasses on, frowning at her cellphone. "Dead battery," she reported.

I dug in the satchel where I kept necessities: ChapStick, a tube of hand cream, nail clippers, hair comb, Swiss Army knife . . . "Try this one," I said, and while she left a message on her home phone to say she was staying another night, I got out my to-do list, noting unhappily that fewer things were crossed off it than I had hoped.

Still, we had accomplished a lot: measuring, check, I noted mentally; digging, likewise. We'd gotten the concrete-block foundations lugged over and squared up in the holes, too, and filled them in with the gravel we'd hauled.

And finally, we'd enclosed the space underneath the deck by nailing up sheets of wooden lattice. The job was much easier when one person held the sheet in place while the other did the hammering, so I'd been eager to complete it while Ellie was still here to help.

But the road-repair guys had never arrived, and as a result, it seemed the lattice could've waited. "I could still drive you out to your car, though," I offered. "By now the road must've dried up a lot. We could get over the washed-out place if we were careful, and you could go home tonight."

"Forget it," Ellie replied, not even looking up.

That thumping we'd heard in the gravel pit, I now felt sure, had been the dead pine tree's enormous roots snapping one by one as the earth gave way beneath them, not someone trying to start an avalanche. But Ellie still wasn't so certain.

"I'll go if you will," she added. "But I'm not leaving you here alone."

Retreat wasn't in my plans, though; leaving aside the big bet I'd made with Wade, Bella's need for a little quiet time, *and* that newspaper piece I'd said I would write, I could just hear my family when they heard I'd been too scared to stay alone at the cottage. The phrase "never live it down" didn't even begin to cover the kind of razzing I would get.

And anyway, tomorrow I planned to put the deck's floor on, so in the evenings I could sit out there, and after that just the railings and steps would be left to finish.

If you could call that "just." "I ache all over," Ellie reported.

"Me too." It occurred to me that I ought to phone home, as well. It wouldn't kill me to let Wade know I hadn't thrown my back out by lifting the lumber or cut my arm off with the chain saw. Speaking of my back . . .

"Oof," I said, wincing as another twinge from my sacroiliac pulsed up toward my neck.

"Roger that," Ellie agreed with a grimace as she handed me the phone. "I never knew building a deck was so . . . exertional."

No one answered at my house, so I left a message saying I was fine; then, after another good dinner made by Ellie—fried steaks and mashed potatoes with canned butter beans, a veritable feast—we dosed ourselves with whiskey and two aspirin apiece.

An hour later we were tucked into the daybeds, propped up with pillows and wrapped in down quilts while the fire crinkled softly in the woodstove, and the radio, tuned to a jazz station out of Montreal, played old Dave Brubeck tunes and torch songs whose lyrics sounded especially good when crooned in French.

Rain tapped the windows; mice scampered in the walls before settling, finally, into the nests they'd made of old newspapers and torn-up insulation. A boom of thunder rolled and deepened; then another one nearer by. A lightning flash lit the lake, making skeleton arms of the tree branches and turning the water's surface briefly to silver.

Ellie looked up contentedly from her Kindle, a dandy little electronic gadget on whose bright screen she was reading an eight-hundred-page novel about life in suburbia.

Personally, I like paper books with bindings and cover art and different typefaces, and the smell all books have, even the bad ones, like a cross between libraries and print shops with a little bit of glue-scented perfume thrown in.

On the other hand, eight-hundred-page books are heavy, even if they are about life in suburbia, and Ellie's Kindle was light. Also, if she decided she didn't like the book, she could download some other one, even from way out here in the woods.

"Nice that the storm can't take our power out," she said a little drowsily.

"Yeah." From my snug nest of pillows and quilts in the daybed, I looked around through eyelids that I could barely manage to keep open. Only the intense pleasure of lying there not having to do a single thing kept me awake; it felt too good to end it by going to sleep.

"Solar power," she said and sighed. "It's fabulous." She'd had just a teensy bit more Bushmills than she was used to.

But she was right; in its wooden stand by the door, the small electrical converter that turned the sun's collected rays into something our lamps could use hummed quietly to itself. The solar-collecting panel was way uphill on the outhouse roof, next to the water tank, but even if the wires linking it with the cabin got torn down by high wind or falling branches, the battery we used for a power reservoir held plenty.

That meant we'd be fine for the night, or so I was thinking—a bit smugly, for it was a sizable storm coming, and here we were all this way out in the woods with no so-called modern conveniences, yet we were as snug as bugs in a rug, as Bella would've put it—when without any warning at all, the percussive boom of a shotgun being fired right outside was followed by a deadly sounding *crack!* and the bright, sharp tinkling of falling glass pieces as the windowpane by my head exploded inward.

At the same instant I felt a quick *zzt!* of pain in my right cheek, and the lamp on my table went out with a hot *pop!*

Ellie sat up fast. "What the—"

But before she could finish, another crash blew in, this one through the window behind her, and we were suddenly in the dark.

Very dark.

Sam spread his hands. "Hey, man," he began placatingly, but he could already tell that in his present mood, Richard Stedman was not to be reasoned with.

Richard was still aiming the gun at Sam from the motel room doorway, looking very different from the guy who'd accidentally poked a hole in his own boat the day before.

Then he'd been genial, friendly, and fumbling, a fellow who was trying hard but who was clearly out of his element. Now with the gun in his hand, though, he seemed comfortable: angry but calm, as if maybe this wasn't the first time he'd ever pointed a weapon at someone.

As if maybe he'd done it a lot. Sam turned to Carol, whose sweet, wholesome-appearing face was surprised but not nearly as shocked at the sudden turn of events as Sam would've liked. He put his hands up higher in what he hoped was a calming gesture.

"Look, Richard, I don't know what's going on here, but . . ."

Richard looked past him at Carol. "Get your stuff together."

He twitched the gun barrel unpleasantly at Sam. "You. Go sit down over there."

And when Sam didn't move right away, "Hey," he added, "you think I'm kidding?"

In three steps he was in the room with the gun's barrel up under Sam's chin. "I like you, Sam. I really do, you're a good guy. But things haven't gone well here. They just haven't."

Behind them, Carol was throwing things into a duffel bag. "And now," Richard went on, "we have to leave in a hurry."

The gun was a .38, the kind of weapon people had when they were in the habit of concealing the fact that they were carrying a gun at all. Sam knew that much from his stepfather, Wade, who was a firearms expert.

Also he knew that from where it was lodged right now, the gun would blow half his face off if Richard fired it, and the half face he'd have remaining would be useless to him because he would die of blood loss, in the unlikely event that the bullet hadn't bounced around inside his skull a few times before exiting the back of it, pulverizing his brain in the process.

That part he'd learned from his biological father, the late Dr. Victor Tiptree. *Thanks, Dad,* he thought sardonically at the long-dead brain surgeon. *It was just great of you to let a little kid like I was listen in on your shoptalk.*

He put a hand on the dresser to steady himself. "Richard, put the goddamned gun down, for Christ's sake."

Because that was the other thing Victor had taught him. Sam could hear his father even now, all this time after the man's death; all this time, too, after what seemed to Sam like a life on some other planet. Back then he'd been a surgeon's son living in a fancy apartment in Manhattan, wealthy and privileged and so spoiled, hardly anything that anyone said to him ever sank in.

But one thing had. He heard it again now: Victor's voice, explaining to his young son how he dared cut into a human being's head:

Sam, you can do a whole lot more than you think you can if you just never lose your nerve.

"Put the gun down," he repeated, and Richard appeared to be thinking about it while Carol went on hurriedly packing.

Just don't lose your nerve. . . . At the time, he'd thought his father's words were a license to drink and run wild in the big city, a nonstop search-and-destroy mission for a teenaged misfit.

But now . . . Slowly, Sam put a hand up to the weapon and pushed it away from his face. "Chill, buddy," he said.

Richard let the gun be moved. But when Sam took a step toward the motel room door, the weapon jerked up sharply again.

"No. I'm sorry, Sam. You can't leave yet. Over there."

Richard waved Sam to one of the chairs by the table near the sliding glass door. The big freighter had long gone by, and now all Sam could see were the tiny lights in the houses across the bay, on Campobello Island.

"So, what's all this about?" he asked. Carol hadn't looked at him since Richard arrived. She didn't now, either.

"Look, I just about got my head knocked off helping you with your boat yesterday." He thought for a moment, then added, "And I spent today working with the guys trying to get *Courtesan* off the bottom," he lied. "Which was a job that I notice you didn't stick around for," he added, hoping he was right and Richard hadn't.

Nothing in Eastport was big enough to lift the vessel, full of water and heavy the way she was, and there was no way to seal her off well enough to pump her out, either, especially with all those ragged holes Richard had unwisely bashed in her. So the boatyard had called in a rig that specialized in bigger jobs.

Its crew hadn't needed supervising—fortunately, since Sam had been on the Bangor errand. But now he figured he needed all the moral high ground he could get, and from Richard's face he saw that he'd guessed right in the you-weren't-there department.

"I don't understand why you wanted a boat at all," Sam went on, thinking *Keep him talking,* "if you're not interested enough to stick around for that."

Carol glanced pityingly at Sam. "You really don't get it, do you?" Then Richard spoke up again, impatiently.

"Hey, I bought it, okay? I didn't adopt the thing." He made a face as if Sam's question had been obtuse. "I wanted to see what it was like. We were here, there's plenty of water, I wanted to try it."

And now I don't anymore, his shrug added. *Easy come, easy go.* As if Sam had been stupid ever to think otherwise, which was what caused him to push his luck, to tweak Richard a little bit.

"Yeah, well, I hope you left your credit card on file at the boatyard. That salvage crew doesn't come cheap."

But then he saw instantly that he'd made a mistake; at the mention of a credit card, Richard's look darkened. *So that's what this is all about,* Sam thought. *The card, someone's already after them about it.*

Richard stuck his hand out; Carol took a roll of silvery duct tape from her duffel and tossed it to him without comment, as if they had done all this before, to someone else.

Maybe a few times, Sam thought. Or things like it. Richard himself looked different to Sam, too, his confidence more like impulsiveness, his energy a kind of jumpiness, an inability to be still. Richard had bashed those holes in *Courtesan,* Sam thought now, not to save her but because in his frustration, he couldn't stand *not* hitting something.

The one thing Richard did seem calm about was the gun, holding it in an easy, competent-looking way with his right hand as with his left he began wrapping the duct tape around Sam, securing him to the chair.

"You and your great ideas," Richard told Carol. "You had to go get a crush on Mr. Country Boy here." He wound more tape. " 'Ooh, he's cute, let's get him to come with us,' " Richard mimicked nastily.

In answer, Carol only huffed out a breath. When he finished wrapping the duct tape a dozen or so more times, Richard tucked the gun away, sliding it into the nylon shoulder holster that he wore under his jacket.

Sam let out a sigh of relief. In response Richard ripped off another piece of tape and slapped it over Sam's mouth. "Sorry."

Yeah, but not sorry enough. Sam wished intensely that his hands were free so he could show Richard just how very sorry a person could get. The clearest thought in his head at the moment, though, was gratitude: that somehow, he hadn't sunk so low as to have a drink with these people.

Or a drink at all. *Thank you,* he thought to whichever god had been in charge of granting him this bit of undeserved luck; he'd done everything but lie down openmouthed under a beer keg's spigot, he knew, to ensure having a slip.

"Last night at the restaurant, there was a wedding dinner," said Richard, apropos of nothing. "And do you know who's always at a wedding dinner, Sam?"

He turned slowly. "A photographer, that's who. And to get the candle glow in the pictures, the *atmosphere,*" Richard grated the word out, "he used available light. Which means no flash, and that means I didn't know *pictures* were being taken."

He turned to Carol. "Pictures of us. There's one taped in the window of the Rusty Rudder right now. So, are you ready?"

Hoisting the duffel, Carol indicated that she was. "Go on, get in the car, then," he told her. "Silver Saab," he added. "I found it with the keys in it, can you believe that?"

But when she'd gone, he paused once more. "Look, you seem like a nice guy," he told Sam, and then at the look Sam gave him in reply, added, "Yeah, and I'm not. But that's the thing, see."

Sam shook his head, to indicate that he didn't give a flying Fig Newton what Richard had to say. But Richard kept on talking:

"The thing about you is, you live in a fairy-tale world."

Yeah, yeah. The only thing Sam wanted out of Richard's mouth was his teeth, knocked out by Sam's fist.

"But out in the real world, it's not like here," Richard said. "So take this as a lesson, you know? You're too trusting. People here in East-port seem decent, from what I can tell—"

Yeah? And how would you know? Sam thought viciously at him. *All you did here was sink a boat.*

And what that had been all about, Sam couldn't imagine; just a whim, probably, something to pass the time. Another adventure, as Carol had put it, combined with another way to put something over on someone. Some guy somewhere was almost certainly counting stolen money at the moment, Sam realized, or trying to cash a bad check.

"So I can see how you might get the idea that most everyone is on the up-and-up," the man standing in the doorway said. "But away from here, out in the real world . . ."

Richard's voice took on a patronizing, let-this-be-a-lesson-to-you tone that Sam somehow found more infuriating than anything else so far. He hoped what showed of his face conveyed to this lying piece of scum that there were two men in this motel room at the moment, and the wrong one had duct tape over his mouth.

". . . in the real world—and it's important that you remember this, Sam—in the real world, there are real bad guys. Like me."

Richard walked out, closing the motel room door behind him.

Half a block away in his office in the old Frontier Bank building, Bob Arnold settled his duty belt loaded with his gear around his middle, which he noted ruefully was expanding again. He'd been living on Hungry Man frozen dinners and takeout since six weeks earlier, when his wife and daughter had gone to stay with his in-laws in Boston so the child could get treatment for her asthma.

The wheezing had been getting worse, despite everything that Maine doctors had been able to do for her. Bob was afraid the Boston specialists would end up recommending a warm, dry climate, someplace where the ice crystals didn't freeze in your nose hairs in late November and stay there until May.

Arizona, maybe, or the Southern California desert. All new crimes, all new criminals and informants, after a long career of being so familiar with all the crooks around here that if one so much as snif-fled at one end of town, Bob reached for a tissue at the other.

Not that he wouldn't have moved to Mars if it would help, but he didn't know how to make a living there, either. Policing, he reflected as he buckled his weapon into its holster, was like being a salesman; you had to know the territory.

Sighing, he pushed open the big glass front door of the old bank. By next week he'd be in the department's new quarters.

The thought, he admitted to himself as he stepped out into the night, depressed him. New facilities, new equipment . . . it all seemed to be shoving him toward an unwelcome realization: that he was up against new crimes and new, much more technology-savvy criminals, too.

More and more—with identity theft, electronic stalking, email scams, and who knew what other varieties of illegal stuff he didn't even know about yet—just rounding up the usual suspects was a thing of the past. Even this latest situation with the two credit card criminals proved it: nothing, not even Eastport, was as far off the beaten track as it used to be, and ready or not, criminal behaviors he'd never had to worry about before were now coming soon to a crime scene near him.

He inhaled a deep breath of the night air, smelling of the storm that was coming, the breeze laden with seaweed, creosote, and the french fryer bubbling in the kitchen of the Happy Crab sports bar, across the street. A plate of fried haddock would go good for dinner later, he decided; better than chef's salad with "lite" dressing out of a packet, that was for sure.

But for now, he'd take a spin around town before packing it in for the night. Calories must be what the Almighty put in food to make it taste good, he reflected as he got into the squad car, noting with sor-row the way his belly nearly touched the steering wheel; if his wife, Clarissa, were at home now, he'd be on his way to having dinner with his family.

Instead it would be another solitary evening of sports on the TV with the scanner on low on the coffee table, just in case. Thinking this, he drove up Washington Street past the post office and, straight across from it, the remodeled A&P building where his own new professional quarters would be, once he'd moved in.

As he drove he watched for young Sam Tiptree, who'd been at work today according to the boatyard guys but hadn't shown up here in town yet. Not that Sam was at the top of their worry list at the boat-yard; as if Bob didn't have enough to concern him tonight, there'd been a break-in at the yard's office just a few hours ago, and a whole lot of money was missing along with a customer's car.

Bob hoped Sam hadn't fallen off the wagon too hard; the kid had been sober for quite a while, and Bob would've bet by now that he wasn't going to fall off at all. So in the gloomy back of his mind he was beginning to wonder what else might've happened, and whether or not recent events–Sam's slip, the credit card thing, and the boatyard break-in–were somehow all connected.

That being another of the chronic side effects of small-town polic-ing: actually caring about what happened to the people whose welfare you'd sworn to guard. Turning left onto High Street past the old wood-frame city hall building with the flags–American, Canadian, and State of Maine–flapping in the floodlights in front of it, Bob won-dered if he would feel the same way about the people of Phoenix or San Diego, once he had gotten to know them.

Probably not. Eastport, with its saltwater-soaked air and its stub-born pride, rah-rah boosterism staggering companionably along be-side pockets of crushing poverty, was in his blood as surely as the fat globules that floated off his meals of fried fish.

Left on High Street, left on Battery Street, out to South End and back, then out County Road to the town garage . . . when he'd fin-ished his routine, he decided on the spur of the moment to do it over again. But even on the second go-round, there was no sign of Sam anywhere, or of Wade Sorenson, either, and no one seemed to at be home when Bob drove by their house on Key Street.

Jake and Ellie were probably still up at the cabin. So maybe the two old people who lived there—Jake's father, Jacob, and his wife, Bella—had gone somewhere, too: shopping in the market town of Calais, maybe, thirty miles distant. Lousy night for it, the smears of rain on Bob's windshield alternating with streaming downpours as he drove, but it was the simplest explanation, and so probably the correct one.

Bob hoped that later when he went to the Happy Crab he would find Sam and Wade enjoying their own deep-fried dinners. Probably he would; thinking this, he reached for one of the sugar-free candies he kept in the car's cup holder, unwrapped it, and popped it into his mouth.

The sour watermelon taste had begun spreading on his tongue when the squad's radio blatted out a burst of static. Then a tinny voice out of county dispatch began relaying the information that there was a vehicle off the road, back in among the trees on Route 190.

Bob recognized the location, a mile or so past where he had just turned around and driven back into town. A passing motorist had called it in, the dispatcher said. Bob depressed the speaker button, bit down on the watermelon candy, swallowed the pieces, and hit the gas pedal, swinging the car around hard and flooring it as he spoke, identifying himself.

"On it," he added, thumbing on his light bars and siren as the car's speedometer leapt to sixty, wondering as he swung into the curve past the Mobil station whose family he would be either calling or visiting later this evening, depending on how bad the news was that he would be obliged to deliver.

The last thing Jacob Tiptree remembered clearly was seeing a deer step out of the brush by the side of the road. It was a doe, plump after a summer of garden grazing, mowing down lettuces and nipping off dahlias; now in autumn the deer herd had mostly moved to their wintering grounds, out here along the highway.

He might not have seen her at all if she hadn't turned, her eyes reflecting redly in his pickup's headlights in the moment before she leapt.

He didn't know how long ago that had been. Someone moaned in the darkness beside him. *Bella* . . .

He couldn't speak, understood distantly that it was because his face was jammed up against the steering wheel. It was cold in the truck's cab, which felt unnaturally small and closed in, so they might've been here awhile.

Crushed in here . . . He tried to reach out for his wife, with him in the demolished pickup truck. But when he tried to move, a pain like a lightning bolt shot across his shoulder and into his chest. Something held him tightly between the wheel and the seatback; after a moment he realized that it was the engine, halfway into the passenger compartment.

Now he could smell motor oil, the sweet chemical stink of antifreeze, and the acrid reek of burnt electrical insulation. But not gasoline, thankfully. When he wiggled his face to try to free his lips, at least, he felt stuff crinkle from his forehead. A bit of it fell to his mouth, and when he tasted it he realized it was dried blood.

So they *had* been here awhile. Hours, maybe . . . There'd been no one in sight when they went off the road.

"Bella," he whispered.

Silence. He couldn't tell if she was breathing or not. Fear poleaxed him, turning his blood to cold sludge and his gut to a lump of ice. Then:

"I'm here, old man," she whispered "But I can't . . ."

"Don't try to move." Talking set something inside his mouth to bleeding again; he tried to spit, couldn't, and swallowed the blood instead, felt he was going to vomit and knew he mustn't.

He could feel her gathering herself beside him, getting her wits about her, her voice a little stronger when she spoke again. But what she said scared him more than anything so far:

"There's a lot of blood." Then she coughed, a wet, bubbling sound that could not mean anything good, that went right through his heart like a sword. "Jacob . . ."

"Shh. Just hang on now, old girl, we'll be all right. We're not far off the road; somebody will see us. People go by here all the time. Someone," he promised, "will come."

But the truth was, he didn't know how far off the road they might be. He didn't remember swerving to avoid the deer, or if he had; he didn't know whether they'd hit it or not, or how far the truck had traveled before striking something, a tree or a granite outcropping.

The crash had burst the truck's windows, scattering glass pellets. He could feel them in his hair and on his face, stuck to his skin. Rain began, slanting in coldly, drenching and chilling him to the bone, and when he shivered, the pain went through him once more, worse now that he was awake and alert.

But the worst part was that Bella had fallen silent. Jacob couldn't get an answer out of her anymore, and pretty soon he quit trying, fearing that any effort she made might be the thing that used up the last of her reserves, or nudged something wounded to bleed again when otherwise it might've stopped.

Maybe she was unconscious, or maybe she was just saving her strength. He hoped it wasn't anything worse, and he had no way of finding out. Eventually he let his neck relax, resting the bridge of his nose against the wreck of the steering wheel, letting the pain wash over him. The pain, really, was nothing to him if Bella didn't make it all right.

He still couldn't move, though, and now his neck and back were stiffening up, freezing him rigidly into position. He sat that way for a long time in the cold and wet, in the darkness of the smashed-in truck cab. Thunder began rumbling, getting nearer; soon lightning flashes whitened the crazed safety glass of the truck's windshield.

If Bella had a cellphone in her bag, he didn't know about it, and he wouldn't have been able to reach it, much less work it—he couldn't feel his fingers, and his feet seemed not to be down there below the busted dashboard anymore, either—if he had.

He whispered her name again, and got no answer. Outside, the rain came down steadily. He lost consciousness once more, and sometime after that when he awoke to a siren's wail and lights flashing, he hardly cared, certain that they were already too late.

By the time glass had finished falling out of the cottage windows, Ellie and I were on the floor, crawling together toward the woodstove and the chimney behind it. From the chimney, it was a quick scramble around and into the kitchen alcove.

Neither of us could breathe right, we were so scared, and we couldn't see, either; the lights were shot out, it was pitch dark and raining outside, so there was no moon, and we couldn't turn on a flashlight even if we could find one, because then whoever was out there could see us, too.

"Who?" Ellie whispered when she'd gotten her wind back.

"No idea." Except for the rain still pattering down, there was only silence out there now. "But if whoever is out there gets in here with the shotgun," I said—from the way the windows blew in, I thought it must be one—"we'll be sitting ducks."

I felt her nod beside me. "As small as this place is, just shooting randomly around a few times'll do it," she whispered.

How, I wondered, could this be happening? Two minutes ago I'd been tucked into a bed, tired from a day's work, and now . . .

"Okay. My bag with the phone in it is on the counter," I said.

Because we had to get out, and we had to let somebody know what was happening. Toot sweet, as my son, Sam, would've put it.

And the truck was right outside. "You run for the passenger door and I'll jump in and start it," I whispered.

"Uh-huh." A pause, then, "We should call someone *before* we go. I mean, so they know what happened in case . . ."

In case we don't make it. That feeling of unreality washed over me again. But: "No. My phone's turned off."

I'd checked for messages after dinner, found none, and had

planned to do so once more before I fell asleep, just in case someone from home really needed to talk to me. In between those times, though, I'd turned it completely off to save the battery.

"It chimes when it powers up," I added. Which we obviously couldn't let happen. In all this quiet, the sound would be plenty loud enough to betray where we were.

Ellie sighed. "Okay. We can do it on the way out."

Of the woods, she meant; in the truck. I snatched my bag off the countertop, hunkered back down. No sound came from outside, and neither did another shotgun blast.

Keeping low, we crept quietly from behind the counter, past the chimney on one side and the steep open stairs leading to the cottage's second-floor loft area on the other. At least whoever it was hadn't caught us up there, where we'd really be trapped.

Small comfort, but by that time I was willing to take whatever I could get.

Putting my hands out blindly, I found the doorknob and turned it silently, then swung the door open, fast. "Go, go, go," I chanted, and Ellie flew out with me right behind her.

We scrambled into the truck, and I found the key in the cup-holder and jammed it into the ignition. The engine roared and the headlights came on, a sudden blare of illumination: trees, boulders, and brush but nothing and no one else.

I stomped the gas and we shot out of there like our hats were on fire and our tail ends were catching, as my dad would've put it, out through the open gate toward home.

"Damn," said Ellie as we bounced along the dirt road.

"What?" I glanced over at her. She was frowning at her cellphone, which she'd plugged right away into the dashboard charger.

"Battery's dead again. Maybe it's . . ."

The truck's glaring headlights turned the forest into the set of a low-budget horror movie, garish and stark. I flung my bag sideways at her, grabbed the wheel again as we hit a rut.

"Use mine." She took it; the familiar chimes tinkled as its screen's greenish glow lit. Which was when I realized what it was that I hadn't noticed when we first got into the truck.

"Ellie—" Her scream cut me off; I slammed on the brakes. A man stood in the road smack in front of us, grinning.

Holding a shotgun. The sudden stop jolted us both forward; I felt the steering wheel slam my rib cage, heard Ellie's hands smack the dashboard's hard plastic.

And when I looked up again, the man was gone. "Ellie, when we got in the truck there were no . . ."

Lights. The interior cab light hadn't gone on. Neither had the two little bulbs by the rearview mirror.

"I can't find it," said Ellie frantically, scrabbling around on the floor and then patting at the seat around her. "The phone, it fell when we stopped so fast, and now I can't—"

Great. I hit the gas again. "Well, we'll just have to make it out of here on our own, then, won't we?"

From beneath the truck came a loud bang and then the *clank-clunk* of the muffler getting knocked off the undercarriage by a rock we'd have cleared if we hadn't been going so fast.

A bolt of fright went through me; at first I'd thought it was a shotgun blast. Luckily, though, by then my hands were clamped so tightly to the steering wheel that a bomb couldn't have loosened them.

So we managed to stay on the road. "Who the hell was that?" Ellie breathed, twisting around to peer out the back window.

"No idea." Actually, I did have one; I'd gotten a halfway decent look at him. But that wasn't the important thing now.

"Ellie, the cab's interior lights aren't working." Outside, the night flew by; if I drove any faster, I risked losing control on the rough road.

But we had to get out of here, to where there were people and . . . "He must've disabled them," I said.

A porcupine waddled out in front of us; I braced myself, but he made it across somehow. We were nearly to the culvert; past that there was still plenty of rough road between us and safety, though.

Ellie found the broken dome-light plastic with her hand. "Why would he do that?" she wondered aloud.

"No idea." The headlights picked out the metal culvert's rim and then the pond's surface. I recalled Bob Arnold's warning on the dangers of flooded roads.

The road itself was dry, however, and we'd be across the culverted section in moments, slowing only for the gulley that the flood had cut in it earlier. And that would be no problem if I was careful, or so I thought, but then a number of things happened fast:

First, in the reflection of our headlights off the pond, a dim shape upstream began *moving,* sliding sideways and then up out of the water entirely. That big log, I realized, that the Calais cop had said was damming the stream . . .

He was removing it. But even before I understood this, water began pouring through; a *lot* of water, straight at us. A *wave* . . .

And then we were in it. In the headlights the water roiled, swirling and gushing. The tires slipped, fighting for purchase on a road now turning liquid underneath us.

We hit the gulley before I could brake. Suddenly the water was much deeper; the truck began moving sideways. "Ellie, we've got to get out."

She was ahead of me, already reaching for the passenger-side door handle. But it wasn't there.

Mine, either. I could feel the sharp edges where it had been sawed off; we'd have heard him doing it, maybe, but we'd had that music on, so . . . As I thought this, the tires caught on a low scrim of brush lining the road, and the rushing water carried us over.

Headlight beams strafed the sky; then we were pressed together against the passenger-side window, which unfortunately had hit a rock or something when it landed.

Something hard enough to *break* the window. The truck was on its side in the part of the pond that the culvert drained into, I realized, and a thud of real fear hit me; that part was *deep*. Cold, muddy water began gushing in, filling the cab. I hauled my weight off Ellie as best I could by grabbing the steering wheel.

But that wasn't going to work for long. In the few instants we had been down here, the cab was half full and the water level in it was still rising fast. "Ellie . . ."

She snapped on a flashlight she'd miraculously managed to snag out of the glove compartment. A blessing; at least we were not going to drown in the pitch dark. But my relief was short-lived; the water was freezing cold, stinking of swamp muck, and still bubbling up through the broken window with a force like an out-of-control fire-hose.

Too bad that safety glass was smashed enough to let water *in* but not enough to let us *out*.

"Okay," gasped Ellie. "Okay, okay . . ." She hauled herself up and over, into the truck's vestigial back seat, feeling around for . . .

"Got it," she managed triumphantly, coming up with a red plastic toolbox. I recognized the cordless drill's carrying case. "Here," she said, shoving it at me.

"Oh, Ellie." My heart sank, knowing how useless that drill was going to be, how I was going to disappoint her. She thought I was handy with tools, a notion I'd done little to discourage; it was fun, having people think I was good at something when mostly I was just stubborn and lucky.

She thought I could do something useful, like maybe drill us out of here somehow by using my handy-dandy, mostly self-taught house-repair skills, or maybe my deck-building abilities, which to tell the truth weren't any great shakes, either.

Real tools might've made a difference, a sledgehammer or a pipe wrench. But the drill bits were tiny compared to what we'd need to cut that windshield. And while I thought this, another huge *bloop* of muddy water came in.

"Okay, gimme that," I said. With shaking hands I slotted in the biggest drill bit we had and tightened it. "Here goes . . ."

The sound was ear piercing, as if the dentist had to go in through your eardrum to reach your wisdom tooth. But it wasn't windshield piercing.

And then the drill's battery died.

"Oh, no. No, no, no . . ." The water was to my waist, and as the truck's weight sank it deeper and deeper in the mucky pond's bottom and more water came in, the cab would soon submerge.

She grabbed the drill.

"Ellie, the *battery* is—"

Ignoring me, she shoved past me. "Get back." I'd never heard that tone out of her, before: deadly, and utterly focused.

She gripped the drill by its nose, the heavy battery pack section aimed like a hammerhead. And then she *swung* it—

But not at the windshield; at the driver's-side window above us. And although it didn't break out completely, it shattered, spiderweb cracks spreading through it.

Wiggling around, she braced herself against me, drew her knees up, and—

Wham. The weakened safety glass made a harsh ripping sound as it tore; she kicked it again for good measure and it tore out in one flexible piece, like a sheet of rubber.

"Go!" With me pushing, she wiggled up and out through the opening, and I tried to follow, but instead the truck gave a mean lurch sideways, then sank suddenly much deeper.

Water *boiled* up into the cab, up over my head so fast that I lost my bearings; flailing, I tried to find the window, couldn't, and got panicky, grabbing around but not finding anything.

Then something grabbed my hair, yanking and tearing at it. I reached around wildly, trying to free myself from something that gripped back. It was Ellie, and she was yelling at me.

"Don't fight. Just let me pull you! Get your face up here!"

For once, I obeyed without an argument, noticing a sudden improvement in my situation once my head was up out of the water.

Cold, wet, and more scared than I'd ever been in my life . . . but I could breathe, and once my arms and shoulders were out, I could wiggle onto the truck's door, and from there to the pond's edge.

There I collapsed. Beside me, Ellie fell, too, catching her breath. Around us, everything was quiet and dark. No owls hooting or animals scuttling . . . nothing at all, as if the night itself was holding its breath, waiting.

"Ellie," I whispered, "we can't stay here like this."

Unarmed, I meant, and with nothing between us and whoever it was who was trying to kill us. Walking two miles out to the paved road, soaking wet in the freezing dark, wasn't an option I liked, and especially not with that guy-with-gun factor added in.

But from here we might be able to make it through the brush in the other direction, stay off the road and maybe out of his sight long enough to get–

"We should try to get to the cottage," Ellie said, echoing my thought; God, it was cold out here.

"Upstairs," she managed through teeth now practically together, they were chattering so hard, "and push some furniture over onto the landing, to block it . . ."

The gun I'd brought along was still up there, too, since of course I hadn't thought fast enough to get it as we fled.

"Come on," I whispered, hauling myself up. My back felt as if fire ants had set up housekeeping in it and were biting their way out. Everything on me was cut, scraped, or torn; parts of my scalp felt as if Ellie had used a razor knife on it; and my nose, mouth, eyes, and ears were clotted with stinking mud.

Also, probably a very bad guy was still around here, wanting to kill us; with each soggy-shoed step through the weeds, bushes, and brambles between the pond and the cottage clearing, I expected another blast from a shotgun to explode out of the dark at us.

But none did.

For now, anyway.

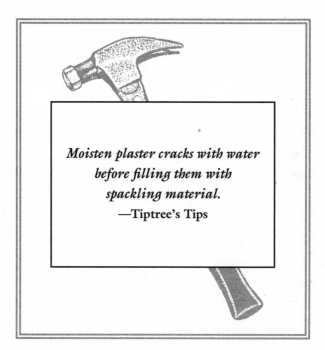

CHAPTER 8

*Moisten plaster cracks with water
before filling them with
spackling material.*
—Tiptree's Tips

At the Motel East, Sam Tiptree hitched himself and the chair he was duct-taped to across the floor to the motel room's door. The room was on the first floor, so if anyone went by outside they'd be able to hear him.

Next he tipped the chair over, banging his head quite hard on the door frame as he did so. But seeing stars didn't matter to him; what mattered was that when he stopped seeing them, he was as near as possible to the door itself.

He couldn't kick it, or pound on it with his fists. The tape took

care of that. He could've hammered on it with his head, but the way
it still felt after hitting the door frame made him think it was probably
a better idea to save that tactic for later.

After all, he couldn't make any sound at all if he was out cold.
"Mmmph! Gnrr! Mmmph!" he yelled, hearing footsteps outside.

Or it would've been yelling if the duct tape weren't tightly covering his mouth. "Gnnr! Gnrr!"

As he'd hoped, whoever was out there paused. Maybe it was a
housekeeping person or a motel guest. But what he heard next was
not what he had hoped to hear.

Not at all. "Hello?" *Hewwo?* It was a small child's voice. Sam stepped
up the urgency on his grr-ing and mmmph-ing as well as he could.

From outside: "Mama, the monster is in there." *Monstew.*

From a distance came a woman's voice, harried and impatient:
"Crosley, get over here. Whoever's in there doesn't want—"

Yes! Yes, I do! But it was no use; the child let himself be summoned
away. Moments later everything was silent again.

Outside the sliding glass door on the other side of the room, the
sky was dark. From where he lay on the floor, Sam could see through
the railings on the deck outside—the motel was built into the side of a
steep hill, so the deck was thirty feet off the ground—all the way to
Campobello Island across the bay.

Lamps came on in the houses over there as people got home from
work and began fixing dinner. Headlights flickered along the shoreline road. But then, after a while, the lights went out again one by one;
TVs, too, and the headlights along the road grew more infrequent
until there were hardly any.

Sam tried to kick the door—or anything, really—with his bound-to-
the-chair feet, but all he could produce was scuffling, not loud enough
to be heard by anyone more than a few feet away.

It might have been enough to alert tenants in the rooms on either
side of this one, if any had been in them. But business was thin at the
Motel East that night, so the rooms were vacant.

The glowing red numerals of the clock on the table between the room's pair of queen-sized beds read 11 p.m., the last time he looked. After that, having had no luck in attracting attention to his plight and feeling that he might as well resign himself to waiting for the maid to come in here in the morning and find him, he decided to try to sleep.

But the nightmares he began having as soon as he succeeded jerked him awake again. There was a chilly draft coming under the door, too, and his head hurt, not to mention the fact that he had to use the bathroom rather badly; also, he was hungry.

A surge of frustration overwhelmed him. Damn, how had he let himself get hornswoggled so thoroughly, as his grandfather Jacob would have put it?

And all over a woman. *Let that be a lesson to you,* he told himself wryly, feeling his muscles begin cramping as he lay there tied up on the cold floor. *Quit thinking with your . . .*

The motel room door opened suddenly, smacking him in the head. The sound he made caused whoever was on the other side of the door to pause, then open it again more cautiously.

A hand came in, flipping on the light switch. A face peered down, grimacing in consternation and surprise. "What the—"

It was Sam's stepfather, Wade Sorenson. "Oh, Christ."

The big man pushed on the door, sliding Sam's taped-to-the-chair body just far enough back so he could squeeze inside. A few minutes later they were leaving the motel room, Sam staggering a little on legs that were still stiff and prickling.

They got into Wade's pickup. But they didn't turn up Key Street toward home, instead heading through heavy rain on down Water Street past the fish pier.

"Where are we going?" Sam asked finally. In the glare from the lights out on the pier, big waves slopped the pilings. Wade seemed angry, his eyes intent on the street ahead and his face expressionless. He hadn't even asked Sam how he'd managed to end up bound and gagged in a motel room.

"Hospital," Wade replied tersely. "Bella and your granddad were in an accident."

They headed out of town, Wade squinting past the wipers into the streaming dark. "Are they all right? What happened, what kind of accident?"

Wade pulled to the side of the road, put the flashers on, and pointed wordlessly to a set of tire tracks leading from the pavement through some brush and into the trees. In the darkness the marks were hardly noticeable unless you knew where to look. Hoof prints in the soft shoulder told the rest of the story.

"Looks like your grandfather must've swerved to avoid a deer in the road." Wade still sounded angry; Sam thought it was because he was upset about the accident, until another thought hit him.

"You're not up there with them. At the hospital."

They reached Route 1, turned onto it. Wade hit the gas hard. "That's right, Sam, I'm not. I was out looking for you, instead."

In the dimness of the truck's cab, he turned furiously. "So, was it a fun evening, Sam? Was it worth it to you?"

And when Sam must've looked puzzled, Wade added, "What, do you think you can drink in this town without people talking about it?"

Enlightenment washed over Sam, followed by anger of his own. But then he realized: of course. Why wouldn't they think that?

They sped in silence down the dark, rain-swept highway, hemlocks and white pines looming on either side, Wade frowning as he drove, alert for wildlife: moose, deer, even bears, although it wasn't common to see them out near the road. Finally:

"Wade. It was lemonade. I went back and told the bartender not to put gin in it. No one else knew, though."

Wade said nothing. But he was listening. It didn't escape Sam, either, that Wade had spent a long time looking for him.

That he'd cared. Then, "Okay, let's hear it," Wade said, and added, "There's a can of Coke on the floor there somewhere."

Sam found it, guzzled gratefully from it. "See, there was this girl," he began when he'd slaked his thirst somewhat.

The whole complicated story of Richard and what happened on his boat *Courtesan . . .* all that could wait, he decided.

The girl was the important part. "I didn't want to tell her that I don't drink. I don't know why. . . ."

Yes, I do. He started again. "I was embarrassed. To say so, I mean, that I don't drink alcohol. I should've known what a bad sign that was, that if I couldn't tell her, then . . ."

Then it was hopeless. Once Sam had blurted that part out, the rest of the story poured forth until the next thing stopped him.

During that very short pause, he decided not to talk about the hallucinations he'd had, either. Or whatever they were; he just didn't think that part of his recent experience would go over very well right now. Instead, he ended with Richard showing up in the room and tying him up, and after that a brief summary of the time he, Sam, had spent on the floor.

"I'm really sorry, Wade. Like I say, I just . . ."

"They robbed the boatyard office."

A cluster of small houses lined the shore in Red Beach, the windows mostly dark. Sam found his voice. "What?"

But it already made sense to him. After getting burned by bad checks too many times, the boatyard's owner had gone to his new policy: the sign reading "No Cash, No Splash" over the office applied to all sales and service, not just launching.

And there'd been a lot of cash in the office. Sam's heart sank, realizing why.

"Alarm went off after the shop closed," Wade said.

The alarm was just one of those big brass fire-alarm striker mechanisms, wired up to a motion detector. But the bell was loud; on a quiet night, you could hear it all the way into town.

"Bob Arnold says that by the time he got out there, no one was around. Door hanging open, cashbox gone."

Sam added it up in his head: a couple of fishing boats had been hauled out of the water, and one put back in after repairs. A few sales of parts and small equipment, dry-dock rentals . . .

All of which was bad enough. But there'd also been a bunch of summer people in, settling their seasonal accounts. And . . . the credit card slips, he remembered suddenly. A whole month's worth of them, because the boatyard took credit cards but it didn't have an electronic card reader. Instead they used an old manual card imprinter, saved the slips from it to turn in all at once to the bank for payment.

And whoever had those slips also had all the card owners' credit information. . . . Oh, Sam thought glumly, he was going to be in so much trouble. It had taken a long time to earn the level of responsibility he enjoyed at the boatyard, and now he'd blown it.

"So did they catch them?" he asked. "Richard and Carol?"

"Not yet. State cops're on it, though, shouldn't take 'em long. Car they stole for their getaway had a LoJack tracker in it." Wade glanced sideways, saw Sam's face.

"What's the matter? You don't want them caught?"

"No, no. I do." He sighed heavily. "Man, do I ever. It's just that . . ."

Swiftly he explained his fresh misery: that it was his job to make the cash deposit at the bank after work. But he'd put it off until tomorrow because he had a date. Hurrying back from Bangor, he'd been in a rush to meet up with Carol.

Then another thought hit him. "Is Mom at the hospital? And how bad are Bella and Granddad hurt, anyway?"

Wade drove fast, the truck plowing along in the rain, and that wasn't like him. "I haven't called your mother at the cottage yet. I wanted to find you, first. Your grandfather's just bruised up a little."

Shame flooded Sam. He'd been a damned fool, and as a result not only had the boatyard been robbed but Wade had been dealing with all of this by himself. Then another thing hit him:

"How did you find me, anyway?"

Wade squinted past the wipers beating aside the slashing rain. "Desk clerk at the motel saw the picture of you and your two dinner companions in the Rusty Rudder's front window."

Sam sighed as Wade went on. "She remembered them checking in a couple nights ago, called Bob Arnold. And he called me."

A sudden downpour obscured the windshield; Wade waited until it cleared. Then: "She told him she thought they were gone, but I decided to have a look anyway, just in case."

Wade turned the truck's heat up. "Bob," he added, "was at the accident scene already, so he couldn't."

Sam puffed a breath out: what a mess. "Is Bella okay?"

The lights of the town of Calais glowed murkily ahead. "She was going into surgery, just before I found you."

They passed the community college's collection of dorms and classroom buildings, surrounded by the crumbling remains of what had been, just a generation ago, small working farms. Next came a row of old sea captains' mansions, once the homes of the town's most prosperous families but now in need of maintenance and in some cases even of tenants; over the decades, rail had taken over from shipping, and then it, too, dwindled as a source of wealth for the local gentry.

Wade turned left at the convenience store where youngsters in torn jeans hung out smoking cigarettes under the canopy, then left again into the hospital's parking lot. It was late, so most of the spaces were empty, and the lobby lights had been turned down low inside. Only a few people were in the waiting area.

Sam smelled cleaning products and rubbing alcohol, and told himself again that it wouldn't have made any difference if he'd been at home. But he knew it would have, that he could have done what Bella and his granddad had set off to do, whatever it was.

Then none of this would've happened. But instead, he accused himself bitterly, he'd been panting after a strange new female, as stupidly single-minded as a dog chasing a bitch in heat.

"Bella's in the recovery room," Wade said when he came back from the information desk. "So far, so fine."

Sam let a breath out, then out of the blue felt another wave of foreboding wash over him. He reached out for the railing that ran waist-high along the wall of the hospital corridor.

Wade turned, looking concerned. "Hey, you all right?"

But Sam barely heard. Instead it was his father's voice, his father's face capturing him. The late, great Victor Tiptree was suddenly there in all his long-dead, impossibly present glory, and not only that, he had *something to say, something to warn Sam about.* . . .

"Sorry, Dad." *You're too late as usual.* . . . Then, realizing that he'd muttered it aloud and that Wade was staring curiously at him, Sam gave himself an inward shake.

"Got another chill or something for a minute there. I'm fine," he told Wade as the apparition—or whatever it was—vanished.

He followed Wade through a set of swinging doors to the patient area. The corridor was hushed and dim, most of the doors open only a crack so the sick people could sleep.

At the corridor's far end, the nurses' station was an island of light. Wade nodded back at the nurse who waved him on into the one room with its lights still on, and they entered it.

In the big white hospital bed, Bella lay asleep. Wires led from her chest to an EKG machine. IVs ran in; tubes ran out.

"She'll sleep for another few hours," the nurse told them quietly from the doorway. "She had a broken rib and a punctured lung, but they're fixed, and everything went fine."

Bella's hair, henna-dyed purplish red, stuck out from under the paper cap she still wore. Her face, all angles and sharp edges, looked rougher and bonier than Sam had ever seen it before.

Her hands lying atop the sheet were mottled and lumpy with arthritis. Tears prickled Sam's eyes at the sight of them so still; blinking them away, he accompanied Wade out to the hall.

"Can we see Granddad?"

Wade nodded. "Guess I can call your mom now, too."

Sam said nothing, another rush of shame coming over him, but this time Wade noticed.

"Hey, Sam? Cut me some slack if I'm wrong here, but . . . this is the kind of thing people drink over, right?"

Bummed out as he was, Sam still had to smile at Wade's use of the recovery terminology: *drink over.* Also, Wade was right, and it surprised Sam, though he supposed it shouldn't, that his stepfather was so perceptive. Sam had always thought of him as a hardworking good guy with a major talent for making his mother happy, but not anything more.

Until now. "Uh, yeah. If a person was inclined to drink over things, this might be one of them. Doing something stupid, so he wasn't there for his family when they needed him."

Wade reached out and gripped his shoulder hard. "Listen, we both made some errors tonight, okay? This Carol and Richard, they were real con artists. It's no surprise they were so believable to you; that's their job. And . . ."

He hesitated. "And I'm sorry I jumped to the conclusion that you were drinking, Sam. I'm not usually that gullible, either."

Wade pulled his cellphone out. "If I wait until morning to tell your mom all this, she'll have my head on a platter."

He pressed the keys, then stood with the device to his ear. But from his face as he waited, Sam could tell that no one was picking up. No surprise, really; the clock in the nurses' station said it was 2 a.m., and if she'd left the phone in her purse, as she often did, his mother probably wouldn't even hear it.

All of which Wade knew, too, and with everything now under control and Bella resting quietly . . . Snapping the device shut and stowing it, Wade shrugged. "We'll catch her later."

Sam understood the relief in Wade's voice; his mother would be worried, full of questions, and he and Wade were for different reasons both thoroughly exhausted. But even as he thought this, another flashback—*Is that what it is?*—hit Sam: the dark water in the bilge, the urgency of the nightmarish apparition swirling in it, all mingled somehow with Carol's red lips . . .

"Or take a ride out there when it gets light," Wade added.

"Yeah," Sam said faintly, still in thrall to the bad-dream howl of impending doom ringing in his ears. *What's wrong with me?* Dead people didn't lunge up out of flooded bilge compartments, dripping and screaming. They didn't *warn* you about . . . something.

He was just really messed up, he decided, his near slip now showing itself to him for what it was: another step in a gradual downward trend he simply hadn't been mindful enough to notice.

His vulnerability, his yearning for acceptance from Carol and Richard . . . they were part of it, and so was his not having taken that bank deposit in, a bit of carelessness he was going to have to work off forever, he supposed miserably, to pay the money back.

"Thanks for finding me," he said. "I mean, you kept looking for me. It would have been easier for you to . . ."

Give up. Decide I deserved whatever mess I was in. Fill in the blank, Sam thought.

But Wade only shrugged, and then the two of them went off to find Sam's grandfather's room, to see with their own eyes that the old man was okay–he was, but sedated and sound asleep–before heading to the cafeteria for coffee and a vending-machine pastry to keep their energy up.

To keep them, as Bella would have put it, bright-eyed and bushy-tailed.

Ellie and I didn't talk as we stumbled in darkness down the dirt road back to the cabin. We couldn't; it was raining too hard, and besides, we didn't want to make unnecessary noise.

We'd been attacked, first deliberately driven out of the cabin toward the culvert and then nearly drowned. If Ellie hadn't summoned the strength to bash that window out and drag me through it, we'd still be in the flooded cab.

Now she tramped grimly beside me, smothering a sneeze every so often; besides being soaking wet, we were cold, exhausted, and scared half out of our wits. But *only* half out of them; when we got to the gate, we both stopped at the same moment without having to consult each other.

"It was him, wasn't it? Dewey Hooper," Ellie whispered.

"Yeah." I'd had a decent look. "It was him, all right." And what that meant, I wasn't sure. But it couldn't be good.

"Maybe he thinks we're dead. Drowned back there."

"Maybe." But I doubted it. We'd made a lot of noise getting out of the truck, and even if he hadn't heard us, I didn't think he'd take that kind of thing for granted.

The rain was slacking off; I tried cheering myself with that fact and with the knowledge that in a way, we were lucky.

After all, it could've been snow. But I'd still never been so cold in my life; last time I'd seen the thermometer outside the cottage window, it had read forty degrees.

"Anyway, it doesn't matter what he thinks. We've got to get inside and get that fire blazing."

We walked some more. Then it hit me: "Accident. It was supposed to look like an accident."

It was why he'd shot the windows out instead of shooting us, which he could easily have done. Still could, actually.

Ellie nodded in the darkness beside me. "And afterwards he'd have plenty of time to come back here, make this place look like— what? A fire? Or an explosion, say, if the gas stove blew up?"

"Yup." Ahead, the cottage was just a big, dark shape in the dripping gloom.

"And while we were escaping in the truck, we had a mishap," I added. "That would be the theory."

Of how our deaths had happened, I meant. A shiver that had nothing to do with the temperature went through me; it could have worked. Would have, if we hadn't been lucky.

Now I hoped our luck wasn't all used up, because we were going to need it. We wouldn't have come back here at all if we had anywhere else to go, but the dirt road out was too exposed and bushwhacking through the woods that far at night was out of the question; either we'd get lost or he'd hear us crashing around in the undergrowth and find us out there, or both.

Or we'd get lost and die from exposure. So we really didn't have a choice. Inside, the cottage smelled like rain, cold ashes, and a whiff of gunpowder. Hurrying to the stove, Ellie put her hand inside and snapped a lighter on. The tiny flame lit her face:

Scared. Like mine, I imagined. But she still wasn't giving up. "Get me some kindling and a few sheets of newspaper," she said through chattering teeth.

After delivering what she'd asked for, I cautiously pulled a shade aside and put my face to a window. I didn't see anyone out there, but the darkness was so complete that an army division could've marched into the clearing and I might not have seen it.

Which presented me with a choice: I could leave things the way they were, no lights at all in here, hoping that in the dark our attacker really hadn't noticed our escape from the truck.

But that was probably the worst kind of wishful thinking; the kind that could get us killed. More than likely, he was just putting another, worse plan together.

Thinking this, I checked all the solar equipment, took the lamps that had gotten broken during the shotgun attack out of the circuit, and snapped the outside light switch. In response a pale fluorescent glow lit the clearing, picking out the chopping block with an ax still stuck in it, and the toolshed.

Drat, I hadn't meant to leave the ax out in the rain where it would get rusty. Or where Hooper would come upon it, either . . . but there it was.

Also, I always shut the shed door at night so wild animals wouldn't gnaw the salty wooden handles of the implements stored inside. But now the door hung open, which answered the question of how our assailant might've gotten the tools he'd needed.

Among the other items out there was a small hacksaw with one of those space-age-metal blades on it, the kind that the TV ads said would slice through anything from tomatoes to concrete.

Or through the door handles of trucks. Behind me, Ellie kept feeding small sticks and bits of bark into the stove. "Are you thinking since he probably already knows we're still alive, we might as well have lights on?"

It wasn't an objection, just her making sure we were on the same page. The one, I mean, where it said hiding probably wasn't going to work.

"Yeah." Grabbing a battery lantern, I climbed the stairs to the loft area. The stove's concrete-block chimney ran up through the center of the big, open room; behind it I found the lockbox with my gun and the ammunition in it. Next I quickly rummaged the old thrift-shop dresser tucked in under the eaves, coming up with pairs of socks, a couple of heavy shirts, and sweatpants.

Not that it would make any difference whether we were wet or dry, cold or warm as toast, when the guy shot us. Or drowned us, or burned us up in a—

"Ellie," I whispered down the stairs. "Find those new fire extinguishers we brought."

The stove door closed with a faint creak. "Got them," Ellie reported.

I hurried back downstairs, and while we pulled on as many layers of the dry clothes I'd found as we could, I told her what I'd seen just before the flood hit us. "Remember the log stuck in the stream?"

Enlightenment dawned on Ellie's face. "So when he pulled the log out . . ."

"Uh-huh. It opened up the blockage. And with the stream so swollen from all the rain . . ."

The dry clothes felt better; too bad they didn't include a bullet-proof vest. Ellie crept to the kitchen area, where a pan of already brewed coffee still sat on the gas stove, miraculously untouched amidst the chaos created by the shotgun blasts earlier and our hasty exit afterwards.

Snapping her lighter again, she lit the burner; the sight of the low blue flame, so normal and domestic, was oddly comforting, and so was the hot coffee she handed me moments later.

"So he's a creep, but he's a clever, resourceful creep," I said as I wrapped my cold hands around the mug. Ellie had the woodstove blazing, but two windows were still broken and no stove could keep up with that much chilly night air coming in.

Outside, the wind and rain were finally ceasing as the storm passed by, and when I peeked again, nothing moved. In my sweater pocket was the gun I'd brought downstairs, and more bullets.

But having them didn't make me feel better. For one thing, the solar porch lamp only lit a small circle, fifteen or so feet from the cottage door; meanwhile, a shotgun's range is measured in hundreds of yards. Our assailant could stand in the darkness beyond the lamplight and hit us easily.

And the thought of a direct attack was bad enough, but even worse was the mental picture I was starting to get of this guy: smart, stubborn, and for some reason, intent on killing us. What he thought he'd accomplish by that I had no idea; revenge for my testimony against him didn't seem a good enough reason.

Right now, though, the reason didn't matter. "We need help," I said. "Or better yet, to get out of here, fast."

But the cellphones were both lost, still back in the truck. Walking out wasn't an option, either, two miles in the dark while a bad guy with a shotgun stalked us.

Worse, with the road washed out, we'd have to bushwhack around it, and in that direction lay marsh and brush so thick and thorny, it would turn our clothes to shredded fluff in minutes, then start on our skin; also, we didn't have hiking boots, which put twisted ankles high on the list of likely events.

"So how are we going to get out of here?" I asked, thinking she'd come up with some other suggestion. Instead:

"We're not."

"What?" I turned, horrified; she was giving up? "Come on, Ellie, there's got to be a way to—"

But she remained resolute. "I don't like it any more than you do.

But the truth is that we can't get out without exposing ourselves, if not to his shotgun then to some other, maybe even worse, mischief."

She had a point; he might *want* all this to look accidental, but if push really came to shove, who knew what he'd do? "We're exposed here, too," I argued. "We've got to at least try. I don't see how you can just quit."

"Who said anything about quitting?" She turned from checking the fire in the stove again. "I'm talking about *winning*. I'm cold and I'm scared and I don't like being *hunted*. Which we are."

Yup: all three of those things, with emphasis on the *scared* part. Because that water trap he'd sprung on us was crazy, the kind of thing only a real whack job would not just think of but actually try. But it was also very resourceful.

Enough to have almost worked. "And *that*," Ellie went on, "makes me mad."

She marched to the firewood bin, then back to the stove, head high and shoulders straight even under all those clothes. "So I'm for catching him, and after that I'm for making sure he never does anything like this ever again."

She knelt to feed more sticks into the stove's maw, watched the fire blaze up before closing the door on it again. "So put on your thinking cap, Jake, because the fact is, we can't get out of here, at least not tonight, and we have no way to call for help."

She stood, her shape a slim, dark shadow etched on the larger darkness: of the room, the forest around us, and most of all the dark intentions of whoever lurked among the trees.

Not only that, but there was a part of what had happened at the beaver pond that Ellie hadn't thought of yet, or just hadn't mentioned:

Our attacker had gone to a lot of trouble making the truck rollover look accidental, a freak occurrence out in the woods. As Ellie had said, likely he'd meant to come back here to the cabin afterwards, to set things up so it looked as if those windows had been broken by wind,

or storm-tossed branches . . . anything to make it seem like Mother
Nature and not some human culprit was behind our deaths.

But we knew different, and we'd lived to tell.

So now he pretty much had to kill us.

Gotcha, he'd thought as with dark-adapted eyes he'd watched the
pickup truck slide sideways, then roll over into the flooded pond. But
then . . .

Then *she'd* had to spoil everything. The way she always had, the
way she'd spoiled seven years of his life, because of course it had been
her; who else could ruin a beautiful plan like that?

Now as he crouched in the clearing, staring at the cottage with its
glowing porch light and the woodsmoke puffing once again from its
chimney, Dewey Hooper cursed his dead wife, who'd escaped before
he could finish her off. Her and that friend of hers, Jacobia Tiptree . . .
now, he fumed into the rainy darkness, he was going to have to deal
with both of them again. And that meant time and trouble he could ill
afford.

Where the hell was his good luck? he wondered. Somehow it all
seemed to have vanished, probably also on account of *her.* But whatever the reason, now the women knew someone was after them, and
not only that, they knew *who;* in his rush to get back to the stream in
time to pull the log out when they crossed the culverted part of the
road, he'd accidentally allowed them to get a look at him.

So if he didn't finish this soon, they'd tattle on him, and the next
thing he knew he'd be back in prison, where for all its warmth and
safety he did *not* want to go, he did *not.*

Or worse, Marianne herself would find a way to get revenge.

And what that revenge might be like, he didn't want to imagine.
For all *he* knew, she might be able to reach into his chest, grab his heart
with her ice-cold hand, and *squeeze.* . . .

So he had to get rid of her permanently, do it right so that this time she couldn't ever come back. Glancing around at the small, dimly lit area of rustic sheds and lean-tos ranged loosely around the cottage under the big trees, he began taking inventory of the available items that he could use for the job.

Without warning, another attack of nerves hit him; shakily he ordered himself to take deep breaths, wait it out, ignore the idea that life might be like this now, forever and ever: scared. Just . . . he didn't know how people did it, all this having to make decisions. How had he made them before? He couldn't remember. . . .

· But in the light of the rising moon as the clouds from the departing storm began pulling aside, the lamplit area wasn't all he could see, and soon his surroundings gave him an idea: there was a gas can in the shed. And if that failed, there was a propane tank standing on a small concrete pad at the side of the house.

At the sight of it, a smile began curving his lips. The tank was not the fat, barrel-shaped kind that fuel companies installed at in-town residences; instead it was the tall gray industrial-type cylinder used in garages and factories. Back in prison he'd moved these around on metal carts, delivering them to classrooms where inmates learned employment skills like metal cutting and welding.

But even without a cart, one man could move a tank like that fairly easily. He'd need a wrench to disconnect the tank from the gas line that led into the cabin; probably it ran the cookstove, maybe some gas lamps. But there were wrenches in the toolshed.

Then he noticed a homemade outdoor shower setup at the far edge of the clearing. In the summertime it would most likely be screened by an elderberry thicket, but now through the leafless brush he could just make out the big black rubber water bag hung from a tree branch, and a long hose with a plastic spray head at the end of it.

The water bag didn't interest him, but the hose did; maybe his good luck hadn't abandoned him after all. Maybe instead things were all falling together for him at last. . . .

Finally he spotted the pile of kindling, by a chopping block with a long-handled ax stuck in it, and his smile widened to a grin; it was the last piece in the puzzle.

Because that propane tank resembled a bomb, and properly handled it would act like one, too, or at any rate its contents would. So with gasoline or with propane, one way or the other those women were as good as dead . . . but the hardest part of all this would be making sure they *stayed* dead.

Or making Marianne stay that way, anyway. And now even that knotty little problem was solved, because he'd seen enough scary movies to know that if you were having trouble getting a dead person to stay dead, you put a stake through their heart.

A wooden stake . . . And now, wouldn't you know it, here he was practically within arm's reach of a whole kindling pile of them.

Sharp ones, too, he noticed. Long, splintery, and . . .

Gotcha, he thought.

Inside the cottage, Ellie and I sat together on the floor by the stove, away from the windows. I'd hurried back upstairs long enough to grab some more quilts and blankets, and we'd gotten as dry and comfortable as possible.

Considering, I mean, that there was a guy out there in the darkness who was bent on killing us. Also that we had only a single weapon, which in no way matched the firepower of the guy's shotgun.

And of course we had no vehicle. It was quiet, too, no sound from around the cabin except for the usual nighttime-in-the-forest squeakings, rustlings, and the occasional dying shriek as some unfortunate small mammal fell prey to an owl or weasel.

Quiet, that is, until something big hit the outside wall of the cabin. A faint metallic *skreek-skreek* sound followed, then came a *clank!*

Ellie crept to the window, then turned back to me, her lean, delicate face lit sideways by the moon's glow.

I must've been staring. "What?" she demanded, but I couldn't speak, still looking at Ellie but seeing instead an old obituary photo from the *Quoddy Tides*.

I'd last seen the picture seven years earlier, when Marianne Hooper died; it had struck me hard then how much she was like my friend, and now that image rose clearly in memory again.

That face. Those eyes . . . Not twins, not even close, but the same kind of wavy, pale red hair and the same delicacy of facial features, so that an imagination rubbed raw by guilt might . . .

"Ellie." I found my voice. "Maybe I know why." *Why he's doing this.* It was crazy, but when has that ever stopped anyone?

Only I couldn't say so because just then a bundle of flaming rags soaked in what smelled like gasoline flew in through one of the broken panes; suddenly the floor was a pool of flames.

Ellie ran one way for a fire extinguisher; I ran the other for something to help smother the fire. I got to the daybed, reaching out; then my foot caught the edge of the braided rug and I went sprawling, hitting my head so hard on the corner of the bed frame that I saw stars.

And that's all I remember about that.

"Maybe we should go check on them." Sam sat with Wade at a table in the otherwise empty hospital cafeteria, drinking the warm brown liquid that had come out of the vending machine.

"On Mom and Ellie, I mean. At the cabin, make sure they're all right." The powdered creamer had lightened the stuff in the paper cup without improving its vile taste.

Wade looked up. "You think something's wrong there, too?" *On top of everything else?* his tone added.

Sam shrugged, both hands wrapped around the paper cup. If he had been home, Bella and his granddad might not have had to drive themselves wherever they'd been going. Or worse, his conscience added unhelpfully, maybe they'd gone out looking for him.

"I don't know. Probably not. Just a feeling, that's all." A feeling,

Sam didn't add, born of a nightmare apparition: his dead father, on a mission to warn him about something.

Something *bad* . . . Or maybe it was only his own twisted psyche trying to tell him something. Like *Don't let that girl con you.*

He had, though. He'd been a complete sucker, and was now in the aftermath of it, suffering the consequences. So maybe his dad wouldn't appear to him anymore, leering and dripping; maybe the worst had happened, and that last vision had been the final one.

Or maybe not. He felt . . . *disturbed,* like his insides were a hornet's nest somebody was stirring up with a stick. "I don't know," he repeated, and might've said more, but a familiar voice stopped him.

"You two boys mind company?" It was Eastport police chief Bob Arnold, plump and pink-faced in his cop uniform, with a ton of gear hanging from his duty belt as usual.

Equipment jangling and rattling around his ample waist, Bob pulled up a chair. "So. I guess you've had yourself quite a day."

Sam nodded. "I didn't fall off the wagon, Bob."

The chief nodded. "Good. Glad to hear it. Guess I had that part wrong, then."

No apology, though, and why would there be? Sam thought if he lived to be a hundred without ever taking another drink, there would still always be that little question about him.

A *deserved* little question. "You might want to know those two fair-weather friends of yours got nabbed," he went on.

The cut on Bob's forehead, held together by strips of surgical tape, looked fresh. Sam's mind flashed to a mental picture of the metal clasp on Carol Stedman's handbag.

Bob noticed Sam eyeing the cut, put two fingers to it and winced. "Yeah, she got me," he confirmed Sam's suspicion. "When I was helping her into the squad car, she . . ."

He stopped, apparently not liking this memory any more than Sam liked imagining the event. "Would have taped it myself, but I know when the wife comes home she'll ask if I got it looked at."

Sam thought about a woman who was so honest herself that you wouldn't lie to her just on that basis, even about such a little thing. "Huh," he said thoughtfully, and Bob nodded as if catching his thought, then went on:

"I guess they thought we were just a bunch of bumpkins, they could get away with just about anything."

Sam regarded his paper cup. Yeah, and who was the biggest bumpkin of all? Thinking this, he felt suddenly like jumping up from the table, maybe even tipping it over on his way out.

But Wade spoke up and saved him. "Sounds to me like they were a pair of pretty smooth operators."

Bob nodded. "Had enough warrants out on them to wallpaper a room. Made a career out of bamboozling people, charging whatever they could on stolen credit, maybe pulling a few burglaries and then skipping town, on to the next place."

He looked up at Sam again. "Had the boatyard's cashbox in their car, money and credit slips still in it. It's on its way back here now."

Sam sighed, a bigger weight lifting off him than he'd known was there. "Thanks."

He managed a smile, got up from the table without tipping it over. The clock on the wall by the exit said it was 3:10 a.m.

"Guess I'll head home, try for a nap," said Bob.

"Yeah, sounds good," Wade replied, lobbing a crumpled cup at one of the trash receptacles.

It went in. "You know," Sam ventured, tossing his own cup, "on the way home, maybe we could . . ."

Stop in at the cabin. At this way-too-early hour, the idea was ridiculous, but he wanted to see his mother and Ellie.

He just . . . *wanted* to, that was all. In the deserted hospital lobby, he pulled out his cellphone, tried his mother's number, and again got its "leave a message" recording.

And that did it, somehow. Whether or not it made sense, whether he'd had some crazy otherworldly warning or had made it all up in his own head, he was going out to the cottage at the lake whether his step-father liked it or not.

He turned to Wade, striding along behind him, intending to suggest that Wade ride home with Bob in the squad car while he, Sam, took the truck down the dirt road. But before he could say that, Wade's square, regular features went suddenly still and stunned-looking, as if in the shiny black reflectiveness of the hospital lobby's plate-glass windows he was seeing something that wasn't, *couldn't* be there. Something or someone . . .

Then, from behind them both, an alarm began sounding shrilly, a high, abrasive beeping that obviously meant something had gone very wrong somewhere. Beyond the doors leading to the patient wards, people were running, doctors and nurses sprinting toward whatever the alarm was for. . . .

Toward where Sam's grandfather and Bella lay injured and help-less. Wade turned from whatever he'd seen in the window, hurrying toward the alarm's insistent summons, and after a frozen moment—what *had* Wade seen out there, anyway?—Sam ran, too.

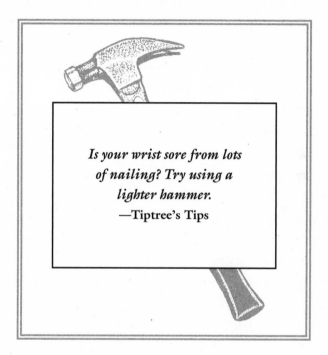

CHAPTER 9

Is your wrist sore from lots of nailing? Try using a lighter hammer.
—Tiptree's Tips

When I came to, I thought I was at home in my bed, safe and sound. But then I realized: Ellie and I were in a cottage deep in the woods, a man with a shotgun was romping around outside, and we had no way to escape.

Or, anyway, I assumed he was still out there, the drowning plot he'd nearly pulled off and the firebomb he'd thrown tending to confirm my belief; if nothing else, the guy was persistent.

Now as I lay on the floor looking up, Ellie peered down at me, relief on her face as she noticed that I was awake again.

"Hi," she said. She'd been fiddling with her Kindle, sitting by me with the device in her lap, but the fire extinguisher stood right next to her on the floor, and when I saw it, I sat up fast, recalling even more of the recent events.

"Ouch." I put my hand to the side of my head, felt a sticky, wet lump the size of a robin's egg that hurt like a son of a gun, from where I'd smacked it on the bed frame.

"Here." Ellie found her way to the cooler, dug out some ice cube remnants floating around in there, and located a dish towel to wrap it in. "Put this on it."

"Double ouch . . ." Ice might make it feel better in the long run, but in the short run, see *son of a gun,* above.

"I've been trying to send an email," she said. She'd put the Kindle back into its case; with the world's most energetic and inquisitive five-year-old at home, Ellie was compulsive about keeping electronic devices in padded surroundings.

Wishing hard that our attacker were in some, I tried opening and closing my eyes a few times, noting that they still worked but that I also wished I'd had some kind of padded enclosure for my head.

"I didn't know the Kindle had email capability." In Eastport it didn't even have a reliable download connection, due to the remoteness of the place; the joke in town was that the island community was the best place to be in the event the world ended, since we wouldn't find out about it until ten years later.

But here at the cottage, Ellie and I were nearer to one of Canada's wireless towers, so the gadget's bells and whistles worked. "It's supposed to be able to hook up to a Web-based mail site," Ellie said. "With the browser."

She frowned, setting the thing aside. "So I tried. But it's really not what the Kindle's meant for, so who knows if it went through. I couldn't tell for sure."

A small, uncertain laugh betrayed how worried she was; like me, I supposed. But there was no point in dwelling on that. "Anyway, while you were out cold, I nailed the front door shut. And the front window shades are all down. He can lurk, but he can't watch us."

The back windows looked out over the deck construction, and after that, sharply downhill through more trees, to the lake. You couldn't see in through those windows unless you were in one of the trees—unlikely, since they were paper birch trees with long, smoothish trunks, difficult to climb—or on stilts.

Or on the deck itself, but of course that wasn't finished yet—it didn't even have steps, much less anything to stand on—so she hadn't nailed that door shut. Besides, if Hooper got up to more tricks, we might need a way to escape.

"Wow," I said, still feeling woozy. "Good work."

She lit a battery lantern, set it on the kitchen counter. A dim golden glow spread through the cabin, half wrecked by gunfire—and by plain, old-fashioned regular fire.

"Thanks for saving me back there," I said. The pain in my head began to ease, but my ears were still ringing. "Back in the truck, I mean. And for the ice, too."

She looked up, the soft red curls framing her face glinting in the lamplight. "For the ice, you're welcome. But for the other part, I'm afraid the only thing you have to be grateful for is my own selfish wish to survive. You were stuck in the truck window, and I couldn't get out until I'd pushed you out first."

It wasn't at all the way I remembered the event; just the opposite, in fact. But that was Ellie, rarely giving herself any credit until everyone else had gotten at least two helpings.

"So listen," she went on. "We need to set a trap. A *sturdy* trap that we can catch him in and *keep* him in somehow until we get help."

Yeah, *somehow*. Glum discouragement washed over me; getting nearly drowned, shot at, firebombed, and bonked on the noggin can do that to a person, or so I've heard.

"Jake." She shoved a mug at me: noodle soup out of a packet. The steam rising from it smelled of bouillon cube, not one of my favorite flavors. "Drink it," she commanded.

Obediently, I sipped. The stuff tasted like chicken-feather stew, liberally seasoned with some kind of onion by-product. But at least it was hot, and I could feel sodium- and MSG-powered strength oozing back into me as I swallowed it.

"The thing is, though, the only traplike thing we've got is the deck we've been building," Ellie went on.

"Huh." I drank more soup. The noodles were like strips of plastic. Little green bits floated in there, too; freeze-dried vegetables, I hoped, since if those were chicken pieces I was in trouble.

"Underneath it, you mean." I tipped the cup up, swallowed determinedly and got the stuff down.

In the dim light, she nodded enthusiastically. "Yes, because we've got it all boxed in under there already with all the wooden lattice we nailed up."

I hate exposed porch underpinnings. Junk gets stuffed in under there, wild animals nest in the dark recesses of the space underneath the house, and spiders build cascading webs as thick as draperies, studded with egg casings and insects' bodies.

Also, two words: hornet's nests. And because of that lattice, right now you could've kept goats or a flock of chickens penned up underneath our deck-in-progress.

Or just one homicidal nutball, especially if you held a gun on him until help arrived; otherwise he could break out just by hurling himself against the lattice, which although it might slow him down some wasn't sturdy enough to confine him for long.

But the way I felt at the moment, I was willing to hold a gun on him forever, preferably with the end of the barrel stuffed an inch or so right up into his ear canal. The only hard part would be getting him in there.

Well, in addition to not firing the gun, I mean; as the soup began taking hold, my discouragement lessened and righteous anger flowed back in; unfortunately, that left little room for even my usual thin quota of intelligence.

"So . . . how do we do this?" If I knew Ellie, she'd already been thinking about it, and her reply didn't disappoint.

"First we put the decking boards on," she said. "We lay them out as if we were starting to build the floor. And then . . ." This was the important part, her tone said. "Then . . . we *don't nail them down*."

In reply I stared dumbly. Because, you see, each end of each decking piece has to rest on a floor joist. Otherwise, it'll fall right through to the ground below. And then you nail them down; if you don't, *you'll* fall through, when one of the pieces shifts off the joist board its end rests on.

"Don't nail them?" I repeated, frowning. "Because . . . ?"

But then it hit me. "Because it's a trap! He chases us until we catch him?"

"Precisely." Ellie looked pleased, either because I liked her plan so much or because, by comprehending it, I'd shown that maybe I hadn't lost quite as many of my marbles as she'd feared.

"He steps on a loose floorboard, it falls, he goes down. At the very least he'll be immobilized with a leg stuck through the floor. Ellie, that's great!"

By "go down," of course, I meant "fall right through the floor entirely" into the latticed-in area below. Whereupon we'd run out there with my gun, which would persuade him to hold still when we told him to do so . . .

"Great," I repeated, hauling myself up; the room took only a spin and a half before stopping, which I regarded as a good sign.

"If he's checked this place out at all"—which no doubt he had—"he knows the deck's there. And he knows that back door is the only way in." Because unless he was deaf, he'd heard Ellie nailing the front one shut.

"So what we need to do is *lure* him." Get him to run up onto that deck, I meant, by making him want to come into the cottage, somehow. And we, of course, would have to be the bait, which was the part of the plan I didn't like. But I really didn't see that we had much choice.

Because right now, we were in *his* trap; just a couple of little varmints, as my mother-in-law, Bella, would've put it. And I had a feeling that the next thing on his to-do list was—

—with a muffled crash, another firebomb flew in, breaking another front window and knocking its shade aside as it came; in response, I leapt for one fire extinguisher while Ellie grabbed the other—

—yep. Varmint elimination.

Half an hour later, we'd put out the second fire—if this went on we would soon run out of fire extinguishers, an idea I disliked intensely but there was no help for that, either—and were getting to work.

"Ouch," Ellie whispered, scrambling up from the ground and dusting herself off in the moonlight.

I squinted down at her. "Gangway," I whispered back, and joined her by jumping out the back door, too, and by the way, have I mentioned how much I dislike heights?

Also, *descending* from heights. And hard landings.

"Listen," I said, climbing to my feet; my ears were ringing again, and my head felt like someone had lopped off the top of it and stuffed in some cotton balls. "This thing about *getting* him trapped."

I scanned the darkness around the cottage for signs of our assailant. But I saw none, and no shotgun blasts or firebombs came out of the bushes at me, either.

So I was guessing he still had his heart set on making all this look accidental somehow. That, or he hadn't noticed us out here in back of the cottage yet.

"I still don't quite get how we're going to . . ."

I dabbed at something wet on my face. Then I dabbed again and peered at my hand. In the moonlight, something dark smeared it. A *lot* of something. But I understood, or so I thought.

"Don't worry about it. I hit that bed frame hard, and head wounds always bleed a lot," I told Ellie, who'd seen the blood, too, and appeared concerned.

I dabbed once more, then got busy trying not to stumble or trip over anything as I located the piles of decking boards I had arranged earlier.

"How are we going to lure him? Is that what you're asking?" Ellie moved the stepladder over to the deck, then scampered up it to perch on the deck's edge.

"I don't know," she went on. "Run around and make faces at him, maybe, or yell insulting remarks. Anything to get him . . ."

Mad. At us; great, I thought. One mistake and our plan could turn us from trappers to trapped, with the extra-attractive additional feature that by then, he'd be royally ticked off at us. *Oh, wonderful,* I grumbled silently.

I touched my head again. The lump was still oozing; that's all the blood meant, I confidently believed.

"You hand the boards up. I'll lay them out," said Ellie very quietly, and held out her hand for the first one.

Which I supplied, and then the next one. And the one after that: bend, stretch, repeat.

The boards weren't heavy, but there were a lot of them; probably my arms wouldn't fall off before we were done. But as I thought this, a hot, dark drop fell onto my hand, then another.

"You know, though," Ellie whispered, taking another decking board from me, "I keep on wondering if maybe we *should* just try sneaking out of here. . . ."

"Uh-huh. So which way do you want to try getting to the dirt road? Across the clearing in front of the cottage? With him right there in it, or near it?"

I handed her another board. "Or through the woods? In pitch darkness, through muck and brambles, over fallen trees, and . . ."

Seriously, I'd been out there in that wilderness and it was darned near impenetrable, even in daylight. "Not only that, but if we run . . ."

Well, he didn't *want* to shoot us. He'd already pretty much proven that. But that didn't mean he *wouldn't*. If, I mean, we put him in a situation where he felt he had no choice.

"Yeah," Ellie agreed in a whisper. "You're right. It's just that . . . Hand me another board," she finished resignedly.

So I did: one more down, another thirty or forty to go.

Or maybe fifty. At least we weren't getting shot at.

He was waiting, that was all. Until things were the way *he* wanted them . . . which probably he was nearby busily arranging right this minute.

Not a comforting thought, but those were getting pretty hard to come by in general, weren't they? So all we could do was try. . . . Another hot droplet leaked down my face; it tasted like salty copper, and as I brushed it away, I realized:

It wasn't from the bump on my head. It was a nosebleed.

Still, no big deal, right?

Wrong.

Once upon a time, the devil wore a red suit, had sharp horns and a pitchforked tail, and spent his time scampering around on cloven hooves doing mischief, never happier than when he could tempt you into doing some, too. But now women had taken over, so no devils were needed to make a man's life miserable.

Or so Dewey Hooper thought to himself as he struggled to eliminate the two females who, if not stopped right here and now, could steal away his hard-won freedom: his dead wife, Marianne, back from the grave to punish him for killing her, and Marianne's bigmouthed pal, who'd already testified against him once.

There would not, he was absolutely determined, be a second time, and now—after another, much more intense anxiety attack, but never mind that, he told himself shakily—he'd decided just how to make certain of it.

He'd tried the small firebombs, but they hadn't been enough.

Those damned women had put them out. What he needed was a fire so ferocious and all-consuming that they couldn't stop it, one that would burn up both their bodies *and* any other pesky evidence of his recent presence.

And as if to reassure him that such a plan really was the answer to his problem, he had the fuel for such a conflagration conveniently at hand: the cottage's propane tank.

There were, though, still two difficulties with the project. First, the tank *was* full of propane, so wrestling it over uneven ground, terrain studded with granite boulders that the tank could hit hard if you dropped it, was a dicey proposition.

Back in prison when he'd had to move such tanks around the complex on various work details, he'd had it explained to him how tanks under pressure spun around like loose rockets when broken; one of them could take your legs clean off. So he was careful as he maneuvered this one across the graveled clearing, toward the cottage's front window.

Then there was the stench of the stuff; he didn't quite know yet how he was going to get around that. The women inside seemed to be staying toward the rear of the building, so he hoped to get a decent amount of propane in there before they smelled it. But he would need luck, too; he hoped his own was still good.

Moments later, though, he found out just how good it still was, even better than he could've hoped. Setting the tank under one of the front windows, he wedged it firmly between two granite chunks sticking up out of the ground like gravestones, then risked a peek through the corner of the window where the shade didn't quite go all the way to the edge.

And got, at first, an awful shock: he couldn't see them.

Stunned, he scanned the interior, what he could see of it. *Where . . . ?*

But then a sound from outside the cabin, through the open back door, sent a spasm of relief through him, followed by a rush of suspicion about what they might be up to. He scuttled downhill on the path alongside the cottage and peered around the back wall only to find . . . what the *hell*?

They were *doing* something. There in the moonlight, the two of them were fiddling around with some boards . . . laying out pieces of decking, he saw with disbelief. They were putting a floor onto the latticed framework of a deck that was in the process of being constructed. And . . . why would they be doing that?

Then, after a moment of puzzling over it, he knew. It was a trap of some kind. All he had to do was avoid it. And that ought to be easy; he had no reason to be going anywhere near that deck.

So—easy-peasy—he simply wouldn't. He would stay away from it entirely. Smiling at his own cleverness, he inhaled the smell of the fresh lumber they were using. With it came the clean pine smell of the surrounding woods and a pungently mineral-smelling whiff of the nearby lake.

They didn't know he was so close. From where he stood, he could just shoot them both right now and they'd never even know what hit them.

But if he did, all hope of their deaths escaping criminal investigation was over. No, it was best that they stay occupied here while he went on with his propane plan. That way he could get even more of the gas into the building in secrecy.

Then, as soon as they went back in . . .

Bang, he thought happily. They'd have an instant to smell the accumulated gas, but before they could do anything about it—

Oh, his luck was just wonderful tonight, he thought as he made his way quietly back to the clearing where he'd left the rubber hose from the outdoor shower setup. With it in hand, he returned to the propane tank wedged under the window.

But when he tried attaching the tube to the tank, he recalled the other thing that was wrong with cylinders like this one: it had a gauge with a fat, threaded connector on it but no handy-dandy slender nozzle to slide the hose onto.

Instantly his good cheer vanished, replaced by anxious fury as he hunched there among the prickly-branched huckleberry bushes that grew around the boulders. Once more he squinted thwartedly at the black rubber hose in his trembling right hand, then at the tank's top.

But he wasn't seeing either of them. Instead the smug face and superior sneer of the prison's guidance counselor mocked him.

Your problem, Dewey, is that you don't think ahead. Instead you just roll merrily along.

Until it all goes bad on you. Again. Dewey's fists clenched. It was all he could do not to give the tank a shove . . . but no.

No. *Look again. Get control of yourself.* The thoughts came with an effort, just as they had when he'd passed on shooting the women where they stood. He hadn't learned them from the smirking harridan at the prison, either. Instead, they were the only useful advice he'd ever gotten from a cop.

From the Eastport police chief, Bob Arnold, in fact, one time when Dewey was being jailed for—he was pretty sure he recalled this—public intoxication and assault. For no particular reason, on their way to the county lockup, the chief had turned and looked through the perp screen at Dewey, in that piece of junk Eastport used for a squad car.

"Dewey," the chief had said—he'd known Dewey for a long time by then, having arrested him often—"from now on when you get mad, I want you to stop. Look again at the situation and give yourself a minute to get control of yourself."

The police chief had turned back to the road ahead. "Can you do that?" he'd asked. "Can you give yourself a chance and do it?"

And of course Dewey had promised that he would, and then had forgotten about it almost at once . . . until now. *Until tonight.* His shaking hands quieted, his constricted throat opening so he could breathe again. *A minute . . . control of myself. O-kay . . .*

What the hell, maybe it was worth a try, even if the hated prison counselor lady had said the same.

Thinking this, he looked at the valve clamped to the tank. He'd unhitched the tank from the cottage's gas line by first turning the valve off via the big round knob at the top. Then he'd bent the slim metal tubing that carried the propane into the dwelling through a small hole in the wall. He'd bent it back and forth until it broke. That way, no clean cut marks would suggest that the tube had been tampered with; instead, the damage would seem like part of the larger "accident" he was planning.

Once the tank was free, he could roll it off the concrete pad it had been stationed on. Next, he'd used a wrench from the toolshed to unscrew the metal tubing's fitting from the valve.

So now he had a tank with a valve on it, but still no way to attach the hose, which was way too small to fit over the valve's threads. And even if it would fit, he realized as he puzzled over the thing, the tank was so pressurized that when he opened it, the outflow of gas would likely blow the hose right off again.

But . . . he stood there, thinking about that prison counselor and how much he wanted to spite her, and about Bob Arnold and what he had said. And the threaded fitting on the metal tube he had removed from the tank was around here somewhere, wasn't it?

The tank still had a threaded fitting, too, matching the one on the tube. So . . . one thought turned over, then another.

So he could *put the metal tube back on again.*

Swiftly he scurried to where the tank had originally stood, under the cottage's kitchen window. By the sound of it, the women were still working out there on the other side of the cabin.

Good, he thought, reminding himself again not to venture out on that newly floored deck. Their plight might be hopeless, but they could still cause him lots of trouble, and somehow their work was meant to do just that.

So let's get this over with. Once they're gone, the chance of any more problems out of them will be, too.

He eased in among the pine boughs to where he'd dropped the slim metal tubing . . . and found it. Still attached to the tank gauge with a metal hex nut, the whole apparatus lay on a mat of pine needles that had accumulated against the building over the years.

Without warning, another bolt of panic pierced him, the sky overhead suddenly too large . . . *wide open*, as if he might float up into it and be lost among all that . . . that *freedom*.

In which anything might happen. But that was *nuts*, he was *here*, he was . . . *Jeeze, just shut up*, he told himself viciously.

The tank gauge still lay at his feet. Bending, he grabbed it.

Laying out decking boards to form a floor is like doing a jigsaw puzzle, except that if you don't put the pieces in just right, they'll fall right through to the carpet beneath the table—or, in the case of our deck, to the ground below.

"Oof." The boards were light when we began laying them out, but by the end they were *heavy:* reach, lift, repeat. But at long last Ellie and I had put each one into its precarious—we hoped *very* precarious, their ends perched so close to the edges of the joists that a chipmunk could kick one off—place.

Then we fell down exhausted, huddled in the lattice-enclosed space under the deck. "Let's remember not to fall through ourselves," I said, and Ellie chuckled tiredly. But:

"Don't laugh," I said. "You'd be surprised how easy it is to forget that the deck boards aren't nailed down. And no, I do not want to talk about how I know that."

Suffice it to say I'd put a new floor on the porch at home, too, once upon a midsummer. And the space underneath that one had turned out to be full of stinging ants, much to my sorrow when I fell through into it.

Meanwhile, with the nailed-up lattice sheets around it and the newly laid-out floor over our heads, the area under this deck felt fairly safe. But it wasn't, so as soon as we'd caught our breaths we confronted the next project: getting back inside.

And that wasn't the only problem. Through the crisscross slats of the lattice, the moon shone in; I looked down at my hands, stained and sticky with blood. My nose was still bleeding in scary, intermittent gouts; I'd been able to hide it from Ellie by dragging my sleeve hard across my face every time it started flowing again.

I wouldn't be able to hide my increasing dizziness for much longer, though, or the bright stars flaring in my vision whenever I stood straight. Clambering up, I reeled as a wave of faintness washed over me, and grabbed onto one of the lattice sections.

"Jake?" Ellie peered worriedly at me. "Jake, you're . . ."

Yeah. All I could think of was that I must've hit my head harder than I'd thought, but this seemed even worse than a simple head bonk. My ears rang, and my whole body had a watery feeling as if I were dissolving.

"Go inside," I whispered, sitting down suddenly. A ladder was our only way up to the back door, and it looked about as climbable as Mount Everest to me suddenly.

"I'll be right in, too." My voice had evaporated. Ditto my equilibrium.

And, of course, she noticed. "Stay right here," she ordered, ignoring the fact that at the moment, I had little choice.

Whatever strength I possessed seemed to have leaked out my nose. Another big splotch of blood fell as I put my hands on my knees, struggling to rise. "Maybe I can . . ."

But that turned out to be a mistake. The world spun, my legs went weak, and a black wave of unconsciousness crashed down.

When I came to again, I was looking up at Ellie's scared face. "We've got to stop meeting like this," I whispered, trying to smile. But she wasn't having any.

"Stay *here*," she whispered. "I *mean* it. I'll be right back." She scampered up the ladder, tiptoed very, *very* carefully across the loose decking to the door, and vanished inside.

Don't panic. Just breathe. Slow, deep breaths. You're going to be fine.

That's what I told myself. But the steady drip of blood from some-where up inside my face said otherwise. To distract myself, I concen-trated on the cold, which now that we weren't busy working had begun penetrating into my bones. I tried listening to the nearby forest sounds, the pattering of droplets from tree branches and the clickings and rustlings of unseen woodland creatures.

But the sounds only reminded me that in the woods, violent death among soft, defenseless mammals like me is commonplace, a method merely for other, toothier creatures to get something to eat.

Speaking of which, the next thing I knew, Ellie was beside me again, holding a mug from which pale, fragrant steam rose up in ghostly puffs. "Drink this."

Shakily I reached out. But I couldn't make my hand grip the mug tightly enough. "This," I whispered, "is *humiliating*."

"Don't be silly." She held the cup to my lips. Hot coffee was some-where in there, not quite overpowered by brandy plus lots of sugar and cream.

I drank, gasped with relief—that stuff was *potent*—and drank more of it, sinking back against her supporting arm. "Thank you."

"You're welcome," she responded briskly, then pestered me to drink the rest until I did.

The aromatic mixture wouldn't cure what ailed me—I was starting to think I'd need expert help, an emergency room visit or even a sur-geon's assistance, for that—but it made me feel better for now, enough so that I could appreciate what we'd done.

It looked like a deck. It *smelled* like a deck; even through my leak-ing, clogged-up nose I could capture the fragrance of freshly cut lum-ber, sharply astringent.

But it wasn't a deck; it was our villain trap, and now all we had to do was set it.

"So now this is the only way in or out of the cottage," I said as Ellie helped me up the stepladder to the door. Crossing the deck was a Zen-like exercise: foot up, foot down, no side-to-side shuffling—or in my case, staggering—whatsoever. But we made it; inside I sank down at once, then rolled over on the linoleum and lay there, panting.

"Right. If he wants us, he'll have to come and get us." She snapped the shades up, grimacing at him, wherever he was.

"That's right, you jerk," she said at the darkness out there. "Get a good look. Maybe it'll make you want to get even closer, hmm?" And when I glanced doubtfully at her:

"Jake, he's had plenty of chances to shoot us, and he hasn't. I'm betting that whatever he wants to do, he wants it up close."

Right: he had, and he hadn't, so he probably wouldn't. That made sense.

Or it did in my addled brain, anyway. Besides, the way I felt now, getting shot would've been a relief. I crawled groggily across the floor to an end table where there was a box of tissues, then pressed a thick wad of them to my nose with both hands. One handful, and then another and another.

From the clearing, where it was getting darker again as the moon began setting across the lake, he could see Marianne moving around inside the cottage, where she'd raised the shades again as if taunting him. Her red-gold hair caught the lamp's feeble glow, igniting brief sparks of brilliance.

Gotcha, he thought again, but then she looked out toward him for a moment, setting his heart thudding; had she seen him?

He ducked behind the toolshed; having her where he wanted her, trapped and at his mercy, didn't keep her from having a few nasty tricks still up her own sleeve, he suspected. And she could still use them on him, too, if she got the chance.

So he had to stop her. Afterwards he would burn whatever remnants of the cottage remained, make sure no telltale evidence—the hose on the propane tank, shells from the shots he'd fired, tools he'd moved, gasoline he'd used, and so on—was left to hint at non-accidental events.

The cleanup alone seemed overwhelming, when considered as a single project; he'd have to put the tank back, too, and arrange the propane feeder tube leading into the cottage plausibly, and no doubt there were more things, ones he hadn't remembered yet.

That missing gasoline, for instance . . . Could he steal some from one of the other cottages, to replace it? He wasn't sure, or even if it mattered.

But I've done this much, he told himself as he crept from behind the shed. *I can do the rest, too, whatever it turns out to be.*

So, slipping around the edge of the clearing to the place under the window where he'd set up the propane tank, he began. In his hands were the tank fitting with the slim metal tubing on it, the wrench he'd found in the toolshed, and the length of black rubber hose he'd liberated from the outdoor shower setup.

The hose fit snugly onto the metal tubing. While the women kept busy at whatever foolishness they'd been engaged in behind the cottage, he'd sat working the hose onto the tubing, bit by bit, until he'd covered almost all of the metal with rubber.

Next he screwed the metal tubing's threaded end back onto the tank's valve opening, then he fed the free end of the rubber hose stealthily in through the window he'd broken with the firebomb, earlier. Now a turn of the valve handle would send propane flowing into the cottage. It had taken longer than he'd expected to set everything up. So they wouldn't be outside when the gas flowed as he'd planned. But they'd worked half the night. Maybe they'd fall asleep.

Maybe luck was still with him.

He stepped away from the window and the contraption he'd rigged up underneath it. Might as well wait for dawn: just enough pale gleam from over the horizon so the glow of the fire against the sky wouldn't alert people miles away, but dark enough still so the smoke wouldn't show much.

A *big* fire . . . Silently he eased back in among the trees surrounding the cottage. When he could see the branches overhead outlined black against the lightening sky, it would be time to turn the tank on. After that, just a short wait more, and then . . .

He pulled a match pack that he'd liberated from one of the other lakeside cottages out of his pocket, fingering it in happy anticipation. *Bang,* he thought again, mouthing the word and savoring it deliciously this time.

Bang and done.

"You awake?" I asked into the darkness.

"Uh-huh." Ellie came over to where I lay shivering on the daybed. No matter how many blankets she piled on me, I couldn't get warm; my inner thermostat, apparently, was stuck at "icy."

"I could fix you a hot-water bottle," she offered.

It was just past 3 a.m. We'd let the woodstove fire go out while we were working on the deck outside, and there wasn't any wood left in the bin to start another.

"Okay," I managed. The room stank of burned stuff; we'd tossed the firebomb-damaged items outside, trying to get rid of the reek of gasoline that they gave off, but it didn't help much.

"And some hot tea, maybe," I added. "If it's not too much trouble." Being short on blood seemed also to have cut down my body-heat-preservation ability. But somehow I had to warm up.

Or at least stop shivering; I had the gun and the bullets for it wrapped up with me in the blanket. They wouldn't do me any good, though, if I was shaking too hard to fire the weapon when something bad happened.

Which I still felt sure it would. No one did all the things our attacker had done and then just quit for no reason. So he was coming; now we could only wait and hope we were ready for him.

"Drat." Ellie turned off the gas stove's knob, then turned it on again and flicked the lighter near the burner, waiting for the familiar *floof!* of blue flame.

Nothing. I closed my eyes and opened them again fast, hoping this was all just a terrible hallucination and somebody would slap me or throw cold water in my face.

But nobody did. "Maybe we're out of propane," I said. "Wade said he would call the propane guy to bring out a fresh tank, but I guess he forgot. Or the propane guy did."

Which was completely out of character for either one of them; Wade was so reliable that if he didn't show up when he'd said he would, you could be pretty sure he was dead. And once in the middle of winter, the propane guy—his one-man operation was called, appropriately enough, Mr. Propane—had strapped a tank to a snowmobile and driven it out here down the snow-choked forest road, delivering it on an hour's notice.

True, there was an ice-fishing party going on at the time and the propane guy wanted in on it; Bella was frying the fish up as fast as people could catch them, and baking huckleberry pies.

The point is, though, that maybe if in the past couple of hours I hadn't been shot at, half drowned, firebombed, and drained of a lot of blood—not to mention scared half to death—it might've dawned on me sooner that my husband never forgot such things and neither did Mr. Propane.

But I had been, so it didn't.

CHAPTER 10

*Painting outdoors? Wear sunscreen,
a hat, and (especially if it's
white paint!) sunglasses.*
—Tiptree's Tips

For an awful hour at the hospital, Wade and Sam couldn't get anyone to tell them what was happening to Bella, because everyone who
knew anything was too busy working on her. So the two stood awk-
wardly in the corridor, too far from her room to hear anything mean-
ingful but near enough to know things weren't going well.

But then, suddenly, they were. A young guy in a green scrub suit
came out, stripping off latex gloves. Behind him came two nurses, one
pushing a cart with a lot of empty glass ampules and vials on it. The
other carried a shiny basin heaped with medical instruments and the
plastic packaging they'd come in.

"Well, that was unexpected," said the scrub-suited guy, who turned out to be the doctor on duty; the hospital in Calais was too small to have more than one MD present this late at night.

Or, rather, this early in the morning; by the clock at the nurses' station, it was 3:35 a.m. Guiltily, Sam felt another wave of fatigue wash over him; if he hadn't been such an idiot last night, he wouldn't be so completely wiped out and exhausted now, would he?

"But she's okay," added the doctor, whose name was Munson and who was, it seemed to Sam, way too young to be in charge of anything, much less an entire hospital full of sick people. "The upshot, though, is that some of the medicine we were giving her didn't agree with her."

"Yeah, no kidding." It came out harshly, more so than Sam had intended. But now that he wasn't terrified, he was angry. "I guess you should've been more–"

Careful, he was about to finish, but before he could, Wade shot him a look that conveyed very clearly just who needed to be careful here, and it wasn't this young physician.

"Sorry," Sam mumbled. Boy, he was just racking up the points in the good-behavior department lately, wasn't he?

But the young doc had dealt with anxious family members before. "Don't worry about it. Anyway, we've got her straightened out now. I want her to rest, but if you feel like just going in for a minute–"

"I'll go," said Wade. "So she knows we're here for her. You go on, wait in the lobby for me, okay?"

Nodding, Sam bit his lip. How Wade had intuited that Sam was on the verge of a sudden, ridiculous fit of tears, Sam wasn't sure, but he was glad to leave the brightly lit hospital corridor behind. Out in the silent lobby–Bob Arnold had been summoned away by a radio call just as all the excitement had erupted–Sam could be alone to collect his thoughts, at least, and try to get a handle on what he was feeling.

But as he exited the ward, he spotted a familiar dark ponytail. Its owner sat in one of the upholstered chairs in the waiting area, flipping through a glossy magazine's pages without looking at any of them.

He stared in disbelief. It was Carol, whom he'd last seen on her way out of the room at the Motel East with Richard. She got up and turned in appeal; shaking his head, he strode past her.

She caught up to him. "Sam, please."

"Don't talk to me, okay?" He kept walking.

"Sam, I'm not here to get anything from you. I just want to say I'm sorry. I made a huge mistake. If I can make up for it somehow, I will. But if not . . ."

He stopped just short of the big glass doors leading outside, still not looking at her.

"If not," she finished, "then I'm just . . . sorry."

"Why aren't you in jail?"

He shouldn't be giving her any kind of opening at all. But he'd had to say what she'd just said so many times, himself, that he'd become a sucker for an apology, he supposed.

"Richard told them that it was all him, that I didn't have anything to do with . . . well. With anything."

So Richard wasn't a complete bastard, then. Or more likely, Carol knew something she could hold over Richard's head, Sam thought cynically.

"I'm supposed to bail him out tomorrow after the hearing," she added.

Right, Sam thought, so that's why Richard took all the blame—so there'd be someone on the outside who could get cash together for him.

"They let you take the car? Walk out of jail, just drive away?"

Something about this still wasn't adding up. A lot, really, and hadn't Bob Arnold said that there were warrants out on both Richard and Carol?

Sam glanced back at the empty waiting area, then out at the parking lot. "How'd you even know I was here?"

She looked at the floor. "I followed you," she confessed. "I was on my way back to the motel in case you were still tied up in there, and I saw the big blond-haired man go into the room. Then, a little later when you both came out . . ."

His face must've betrayed his feelings: confusion, mistrust.

"I was going to get you out of there myself," she went on, "but he got there first. I just wanted so much to say how sorry I am, that I–"

Suddenly her arms were close around him, her cheek warm against his neck, her hair softly perfumed. "Oh, Sam, please help me. I'm scared, and I don't know what to do now."

He let her rest her head on his shoulder. Her shape in his arms felt fine, like it was meant to be there.

Not that he believed her. Once the pleasure of having her in his arms wore off, nothing she'd said would make sense. It didn't now, even.

But it would serve her right if he pretended not to know that a while longer. It was what his father would have done.

Then he looked up, and in the black reflectiveness of the glass doors saw—

That nightmare face. "Dad?" he whispered. It *couldn't* be, but—

And then it wasn't. Carol turned her head to look up at him questioningly when she felt his arms tighten around her, holding her. Outside the glass doors, Bob Arnold frowned as he recognized the woman locked in Sam's embrace, and started in.

Suddenly she caught on. "Let *go* of me, let . . . help! Someone, help me, he's crazy! Help, I'm . . . you *bastard*!"

Rearing back, eyes blazing and teeth bared in a grimace, she reminded him of a wild animal in the moment before Bob Arnold reached them. A weasel like the one out at the lake, Sam thought, and why, he wondered, was he thinking about that right now?

Bob crossed the lobby, popping the handcuffs from his belt. He snapped them onto Carol's wrists as Sam gripped her arms, pushing them down carefully so as not to hurt her.

"All right," Bob said to her, his voice low and calm, almost soothing. "Let's try it again, and this time there's not going to be any escaping from anyone's custody, so save your energy."

Sam watched her face change as she opened her mouth to lie, to argue and try to bargain her way out of this. Suddenly she was an innocent young woman again, caught up tragically in some awful misunderstanding.

Just then Wade came up to them. "What's going on?"

Carol's head swiveled. "Please," she begged, eyes filling with tears. "Whoever you are, please, this is a mistake. You've got to–"

"Save it," Bob rapped out, and she shut up, reddening as if slapped. "That radio call I got?" He angled his head at her. "Girlfriend here sweet-talked somebody into letting her use the john by herself, at that rest stop on Route 9 on the way over to Bangor. God knows what she told him, but it worked."

Sam wasn't sure, but he thought he sensed Carol preening faintly at this description of how well she'd conned even a cop.

Bob went on. "Next thing he knows, he looks around and she's gone, must've gotten a ride back this way from someone out on the highway. Stole another car in Eastport, followed you up here . . ."

Bob stopped, looking disgusted. But Sam got the point. One thing she'd said *was* true, then: with Richard out of the picture at least temporarily, she *had* needed help.

Money maybe, a place to lay low. And she'd thought that to get it, she'd be able to fool Sam again. That was how dumb she thought he was, the impression he'd given her.

"You'll be *sorry*," she spat, twisting in Bob Arnold's expert grip as he guided her toward the glass doors.

"Yeah," Sam said. Yeah, he already was. Bob took her out.

"Hey," Wade said. From the cafeteria entrance now came warm smells of cooking; though it was not yet 4:30 a.m., the earliest morning staffers were already trudging in for their shifts.

"Everything okay?" Wade asked.

"Fine," Sam said. "I'm good." In the cafeteria, a big rosy-cheeked woman opened the tray line by sliding a grate up.

"Then how about we check on Bella and your grandfather once more, then get breakfast and take a ride up to the cabin?"

"Great," Sam agreed. The night wasn't ending too badly after all, he thought, by the time reached Bella's bedside.

She opened her eyes, panic filling them at her first sight of the unfamiliar surroundings. But then she saw Wade, and her fear subsided.

Sam took her hand, forced back tears at the bony feel of it. "Hey," he whispered, and nearly did cry when she gave his fingers a squeeze. "Hey, you look just great to me, you know that?"

She did, too; funny, he thought, how a skinny old woman with dyed red hair and a face that pretty much defined the term *battle-ax* could be so . . . so *pretty.*

Wade took his phone out, laid it on her bedside table. "You keep this," he said. She didn't have one of her own. "Don't use it until they say you can," he added cautioningly, and she moved her head up and down a little to show she understood.

"It'll make her feel better just having it," Wade explained when she was asleep again. They made their way back out along the corridor. "Because you know she wouldn't use the one the hospital provides."

"Right, because it might have germs on it." Back home, her übercleanliness could be a trial.

But now not so much. In fact, by the time he sat down at the cafeteria table with Wade, who was already digging into his eggs, he felt almost cheerful.

Still, he couldn't stop wondering about one detail. "Hey, Wade?"

The big man looked up from his meal, his broad, craggy face mildly amiable now that no one seemed to be in any immediate danger. He wore his usual uniform of a dark sweatshirt over a plaid flannel shirt, jeans, and work boots; Sam thought that at his age, he ought to be less comforted by Wade's presence. But he was very glad he didn't have to do all this alone.

"Earlier, in the lobby," he began, not quite knowing how to phrase the rest of it. So he finally just blurted it all out: about the nightmare face in the bilge water, and the other times he'd seen it, ending with the most recent hallucination.

"So what I want to know," Sam added hesitantly, because if just one person saw something, that was one thing. But more than one was entirely another. "What I want to know is this," he said, and then he asked Wade: had *he* seen Sam's dad, too? *Had* he?

Wade put his cup down, considering the question seriously.

And after a moment, answered.

To store electricity from the solar panels at the cottage, we used a deep-cycle marine battery, plus a converter to change the direct current from the panels to alternating current. That way we could run ordinary appliances on it instead of having to buy special ones.

But not just any household appliances. Fluorescent bulbs for the lamps were mandatory, so as not to waste power, and we didn't bother even trying to operate electricity hogs like toasters. I'd kept planning to rent a gasoline-powered generator and bring it here along with a vacuum cleaner, and give this place a serious cleaning. But I hadn't done it, which was why the cabin's braided rug had so much dog hair embedded in it.

I knew it did, because I'd been lying on it for an hour when light began peeking through the burnt spots of the bed linens nailed up at the windows.

"You're sure those decking boards are the way we want them?" I whispered.

Despite the tea Ellie kept making me, my mouth tasted like old blood, and even with so many panes broken out of the windows, the cottage interior still stank of ashes and gasoline.

"I'm sure." Ellie was on the daybed with my gun in her lap; he'd be coming soon, we thought. For some reason we didn't know yet, and probably wouldn't like, he seemed to be waiting for better light.

And now it was here. I sat halfway up, lay back down again fast. Saving my strength, Ellie called it.

I called it nearly fainting, any time I tried raising my head higher than my feet. But my state of consciousness wasn't the important thing now, I told myself firmly. Getting away with this was the important thing.

So I was having second thoughts about the completeness of our preparations. "Ellie. Upstairs, there's a little electric jigsaw."

I'd put it there when the gas-generator idea was fresh and attractive instead of just something I'd never gotten around to. Besides the vacuuming project, I'd meant to build—if you can believe such a corny notion—a pair of wooden window shutters with the outlines of pine trees jigsawed into them.

Folk art, I'd thought optimistically, ignoring the fact that I am neither folksy nor artistic. Anyway:

"Jake," Ellie began patiently, "a jigsaw will drain all the power out of the—"

"I know." The battery wasn't meant to run tools. But it was all we had, and if we could just get ten minutes out of it . . .

Blood leaked down the back of my throat again, thin and salt tasting; I spat into a tissue without looking. No sense scaring myself; I was already scared enough.

"But do me a favor and go get the saw anyway, will you?" I asked Ellie. "I've just got a bad feeling."

In fact, if my fears were electricity, I could've run that saw for hours, with enough power left over to light Times Square.

Ellie scampered upstairs to the loft; I heard her cross the floor over my head, and moments later she returned with the tool.

"I don't understand, though, what you think we can—"

"Thanks." The saw was shaped like a power drill, only with a place to insert a slim cutting blade instead of a drill bit. But there was a problem with it:

No cutting blade. I'd dulled up the last one notching two posts upstairs, I now recalled, so I could set in a shelf for a mirror and a few toiletries. When I was done, I'd taken the old blade out and discarded it, meaning to bring a fresh one the next time I visited.

But I hadn't. I'd forgotten. A deep, sick thud of fatigue hit me suddenly, like being smacked upside the head with a two-by-four, as my dad probably would've put it.

"Okay," I said. I put the saw down. Then something else hit me: "Do you smell propane?"

Ellie sniffed. "Uh-huh. Probably from when I was trying to turn the stove on. The last of it, that was in the gas line . . ."

"Yeah. That's got to be it, I guess." Since if the tank was empty, what else could it be?

Moments later she'd fetched me the Very Sharp Knife, the kind the TV ads say easily cuts steel or a tomato. Because the more I thought about a second escape route, the more I wanted one. . . .

"Great," I said, trying to sound reasonably confident and cheerful. Although from what I could tell, everything about our situation was about as far from great as it could get, short of vaporization by the explosion of, say, a thermonuclear device.

"The thing is," I told Ellie as I slid across the linoleum to the spot on the floor that I had in mind, "we think we can lure him into trying to come in here after us."

Or get him to come as far as the deck platform, anyway. The plan we had so far was that when it got light enough, we'd slip outside, being careful not to dislodge any of those loose deck boards. I'd go down the ladder and hide in the bushes alongside the path, while Ellie perched at the edge of the deck structure.

And then she would *taunt* him, which of course was the most dangerous part. But he'd had chances to shoot us before, and he hadn't, so we were still betting he wouldn't this time, either.

Betting our lives, actually, that he still wanted somehow to make our deaths look accidental. And that, we hoped, would quite literally be his downfall:

If we could get him to climb onto the deck, a careless step from him would knock some of its boards off the joists they were perched on. When the boards tumbled, he would, too, down into the enclosure below.

The plan wasn't perfect; how could it be? If he had that shotgun with him when he fell, for example, we might have to shoot *him*.

Seeming to catch my thought, Ellie spoke up. She still had my gun with her. "Jake? If I get a chance, I'm going to—"

"Shoot him? No." I'd practiced with targets, but not moving ones, and hitting something that's sitting still is hard enough. So far he hadn't shown himself enough to be vulnerable, but even if he did I had no confidence that I'd be able to take him down, especially in the dark.

And for all her admirable determination, Ellie barely knew which end of the weapon to hold. "We don't want to make him so angry that he forgets what he's doing and just charges in here, blasting," I said.

Which for all we knew he might still do anyway, another reason we needed an emergency exit. I gripped the knife, rolled the rug aside, and scored the floor's elderly brick-patterned linoleum, then tore up a square of the stuff. Underneath was plywood, whose grain goes in lots of different directions due to the way it's manufactured.

That makes it hard to cut. But the knife—a Miracle Blade, the TV ad had called it, and I hoped to hell the name turned out to be appropriate—was all we had. Also:

I looked at the plywood. A hole for me to slip the blade's sharp tip into did not obligingly appear. "Hand me the hammer and a big nail, will you?"

Ellie brought them; I slammed a nail into the plywood and pulled it out. Then I did it again, right next to the first hole.

And again. Six holes later, I had a small circle of holes in the plywood. Perforations: I slammed the hammer down hard on the circle's center. The wood popped out, fell through, down into the blackness under the cabin.

Meanwhile, more ways that our plan could fail kept occurring to me. The deck still lacked stairs, of course, so we'd stationed the stepladder where he could easily use it to get up onto the platform. But what if the stepladder made him feel suspicious, so he didn't use it? Or . . .

"What if he tries to force us out without coming in?" I said when Ellie went on looking puzzled.

"Oh. We're trying to trap *him*, but . . ."

"Exactly." I started sawing with the Miracle Knife, which in fact cut so well, I pitied any tomato unlucky enough to come into contact with it. "This is just in case he tries the same."

The blade was not only better than no tool at all; it was *much* better; sooner than I'd thought, I'd nearly finished cutting a two-foot-square hole in the floor. But by that time my arm was like spaghetti and six or so inches still remained un-Miracled.

Whereupon Ellie *stomped* on it; the wood broke and fell with a clatter to the darkness below. "There," she said decisively. "Now we're good if he tries coming in. . . ."

She turned to the back door. "Or if he doesn't."

Suddenly I smelled propane again, stronger now, and glimpsed a brief flicker of orange flame outside the front windows.

And in that flicker, I saw his face.

His hands were shaking. The match went out before he could light the rest of the matchbook and toss it. And she'd seen him.

Damn it, she'd—Dewey tried again, fumbled it, stamped his foot in frustration, nearly weeping. Now they knew something was up; they were moving away from—*damn* it, why couldn't he make his hands stop shaking?

Back in prison, making his escape plan had been easy. Hell, he'd had nothing else to think about—that's why his plan had been so good. That plus a helping of the good luck he'd worked so hard to cultivate . . .

And then, bing-bang-boom and it was done: quick, simple. But this—it wasn't just the one thing anymore. It was *everything,* all coming at him all at once, every minute. Breathing in ragged gasps, chest thudding as if he was having a heart attack, Dewey cursed his luck—and that, somehow, turned out to be the charm.

The next match flared, igniting the rest of them. As the tiny flare sailed in through the break in the cottage window, he ran, flinging his arms up over his head.

Then from behind him a huge, dull boom full of bluish flame erupted, setting the world afire.

Wade and Sam reached the end of the paved road and started down the dirt portion of it just as the sky changed from black to deepest gray.

Ahead, the truck's high beams picked out ruts and rocks that Wade steered strenuously to avoid, with only partial success. On either side, evergreen branches scraped the fenders and slapped intermittently at the roof of the cab.

"You think they're awake yet?"

Sam drank deeply from a Dunkin' Donuts coffee container and began devouring another glazed cake donut from the box of a dozen they'd bought after leaving the hospital. He hadn't thought he'd be hungry after the enormous breakfast he'd just eaten back at the hospital. But something about not getting demolished by at least three different possible disasters in the past twenty-four hours had made him ravenous.

Wade shrugged. "Don't know. They might still be asleep. But your mother wants to win a bet she made with me, though, that she and Ellie could finish the deck on their own this week."

He slowed for a deer whose eyes glowed eerily in the truck's headlights. "So I'm guessing they're up early to get a good start on the job," Wade finished.

He eased the truck forward again as the young buck stepped deliberately off the dirt road and into the brush. "I'm just glad we can tell them that Bella's okay, and your granddad, too."

"Yeah." A fresh wave of relief hit Sam; funny how you could go along practically dying for something interesting to happen, but what *really* felt good was—

Nothing. No thrills, no drama, just riding down a dirt road in a truck with your stepfather in the new dawn, eating a donut. He rolled the window down, letting in the smell of swamp.

"Listen, Wade," he began hesitantly. "About that thing we were talking about before."

"Yeah." Wade gazed straight ahead, alert for more deer in the road, or maybe a moose. The enormous creatures had no regard at all for vehicles and would step right out in front of you.

"About what you saw. My dad, I mean, at the hospital," said Sam, but Wade interrupted.

"Twice. I saw him twice." Wade steered around a puddle the size of a small pond. Surprised into silence, Sam heard the water splash up against the truck's underside, hissing as steam formed when it hit the hot exhaust system.

"Once outside the hospital. And before that, in my workshop at home." Wade hit the gas, powering out of the puddle.

"I got the feeling it was your mother he was looking for, not me. Or at least that's what made sense to me at the time."

He frowned, calculating the height of a rock sticking up out of the roadbed ahead, and slowed to let the left-hand tires ease up and over the obstacle. "As much as anything did," he added.

Sam found his voice. "So . . . what'd you *do?*"

Wade's lips pursed wryly. "I told him to get lost, that if he wanted to talk, he should talk to her. Maybe apologize for all the BS he put her through when he was alive."

They jounced over a stretch of rough stones washed out by the recent downpours. Sam held on to his coffee and said nothing for fear of biting his tongue on one of the harder bounces.

"Not," Wade added, "that I believed what I was seeing. Not really. I figured it was . . . I don't know. My subconscious. Or some other mental-hiccup type of thing. But not *real* real, you know?"

The dirt road took a left between two huge granite boulders that stood like sentries guarding the way in. Then it ran sharply uphill and to the right, narrowing. "But now . . ."

"Yeah," Sam said again, trying and failing to imagine Wade Soren-son, perhaps the most down-to-earth person that Sam had ever known, sitting in his workshop giving advice to a ghost.

Wade steered around a huge blown-down pine branch that half blocked the road. "I guess now that I know you saw him, too," Wade went on, "I'll have to be more open-minded. Or something," he added, still clearly not liking the idea.

They started downhill toward the culvert and the beaver pond on either side of it. A breeze sent yellow birch leaves twirling past the wind-shield; a rabbit whose fur was already whitening for winter hopped to the middle of the road, froze alertly for an instant at their approach, then hopped back into the safety of a blackberry-bramble thicket.

Then they heard the boom, a massive thud like a boulder that had fallen from some great height, landing hard very nearby. At the same time they rounded the final curve to where the road went over the cul-vert.

Or rather what remained of the road, now a complete washout. What had been a dirt track four feet higher than the water level was a carved-out channel, muck-glistening in the early light, littered with beaver-chewed branches and small wet tree trunks.

Wade slowed, easing the truck down toward the scene of the ca-tastrophe. Sam stared, dismayed; the road over the culvert had *always* been drivable.

Always. Once in a while they'd had to get in there in hip boots to unclog the culvert, working with rakes and axes, because the beavers—their dam and the lodge behind it were only fifty feet up-stream—kept stuffing it full of twigs. But this . . .

Wade looked downstream, and his face went suddenly ghastly. In the next moment he was out of the truck and running, toward the wreck of a familiar vehicle on its side in the water on the far side of the demolished roadbed.

Its driver's-side window was covered completely by debris, and more wet stuff—weeds, branches, thick water plants uprooted by what must've been an enormous torrent—half-hid the fender.

Wade slogged desperately toward the pickup truck. Pumping his arms and hauling his legs up and down in the sucking mire, he reached the vehicle and scrambled onto it.

"Get my cellphone out of the glove box," he yelled back at Sam, meanwhile pulling handfuls of slimy material out of the hole in the wrecked truck's window. "Call Bob Arnold, tell him . . ."

Wade crouched on the ruined vehicle, craning his neck to try seeing in through the shattered glass. He dragged more weeds out, pulling hand over hand until the wet mass of leaves and roots came free.

Somehow, Sam found himself at the edge of the massive mudhole, looking down into the deep, wide channel that some sudden rush of water had cut.

So how had this happened? Sam flung himself back into Wade's truck, yanked the glove compartment open, and . . .

Nothing. Of course; Wade had given his phone to–Sam put his hands to his jacket pocket for his own cell, didn't feel it. He clapped the pocket again, then his pants.

No phone. Suddenly a vivid memory of Carol's arms around him back in the hospital lobby washed over him, and he realized:

She'd stolen his phone. Then he was outside again, rushing toward where Wade was pulling his head back out of the shattered windshield.

"No one," Wade reported grimly, climbing down with his pants and boots sheathed in a thick coating of mud. He slogged back up onto what remained of the road.

Sam felt himself sagging with momentary relief; they weren't dead in there, then, his mother and Ellie. *They weren't–*

Wade leaned forward with his hands on his knees, sucking in big breaths. Around them, the autumn day brightened, the gray sky filling with blue, the stark black trees' shapes softening to charcoal. High overhead, a plane made its way through the frigid air up there, a glint of sun flaring off its swept-back wing.

They weren't dead. Wade took the no-phone news without any comment, straightening.

Obviously they couldn't go on in the truck, but the cottage wasn't much farther. Turning together silently, they headed toward the washout, leapt over it, and continued down the dirt road, deeper into the woods.

"What do you think that explosion was?" Sam gasped, hurrying to keep up with Wade.

"No idea." They sprinted uphill between balsam firs, cedars, and white pine, the trees' sharp scents mingling with the reek of recently disturbed swamp in the chilly air.

At last they reached the cottage's driveway, a narrow cut in among the trees barely visible unless you knew it was there. Sam smelled smoke, but not the familiar woodstove kind; this had a metallic tang that reminded him of the day a bunch of kids in his high school shop class blew up a cylinder of welding gas. . . .

Suddenly a man Sam had never seen before stumbled out of the woods at him. He was nearly naked, and his face wore an expression of pain and fear so extreme that he looked like something out of a horror movie.

Moaning, the man spotted Sam. Lifting first one leg and then the other in a shambling, uncoordinated way, he tried to change course. But the attempt unbalanced him, and as he fell, flailing his arms uselessly, Sam saw the deep, red gash in his scalp.

"Hey!" The shocked shout erupted from Sam's mouth. The man hit the ground hard and clambered up again as, ahead, Wade turned questioningly.

Then Wade's hands flew up reflexively, his legs went out from under him, and his torso twisted sideways as he, too, fell suddenly and lay motionless.

An instant later—from which direction, Sam couldn't tell—came the percussive *crack!* of a gunshot.

The blazing match pack had barely left Dewey Hooper's hand when the boom hit him, warm and massive as a huge wave, lifting him off the ground, through the burning air. When he dared turn, the heat made his eyes feel like poached eggs, his face seared and eyebrows crispy. Still, he *saw:*

Flame *boiled* from the cottage windows, blew the door from its frame, billowed the walls out and sucked them in again. Glass shards whizzed glittering into the trees, clipping branches and slicing pine cones in half; chimney bricks sailed upward as if being juggled by an invisible giant, then fell down through where the roof used to be.

The *blazing* roof . . . he was deaf from the blast, Dewey knew, or he'd be hearing the crackle of flames devouring the structure—and, no doubt, anyone unlucky enough to have been inside.

Damn, he thought. The explosion had been too big. How the hell would he put a stake through her heart if it was already burnt to a crisp? Unless . . .

But there was one way. If he found her before the flames got to her—not at *this* end of the cabin, even now falling to embers as the fiercest part of the conflagration subsided, but at *that* end, where the explosion hadn't been quite so forceful.

If he could do that, find her and finish her the way he'd planned, he still had a chance to ensure that this was the last time Marianne ever tormented him.

And that end of the building was where the women had been when the blast happened; he'd seen them there, through the front window. So it was worth a try.

Wincing, he sat up. The shotgun was underneath him, somehow unruined, and the shells were still in his pockets; rolling over, he knelt on all fours with his head shaking slowly from side to side, like a stunned beast.

Before his eyes, the cottage went on burning merrily in silence, like a film with the sound turned all the way down, its ferocious glow seeming to fuel the brightening dawn. A birch tree exploded very near the structure, flames licking up its papery trunk, and then another.

Dewey pushed himself off the ground with the butt end of the shotgun. A flap of his scalp slid, sending searing pain through him; gingerly he patted the bleeding skin back into place.

Onward, he thought determinedly. Because here, right here and now, was where the rubber met the road: here in this bloody, fiery place where he would finish her at last, or die trying.

One-handed, he jerked the shotgun by its forestock to rack a shell into the chamber; she might still be alive, and there was no sense trying to hit a moving target with a wooden stake.

But with the shotgun, he could stop it from moving. Then he'd put the body back where the fire could eliminate any clue to the real cause of death. Shakily, but still full of conviction—he'd lived, hadn't he? He'd lived through that hellacious explosion, and that right there told him he was still on the side of the angels, no matter what anyone said— he approached the burning cottage, its near end already collapsed onto itself. At the other end, though—

Oh, the other end, he thought with a scorched-feeling smile. That's where he would find them . . . find *her,* and be done with it.

But then something flickered at the edge of his vision. A movement, brief but worrisome, flittered briefly out there at the far end of the driveway, coming closer through the trees.

Dewey swung the shotgun around smoothly and fired without even thinking about it, then continued toward the burning house.

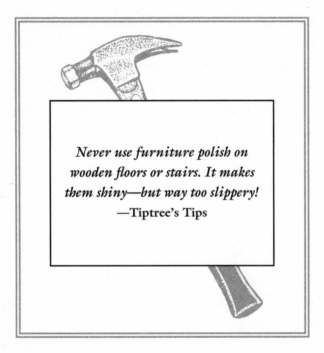

CHAPTER 11

*Never use furniture polish on
wooden floors or stairs. It makes
them shiny—but way too slippery!*
—Tiptree's Tips

The boom rocked the house, blew the glass out of the windows, and set the world alight. Everything at the front of the cabin was fire, roaringly hot and brilliant, flames dripping from every surface and crawling across the ceiling, writhing like bright snakes.

"Ellie . . ." Dark and light, smoke billows rolling chokingly through the flames blazing hotter and nearer. In the instant I'd seen Hooper and understood what he must be doing, we'd hurled ourselves behind the concrete-block chimney.

So we'd missed the full force of it; still, the blast had rocked us from where we'd huddled . . . *"Ellie!"*

I spotted her, flung like a doll against the far wall, where the door out onto the deck hung twisted and jammed. Out of here, we had to get—

"Jake?" Her eyelids flickered.

There was blood on her shirt. A wooden splinter stuck out of her upper arm, shreds of her torn sleeve flapping around it. "You need to come with me."

I tried lifting her as her eyes struggled to focus. "Ellie, come on, we've got to get—"

Out. But I didn't see any way. The whole front end of the cottage boiled with fire now, the hot wind roaring off it making breath nearly impossible. "We've got to get to the back door."

Because in the next few moments, the whole place would flash over. But: "No," she whispered. "He'll be out there. . . ."

She was right. All this had been meant to kill us outright. But if it didn't, of course we would try to escape.

And of course he'd be waiting. With that shotgun . . .

Suddenly I remembered the hole in the floor. From there, we could get out under the latticed-in deck structure, if only I was able to get Ellie moving at all . . . and then I saw why she wasn't.

"Oh, Ellie." The sorrow in my voice alerted her somehow, and she looked at me, wide awake and comprehending. But she still couldn't move, because the splinter in her arm went all the way through, pinning her to the floor.

"Oh, honey," I said, feeling the tears stinging my scorched face. And then, God help me, I grabbed the thing and pulled on it hard. Pulled it *out,* and her scream of anguish felt like that big, sharp wooden dagger had been hammered into my heart.

But then I was dragging her, comforting her and hauling her at the same time across the floor toward the hole, while the hot, deadly conflagration roared ever nearer, chomping and munching.

Wanting to munch on *us* . . . "Okay, down you go." I put her legs down into the hole. "Jump, Ellie. Don't worry, I'm coming, too."

I couldn't remember how high off the ground the floor of the cabin was, how far she would have to fall or what she would land on, whether it was hard or sharp, or—

A sudden exhalation of fire blew straight at us, a blowtorch igniting everything it touched. A chair exploded in flames, then one of the daybeds, each with a low, bright *whuff!*

I shoved her and she fell through, her bloody arm scrabbling for purchase, her hand leaving red fingermarks on the linoleum. A harsh cry of pain from below punched a sob out of me; the silence afterwards was worse.

A gunshot from outside, a sharp, decisive *pow* somewhere out beyond the curtains of fire, hardly penetrated my mind, as if whatever happened there was in another world, one that if I didn't hurry up I wouldn't be seeing ever again. Pressing my arm up to my face to keep the smoke and heat out as well as I could, I took one more wild glance around the place I'd grown to love so dearly.

From over my head a burning timber let out a groan, then cracked through and fell. The whole front of the cottage began collapsing as, sobbing with fright, I hurled myself headfirst down the hole and heard something huge thunder down on top of it, slamming me into darkness.

Above, the crashing and crackling went on, the howling banshee of the fire spiraling through the now-open roof. I could feel the plywood above me getting hotter as the fire advanced across it, sucking air up through the blocked hole. Down here in the dark crawlspace, the breeze it created made the cobwebs all around me shiver and drift against my face.

"Ellie?" Shuddering, I tried pushing the cobwebs away, but my fingers tangled in more of them. Blinded by the blazingly bright light of the flames still printed on my retinas, I fumbled around helplessly, then realized: the flames were real.

At the front of the cottage where the blaze had begun, it was burning through the floor, hot orange embers cascading down in an increasing stream like a flow of lava. Rolling into the dust down here, they extinguished themselves, but soon they wouldn't; soon, there'd be more of them, a hot flood and then an avalanche. We'd be broiled alive.

"Ellie!" Shrouded in sticky cobwebs, blinking and spitting them out, I crawled through old shingles, shreds of tar paper, big chunks of scrap wood—all the things that had gotten tossed back in here over years of fixing and tinkering.

Now they were fuel. As I crawled, feeling my knees shredding on bent nails, stones, and who knew what other tetanus-bearing sharp bits of discarded stuff—*God, I should be so lucky as to live to get tetanus,* I thought irrelevantly—I *knew* there was a way out of here, I *knew* one end of this dark place opened out into the space under the new deck.

I knew it. But I couldn't find it, as a sudden downdraft sucked thick, black smoke under the house, blinding me. Somehow in the panic of the explosion and the fire I'd gotten turned around. Now I was too blinded by the smoke and the awful heat to be able to see the dim, gray dawn that had to be showing somewhere out there, even through the lattice we'd nailed around the deck.

Had to be. Only it wasn't. The smoke kept coming, thickening around me, choking me . . . and I couldn't find Ellie. After she'd landed, she must have crawled, then maybe lost consciousness or worse.

But no. I wasn't going to think that. I just wasn't. I sat up, hit my head on a floor joist, saw flocks of stars twinkling in a sky that was sullenly green and purple, the color of an old bruise.

No, I told myself even as real fright dug its claws into me, *she* wasn't *dead.* She was down here somewhere, and I would find her, and . . . and she *wasn't.*

Fighting back panic, I sat up again more cautiously, pawing away cascades of more spiderwebs studded thickly with egg cases. The smoke thinned, but now stinging tears poured from my eyes; I knew there was a way out, somewhere, but I couldn't *find* it. . . .

The dry, sneaky tickle of a centipede skittered across my neck, the boards above me grew steadily warmer with the awful heat of the swiftly advancing fire just over my head, and—

And then the strong sensation of someone else there with me went through me like an icicle dagger.

Not Ellie. Because Ellie wasn't dead. She *wasn't*.

But when I turned my head—

—slowly, not at all wanting to, terrified and with that sharp, shivery-cold icicle's jab rising up from my heart into my throat—

Ellie wasn't dead. But the person hunkering next to me in the dark, smoke-stinking crawlspace, with spiders and centipedes swarming busily over his gleaming jawbone and prowling his empty eye sockets—

That person most definitely was.

At the sound of the gunshot, Sam dropped flat onto the wet leaves and matted pine needles of the forest floor. He didn't know which way it had come from, or if there would be another.

And he had to reach Wade. Scrambling forward, he peered up and around, spying no one but the man still shambling at him as if nothing had happened.

That smell, though, getting stronger, fire and smoke from somewhere nearby. Through thick, tangled brush and evergreens, the hot yellow glow intensified as Sam watched with horror.

The shambling guy had gotten up. He swung nearer, one arm hanging uselessly and the other waving back and forth in front of him like a blind man trying to feel his way. When he got close enough, Sam saw the bruise swelling the man's left eye shut, the other one wide open, bloodshot and staring wildly.

"Hey. Hey, get down," Sam whispered. But before he could do or say anything more, another shot cracked through the billows of smoke now pouring from the clearing around the cabin.

Rocking on his heels, the man appeared to consider the sound for a moment, a quizzical look coming onto his battered face. Then he dropped once more, first to his knees, finally falling forward, his good hand outflung.

There was a gun in it. Sam's heart leapt at the sight. But if he tried to get it . . . "Oh, God," he breathed, pinned down as a dozen yards away Wade grunted in pain, then lay still also.

"Wade?" But there was no reply. Sam scrambled sideways. No shots whizzed over his head, so he scrambled some more, until he reached the stranger. A .22 pistol lay under his limp hand.

Sam grabbed it, checked it, and found it loaded. Stuffing the weapon inside his jacket, he glanced once more at the prone man, spotted the birdshot pinholing his shoulder. *Sorry, buddy.* But there was nothing Sam could do for him now.

He crawled on his belly over to Wade and saw at once that he was in even worse shape. The shot had caught his upper leg, and the wound was bleeding very freely in gouts that scared Sam more than anything else so far.

Meanwhile, the cottage was burning fast, smoke now boiling furiously from it, flames licking behind the black, reeking billows. Yet his mother and Ellie weren't out here anywhere that he could see . . . so where were they?

Not inside. Please, don't let them be . . . "Okay, guy," he whispered to Wade as he pulled the big man's leather belt off. "Hang in there."

Getting up onto his knees meant getting his head blown off, maybe, but by now Sam hardly cared. He ran the belt under Wade's leg, pulled it tight through the buckle, scrabbled around on the ground until a long, fat fallen branch came to hand.

He twisted the free end of the belt around it. Then, using the branch like a makeshift turning crank, he tightened the belt even more, until the rhythmic pumps of blood from Wade's thigh slowed to a sickening ooze. He bent the branch down and dropped Wade's limp arm over it to keep it in place so the belt wouldn't loosen—he hoped.

But there was nothing he could do to make sure. No shots from the clearing lately, he noticed; grabbing up a rock, he threw it hard in the direction of the cottage, waited for a barrage in reply. None came; cautiously he got himself up into a crouch, then stood, just as a horrendous, creaking-and-groaning crash from over there sent torrents of sparks spiraling up; it sounded as if the rest of the roof had collapsed.

Wade's eyes flickered open. His lips moved. "Go."

Still Sam hesitated, not wanting to leave Wade, until he saw Wade's uncertain hands find the makeshift tourniquet-stick, seize it, and twist it in the right direction to hold the belt tight.

"Don't you let go of that," Sam said. "Don't you let go."

Then, unsure whether or not Wade had heard him—or, if he had heard, would be able to obey for very long—Sam ran.

The reek of burnt gasoline was like a rag pressed to my face as I recoiled from the apparition down there in the crawlspace. Above, the house fell to flaming bits; around me, no light showed the way to safety.

Rearing back from the ghastly thing, I felt my arms flinging out one way, my legs another. Scrabbling wildly in leaf mold and construction debris, my hand touched something softly warm and yielding, like human skin.

It was Ellie, lying limp on her side; I found her pulse and felt it bumping in her wrist, though it wouldn't be much longer if we didn't get out of here soon. Sparks flew from the hole now widening in the floor above; the tortured crashing and fracturing sounds from the burning cottage went on and on.

Ellie moaned, tried to sit up. "What . . . ?" Her eyes widened.

I seized her shoulders. "Ellie, come on. We've got to—"

Back where the sparks were falling, something big collapsed, sending a rush of flaming debris into the crawlspace; briefly the fire above us had been sucking the smoke upward, keeping the air at least halfway decent down here for a few precious breaths. But not anymore.

I didn't know where the way out might be, but as the smoke thickened toward us I knew we couldn't go toward it. And I knew I wasn't going where I'd just seen—*had* I?—my dead ex-husband, grinning and nearly fleshless, with just enough of his face still clinging on so I could recognize . . .

Another huge crash sounded from above. Grabbing Ellie's hand, I began hunching along fast in the only direction that didn't have something bad waiting for me in it.

And for once, that simple strategy worked. Scooching under the floor joists and the big beams they rested on, we went away from the smoke thickening fast around us, toward where fresh air puffed in.

Ellie dropped my hand when we had to duck down hard, crawling through a mess of sawdust, insect bodies, and what felt like a lot of chicken bones, wrapped in a few feathers; an owl's long-ago-deposited leavings, maybe. But when we got through that obstacle course, she grabbed my wrist again.

She'd gotten a look at me in the light we could just make out now, through the lattice under the deck. An expression of alarm she couldn't hide said my nose was bleeding again; it had been all along, really. Sometimes a trickle, other times more; I gathered now was one of the "more" times.

But then I saw the dark puddle forming in the dust in front of me: a *lot* more.

"Oh," I said, realizing suddenly how faint I felt. Drained, actually.

"You know, I might be in trouble," I said, hearing my own voice through the ringing in my ears, like a gong being struck. Also, my legs seemed to have turned to water.

Ellie gave me a shove. "Outside," she gasped, and we ducked from beneath the house, emerging into the enclosed area under the deck. There I sank down onto a rock.

"Oof," I gasped. The fire was still consuming the house, but it began dying down now, the hot snap and pop of charred wood gradually replacing the earlier furnace roar.

Cool air flowed in through the spaces in the latticework I'd nailed to the deck supports. Beyond them, gray dawn brightened over the lake. As if to help celebrate our somehow having lived through the night, a loon laughed out his early-morning call, out on the water.

We crept from under the deck. Blood dripped in blackish splotches onto my pants leg. "I don't get it. You should be . . ."

Dead. The blast, the heat . . . I'd been just sheltered enough, but she hadn't.

"You said to hold my breath," she managed, gulping in more fresh air. "And . . . someone *pushed* me. Two hands."

A strange expression passed over her face. "Really *skinny* hands, like . . ."

The memory of the face under the house, nearly fleshless but still hideously familiar, punched me like a fist. But before I could go any further with that thought, which I didn't *want* to, I definitely *didn't,* the loon called again, nearly.

Only not quite. "Wait a minute. That's not a loon," I said.

The laugh was slightly mad sounding; all loon calls were, I knew. But: "It's too close to be a—"

Yeah, *way* too close. Ellie and I turned together fast toward the lattice enclosing the space under the deck.

Well, *almost* enclosing it. There was a gap two feet wide in the lattice; I hadn't nailed any there because I wanted the deck frame in that area to be accessible later, when I started building the steps. I had to be able to get at it so I could fasten the stringers, which are those long zigzag side pieces that the steps themselves sit on, to the deck frame, and then—

Oh, never mind, the point is that there *was* an opening. And now Dewey Hooper stood in front of it, grinning at us, holding a shotgun.

Close up, at first glance he wasn't what I remembered. Back in the courtroom he'd been clean-shaven, spiffed up and dressed in a cheap suit, no doubt purchased for the occasion. But prison hadn't improved his looks, and neither had living rough, which from the look of him must've been what he'd been doing recently.

Now he was just a small, unshaven, frowzy-haired man dressed in a hodgepodge collection of clothes ranging from a half-decent-looking pair of boots to a jacket so old and moldy-appearing, he might've stolen it off a corpse.

The more I looked at him, though, the more I recalled what had struck me most about him back then, and still did: that he wanted what he wanted, and that's all he cared about, ever.

And that he would do anything to get it, like birds flew and fish swam: naturally, unself-consciously. He held the shotgun in one hand, a long, dagger-sharp stick of kindling wood gripped in the other, and a look of crazed triumph on his bearded face.

Stepping forward, he looked past me, his gaze fastening on Ellie with gloating hunger; for just a moment it seemed possible that his hideous leer might soften into something else.

Regret, maybe, or even guilt. But then, "Marianne," he said. Quietly, the way you'd try talking to a dog you were afraid of. First talking to it, but if that didn't work—

"Marianne, I'm here to kill you. For good, this time."

I got up; stepping past me, he thrust an arm out absently at me and I went down again; now that adrenaline wasn't pumping unnatural energy through me, my whole body felt wavery, like a TV picture that wasn't coming in very well, and my peripheral vision kept fading in and out.

"Stop right there. I'm not who you think I am," declared Ellie, her hand thrust gallantly up in a "halt" gesture. But he just kept advancing on her, while she went on backing away and then around until she was almost under the deck again.

And then she *was* under there, behind the lattice. He took a step and stopped uncertainly, trying to decide if he wanted to follow her into the enclosure.

But no; instead he shouldered the shotgun. "Dewey Hooper," I said to try to stop him, and as I'd hoped, he paused, turning slightly. But what came next, I couldn't have expected:

Seizing the moment, Ellie thrust both hands up through those loose decking boards laid out above her head. Then, despite what must've been agony from her wounded arm, she hooked her fingers over a pair of the joists that the decking rested on, and *pulled*.

Quick as a little monkey, she hauled herself up between the two uncovered joists and then out onto the deck platform. My face must've alerted him; his lips twisted in a snarl. But when he turned back to look under the deck again, she wasn't there.

He peered around with eyes suddenly wide and frightened, even bending to glance under the house. Then he stood straight and spotted her, poised as if to jump from the far end of the deck.

But she didn't; instead came her voice: "Dewey." Crooning it, sort of; crooking her finger at him invitingly.

Luring him away from me. "Oh, Dewey," she coaxed, but now her voice turned taunting.

And that did it. He shoved the ladder over to the deck and began scrambling up, while she went on enticing him, luring him out onto those unstable decking boards. She'd known enough—and even better, she'd remembered—to move delicately, so she got across all right.

But if his step shifted one of the remaining boards so much as a quarter inch, an end of it would slip off the joist and the board would fall through to the ground below, taking him with it.

And that, of course, had been our original plan: trap him behind the lattice. There was one thing, though, that we hadn't anticipated: I no longer had a gun.

I'd intended to be standing there with it in my hand, so he couldn't just run right back out again through the gap in the lattice, or hurl himself through it; the stuff was decorative but as flimsy as matchwood, structurally speaking.

But now the gun was still somewhere in the burning cottage, and the idea of me being upright at all was out of the question. I could barely stay alert, much less hold a weapon steady.

He stepped out onto the deck platform. Any instant now, he *would* fall through. But it wouldn't do us any good. I sat up to try to warn

Ellie, to let her know that once he fell, he'd just get up and run right out here again.

And this time, he'd be *mad*. But instead the loud ringing in my ears rose to a howl, as what little blood remained in my brain rushed down to the level of, apparently, my kneecaps.

At the same time, Dewey Hooper took one more careless step toward Ellie, kicking several of those loose decking pieces aside so that his feet went through suddenly.

As they did, his face changed and I realized just how close we'd come to failure. Because he'd *known;* somehow he'd figured out or guessed what we'd done to the deck. But in the heat of the moment and with Ellie beckoning so tauntingly at him, he'd *forgotten.*

All this went through my head in the instant it took him to understand it, too, surprise changing to a snarl of thwarted fury as he went down. At the same time, though, his hand with the kindling-wood dagger still clutched in it snaked out fast and his arm wrapped around Ellie's neck, dragging her along with him as he tumbled into the lattice enclosure below.

"Oof," I heard him grunt, and then he began cursing as through the lattice I glimpsed him struggling up, which right there was a disappointment: no broken neck.

But what came next was worse.

Leaving Wade behind with the makeshift tourniquet twisted around his thigh, Sam sprinted past the motionless form of the stranger who had appeared without warning out of the woods. Keeping his head low, he ran between the white pines lining the last part of the driveway.

But at the edge of the clearing, he stopped. What had been the cottage was a blackened shell, half-collapsed. The few big timbers remaining were charred like the firewood in a campfire, embers popping hotly and dropping to the smoking ruins below.

His mother and Ellie had been in there . . . but where were they now? He opened his mouth to shout for them, clamped it shut again as faint sounds came from the far side of the cottage wreckage.

First came a clatter, like loose lumber falling, then a low grunt as if the breath had just gotten knocked out of a person. A *male* person, by the sound of the voice, and who could that be?

Not, Sam thought acutely, anyone good. He looked down at the unfamiliar pistol still gripped in his hand. The stranger had been carrying it, and that too was somehow part of all this, Sam felt strongly.

But what the connection was, he had no idea, and right now he didn't care. All he cared about was that the gun was loaded and that it worked.

He crept down the gravel path alongside what remained of the cottage, peeked around the end of the cabin, and saw her. *Mom—*

She lay on the gravel facing away from him, trying to get up by hauling herself with both arms flung across the top of a rock. He'd taken a step out toward her when, at a sound from the shadowy area under the deck platform, he ducked back again.

A man emerged from behind the lattice enclosing the area. He had Ellie White by her hair, clutching it in his fist like the nape of an animal he was determined to control.

In his other hand he held a shotgun, aimed at Sam's mother. When he stopped, the end of the gun barrel was just inches from her head and his finger was on the trigger.

So if I shoot him, the shotgun could go off. Sam shuddered.

"Marianne," the man said softly. "Move an inch, and I'll do it. I'll blow her head off."

He let go of Ellie's hair, and Sam saw what the man held in his other hand: a knife. Or . . . no, not a blade; a long, tapering stick of split kindling wood, like a dagger.

"So here's the deal," the man said almost conversationally.

Sam's mother moaned, tried unsuccessfully yet again to haul herself up onto that rock. Not that it would do any good . . .

Ellie was refusing to cry, biting her lower lip so hard that Sam half

expected to see a drop of blood leaking down from it. Heart pound-
ing, he tried to figure out what Wade would do now.

He couldn't just come out shooting, like in the movies. If he hit the
guy, the shotgun he held could go off and kill Sam's mother. And if he
didn't hit him . . .

Well, that could be worse. All these thoughts went through Sam's
mind lickety-split, as his grandfather would have said.

Patience, Sam counseled himself. Just wait for him to shift that
shotgun aside, even just a little bit. . . .

"You've got to be dead, Marianne," the man said reasonably. "No
more of this coming-back nonsense. So I've got no choice. I have to
put this wooden stake through your . . ."

Marianne? Sam thought puzzledly. The guy's voice took on a plain-
tive note. "Don't you see? There was a reason I couldn't get you out
of my head. It's because I'm *supposed* to—"

He broke off, looked up sharply; Sam shrank back. But it was
something down by the lake that had drawn the guy's attention; he
scowled briefly toward the water, then turned back to Ellie.

"You're wasting time." He jerked the dagger. "Lie down on the
gravel. Do it! Do it or I swear I'll kill her right in front of you. That
what you want? Is it?"

A tiny, broken sob escaped Ellie as she sank to the path. Just one,
but it told Sam that Ellie was at the end of her rope now; ordinarily,
his mother's friend would no more weep openly in front of strangers
than she would strip naked on Water Street.

Which put Sam, suddenly, at the end of his own rope. *Enough,* he
thought calmly, raising his pistol and stepping out into full view of the
angry intruder. "Stop," he said.

A gap-toothed grin stretched the guy's unkempt face. "Yeah? Or
what, smart boy?"

Sam took another step, noting with some amazement how steady
he felt, how calm. But before he could open his mouth to reply, several things happened:

Ellie reared back, shoved the guy's pants leg up to reveal his pale, hairy ankle, then lunged forward and bit down hard on it. The guy howled. He swung the shotgun up and around.

Sam leapt, reaching the guy in a single bound and fastening his hands to the guy's jacketed shoulders, then wrapping him in an imprisoning bear hug. A faint pop came from somewhere, and—

Sam felt the guy stiffen, his back arching and his shoulders trying to hunch forward in a writhing motion. At the same moment, his eyes widened more than human eyes ought to be able to, while his face wrenched in a spasm.

Then, just as Sam understood that the pop he'd dimly heard a millisecond earlier must be gunfire, the bullet exited, taking a large, untidy chunk of the guy's forehead with it.

Sam felt his arms fall to his sides. The guy dropped, first to his knees, then forward onto his face. The gun Sam held fell from his opened hand, made a *chink!* sound hitting the pea gravel around the new deck.

Ellie looked up at Sam, her red hair wild around a face that was unreadable, then past him to where his mother still tried to struggle up.

And past her as well, to a man standing on the shore, behind him a canoe floating adrift on the waves stippling the lake. It was Bob Arnold, and even from here Sam could see that he had his service weapon in his hand.

Struggling to her feet, Ellie staggered toward Bob, and after a stunned moment Sam moved, too, stopping when he got to where his mother lay half-conscious and deadly pale, draped over the rock she'd been trying to haul herself up on. Fish-belly white, Bella would have called that face.

"Mom," Sam whispered urgently, and her eyelids fluttered; it was something. Sam prayed to the silent sky that it was enough, then felt Bob kneeling by him.

"Sam," Bob said. "Listen to me now."

Her face looked as if she'd been punched. But then Sam saw that most of the blood on her was leaking from her nose, not from any wounds he could see, and he dared to feel hopeful again.

"I broke a wheel on the squad car on the way in, and lost control. The car's sitting crosswise in the road, and it's stuck in the mud."

On the rough dirt road, Sam realized, racing the car in here over the rocks and ruts on that—

"Sam, it's *blocking* the road. I radioed for help, but that was before I wrecked the car. They need to know they're not going to be able to get the Calais squads in here. Ambulance, either."

Which must've been why Bob came across the lake. Through the woods, he must have run to one of the other camps that was nearer to that part of the road, found the canoe, and—

"Sam, we need them." Reinforcements, Bob meant. Cops, the emergency medical people.

Especially them. "Now, I want you to get in that canoe," Bob said. "It's the fastest way back to the car, it's right up the hill from the cabin, just across the cove."

Sam knew the place. "Okay," he said dazedly, then remembered that . . . "Wade's out in the driveway, he's—"

Hurt. Maybe dying, or maybe even already dead. "Another guy is out there, too."

And I can't leave my mom, he wanted to add. *I can't—*

Bob shook his head vexedly. "Okay, look. Check Wade on your way. If you can't leave him, don't. But if you can . . . Sam, those Calais guys can come in by boat, get your mother out of here that way. Wade too—but they've got to know about it to do it."

He sucked in a breath. "I'll do all I can here, Sam. You get to the car if you can, get on my radio, you know how to work it?"

For the first time Sam noticed that Bob's uniform was wet. "What about your cellphone?"

Bob bent over Sam's mother to put an assessing finger to the pulse in her neck, withdrew it with a look of deep concern that chilled Sam's heart.

"On the way over here, I fell in, all right?" Bob looked up at Sam. "Capsized, getting out of the canoe. And while I was doing that, I lost my phone somehow. It's at the bottom of the lake, okay? That answer all your questions?" he demanded impatiently.

"Oh. Yeah," Sam said, feeling overwhelmed. "Okay, then . . ."

Ellie bent to Sam's mother. She'd found some water; now she began putting droplets of it onto the unconscious woman's lips, using her fingertip.

"I can work the radio," said Sam, turning to run. But before he could go, Bob said something else to him.

"You're still one of the good guys, Sam. Don't waste it."

"Uh, yeah," Sam repeated, not understanding, and then he did run, first to Wade, who lay just as Sam had left him, bleeding. But the strange, nearly naked guy sat by him now, with the stick holding the tourniquet tight gripped in his hand.

Who the hell are you? Sam wanted to scream at the guy. *Where did you come from?* And—*How can this be happening?* But when he crouched desperately by Wade, the guy spoke up first:

"I'm holding it." Nothing more. But from his hands, which were red with Wade's blood, and the look on his bruised, swollen face—like this was the first time he'd ever been asked to do something *real,* and he would do it or die trying—Sam knew he didn't have to say anything at all. With a last glance at Wade's grayish face, he sprinted away.

To the lake, plunging into the icy water and diving at once to get himself wet as fast as he could. A few long strokes and he was beside the drifting canoe; hurling himself onto it crosswise, he hauled his body aboard, swung his legs in, and sat.

There was still a little water in it, but fortunately, Bob Arnold had rescued the paddle after he'd capsized; grabbing it up, Sam began paddling, putting his back into it. The canoe shot across the icy lake, through the mineral-water-smelling cold air.

But when he was only halfway across, the low growl of a small plane's engine broke the silence. Something big passed overhead fast, its shadow huge, roaring and racing across the lake. Sam stared as at the far end of the lake, the plane turned, descending.

Two pontoons touched down with a splash; only then did it occur to Sam to wonder how Bob Arnold had known to come here at all. A hundred yards from the burned cottage where his mother and Wade lay injured, the plane halted, turned halfway around, then motored slowly toward the shore.

It was a red-and-white Cessna 150 two-seater; two men hopped out, crouching, leapt from rock to rock until they reached the dock, and then ran. One was the plane's owner, Bud Underwood; Sam recognized him and the plane, too, from its slip at the boatyard. The other was Ellie White's husband, George Valentine.

The two men sprinted uphill, out of sight behind the pines screening the shore. Watching, Sam reversed course and paddled hard toward them, weeping with relief that help had arrived.

But he still didn't know if they'd gotten here in time.

It was midafternoon when the Calais cops ferried Bob Arnold back across the cove in their patrol boat.

"Thanks, guys," he said, then stood on the shore watching as they motored away toward the launch ramp, at the far end of the lake. The boat dwindled, then vanished around the tip of Balsam Point, its engine sound dropping away.

Shivering, Bob turned uphill to where his car was parked. In his absence, a wrecker had come out and hauled the vehicle out of the deep mud it was mired in, and put a wheel on to replace the one he had ruined. Then the wrecker guys had driven the car up here and left it for him, the road in to the crime scene by that time being clogged with squad cars, state vehicles, and a fire crew from Calais.

So now here it sat, mud-spattered but drivable; meanwhile, throughout the day, the Calais cops had brought him dry clothes, set up emergency heaters, and furnished him with gallons of hot coffee in an effort to get him warm after his icy dunking. But he still felt like somebody had shoved an icicle up his . . .

Well. Cold was how he felt, and it had nothing to do with the lake. Or the weather, chilling down again with the onset of afternoon, the sky a deep, purplish blue more like February than October and the air smelling ominously of snow.

I killed a guy. Bah-*dum*-pum-pum, the rhythm of the words a repeating drumbeat, not so much in his head as in his heart.

To distract himself, he ticked items off his mental to-do list, even though he was not strictly speaking in charge of the crime scene, or the rescue scene, or even on the teams that were in fact responsible for them. The Calais cops and state guys had jurisdiction, Calais because of where the scene was located and the state because the perpetrator was an escaped prison inmate.

Had been an inmate. Bob returned his mind to his list:

Jake Tiptree and Wade Sorenson were both still alive as best Bob knew, both airlifted to the hospital in Calais, then Life-Flighted to Bangor, check.

Halfway up the path, Bob turned back to gaze across the lake at the cottage wreckage, staties still swarming over the clearing and the woods around it. He knew from the way they'd treated him that he wasn't going to have any trouble about the shooting, that even before he'd given a statement—which he would no doubt be doing all the rest of this afternoon and well into the evening—they'd known it was a justifiable use of his weapon.

That he'd been right to shoot Dewey Hooper in the head . . .

In the head. Bah-da-*bump*. He shook his own head to clear it, went on trudging up the steep path between the big old trees. A vivid picture of his wife, smiling prettily at him, floated into his mind; next time he touched her, it would be with hands that had killed another human being.

Meanwhile, Ellie White had been sent first to the hospital in Calais for treatment, then back to Eastport, where she'd be asked to give the only full account that was presently available of all that had transpired over the past two days.

Check, Bob thought. Ellie's husband, George, had argued protectively that Ellie ought to give her statement later, when she'd had a chance to get her thoughts together; tomorrow, maybe, or even sometime next week.

But that of course was just what the investigators didn't want, her memories tamed and civilized into something more coherent but perhaps less accurate, and so not as useful for the official record. Either way, though, Bob thought she already had herself together just fine.

That she'd be fine. Which left only the unidentified, nearly naked man who had stumbled out of the woods at Sam Tiptree hours earlier, and then saved Wade Sorenson's life. When Bob got out to where Wade lay unconscious and bleeding, the unidentified guy was there putting pressure on the gunshot wound to the thigh Wade had recently suffered, and once he got warm enough to talk again, Sam had backed up the guy's story, that he hadn't been the shooter.

But that part of Wade's savior's tale had been complicated; Bob figured it would all come out in the wash later, once the man had been treated for his own injuries and was able to give more of his own story.

If Wade had been saved, Bob reminded himself unhappily; that part wasn't for sure yet. He flattened his hands on the fender of the old Crown Vic. "To Serve and Protect," the vehicle's decal proclaimed in black letters that were beginning to flake off in patches, exposing the white paint beneath.

Leaning over the hood, Bob felt the forest all around him slowly expanding and contracting, as if it were breathing. Above him a woodpecker's rat-a-tat-tat echoed hollowly; a fish jumped, landing in the lake with a flat slap.

Turning, he let all the coffee he'd drunk come up. They'd taken his service weapon; a formality, they'd assured him. But Bob hoped it would all go as smoothly as they said, and thinking this reminded him once more of Dewey Hooper.

Only this time, not of the act of shooting him. Instead Bob recalled a night a long time ago, when he'd driven a rowdy, uncooperative

Hooper to the county lockup after grabbing the man up on yet another drunk-and-disorderly.

Dragging the back of his hand over his mouth, he remembered what he'd told Hooper that night:

That Hooper should slow down, think things through before going off half-cocked. That things would work out better if he did. Bob wondered now if Hooper had even heard this, much less remembered it.

Probably not. Straightening, Bob got into the car, and once he'd settled behind the wheel he felt better. Sam Tiptree had been driven to the hospital by one of the Calais cops, to be assessed in the emergency room, and shortly after that word had come back that he'd been released, shaken but otherwise okay.

So, check. Bob put his hands on the wheel. The unidentified man had been taken away, too, wrapped in blankets for his own trip to the ER. What would happen to him after that depended on what the rest of his story turned out to be.

Some big-time head trauma, there. Gash the size of Idaho in the guy's forehead. But he'd been walking and talking, so there couldn't have been too much wrong beyond the obvious beating he'd taken, the flesh wound to his shoulder, and the effects of being practically bare-assed out here overnight in the freezing woods.

Bob pulled the car out onto the dirt road. He would go home, take a hot shower, change clothes, and then go give his statement to the state boys, and after that maybe have a beer.

God knew he could use one. For now, there was a half-full bottle of water in the cup holder; he spat the first mouthful of the stale, warmish stuff out the car window, then drank.

He started off down the dirt road, bumping through the ruts slowly so as not to damage the squad car's muffler. A loon called somewhere out on the lake behind him, the mournful-sounding *ha-ha-ha!* bringing a fresh lump to his throat.

I killed a man. But he swallowed it down, let the squad's tires roll over the humps and gulches they encountered. The trees went by, some leafless, some evergreen, the huckleberry brambles and the cat-tails, dark brown and velvety looking. The flat, bright surfaces of the streams and beaver ponds where they came up to the edge of the weathered roadway were glassy and silent.

As he drove he thought of all the things he would say if the deadly shot had been fired by someone else; by Sam Tiptree, for instance. In that case Bob would take pains to reassure Sam, to tell him he'd had no choice. That he'd done the correct thing.

That tomorrow was another day, and that everything would be all right. All those things were true, Bob knew. But as the Crown Vic's wheels kept turning, the tires rolling over and over the bumps in the dirt road, he couldn't stop thinking:

Bah-*dum*-pum-pum. *I killed a man.* Shot him.

In the head.

CHAPTER 12

*To eliminate a small dent in wood
(floor, banister, furniture, etc.)
steam it with a damp cloth and a
steam iron (you might have to do
this several times.)*
—Tiptree's Tips

"**Y**ou mean it can just break like that? A blood vessel, with not even any warning?"

Bella Diamond's voice sounded outraged, as if this sort of betrayal by a person's own body should not be allowed, and if I'd been in the mood to talk I'd have agreed.

But I wasn't; in the mood, that is. Not yet, and maybe not ever. Eyes closed—they all thought I was still asleep—I was sitting halfway upright in a hospital bed with what felt like a cotton wad the size of Manhattan shoved so far up my nose, it was bumping against my tonsils.

Also, I was pretty sure that Ellie and Sam were dead, since the last time I'd seen them a guy with a shotgun had been aiming it menacingly at them, ready to fire.

The cottage was gone, too, and who knew what—or who—else. So I didn't open my eyes. Why bother? But then came Sam's voice.

"Ellie was the real hero," he said. "Can you believe she not only sent an email on a Kindle, she was smart enough to send it twice? Once to George, and a copy to Bob Arnold."

"Oh, well," Ellie remarked self-deprecatingly. "What was I supposed to do, send up smoke signals? Although," she added, "I guess Dewey Hooper did a pretty good job of that."

A tear leaked down my cheek; they were alive. But I put the brakes on any serious weeping, since I was fairly certain blowing my nose would be catastrophic.

"So, what was the guy's story, anyway?" my dad asked. "He thought Ellie was his dead wife?"

"Not just thought so." Sam again, sounding tired but okay. "He was obsessed with her. Bob Arnold says that back at the prison they found a pile of notebooks, seven years' worth. Full of her name written over and over again, pages and pages."

"Hmph." Bella Diamond's contemptuous snort conveyed what she thought of that. "If he was so crazy about her, he shouldn't have murdered her. Seems to me some people don't *deserve* wives."

Amen, I thought. The faint scrape of a chair told me she had come over to sit closer to me.

Her work-chapped hand took mine and held it comfortingly. "Poor thing," she murmured. "What did those surgeons do to her in that operating room, anyway?"

Sam replied eagerly. "Actually, it was kind of great. What she had is called an intranasal arterial hemorrhage. It means a burst artery, not a big one, and really it can happen to anyone, no warning, and it wouldn't stop because an artery has pressure in it, see? It has your blood pressure in it."

I smiled inwardly; Sam had always liked listening when his brain-surgeon father explained medical things. He went on:

"So what they do is, they stick an electrocautery wire—a hot electrical wire, basically—way up there where the bleeding is, and then they *zap* it—"

Ouch. No wonder my face felt like a truck had hit it. They'd electrocuted my nosebleed.

"What I still don't get," Ellie put in, "is who the guy was, who was wandering around nearly naked in the woods."

"*That* guy." Ellie's husband, George, laughed without humor. "*That* guy was just a late-season tourist who'd wandered in there, thought he was going for a hike. A walk in the woods."

Another chair-scrape as George pulled up to my bedside, too. "Instead, he ran into Dewey Hooper. And *he'd* just found the body of that hunter who went missing, remember him? Bentley Hodell?"

I did remember, sort of. There'd been a search for him, but an unsuccessful one. Bella tsk-tsked as George went on:

"Guess we'll never know for sure what he was thinking, but Hooper must've wanted Hodell's clothes. Pretty decent jacket and a pair of lined pants."

I remembered those, too. "So when the smoke cleared, Hooper had the boots and jacket on, *and* he'd hit the tourist guy on the head with a rock, took *his* clothes, too, and put them on Hodell."

"But didn't take his gun?" Bella asked acutely. A stickler for detail, Bella could find a toast crumb on a kitchen counter that was otherwise so clean, Victor could've done brain surgery on it. "The tourist's gun, the one Sam had, there at the end?"

"Right. Hooper didn't know about it." It was Bob Arnold's voice now. "Tourist guy was trying to get it out, he fell on it when Hooper clobbered him, and then it was lying under him, in among the fallen leaves, so Hooper never saw it."

Footsteps entered the room. "Hooper put the tourist's ID on Hodell's body, and the tourist's clothes, too. Bashed him up so he wasn't recognizable otherwise . . . maybe he figured that there'd be an-other search if a visitor went missing, but not so much for Hodell since he'd already been searched for."

So it was Hodell who'd come floating down the stream at us, dur-ing that first flood. Bob pulled a chair out, or someone did.

"Hooper took Hodell's clothes for himself, left the tourist for dead. His name's Harold Brautigan, by the way," Bob added. "And he's right down the hall here, getting over a skull fracture and some bird-shot to his arm."

"What I'm wondering," said Ellie quietly, "is why the blast wasn't bigger. I mean, a propane explosion–"

"Uh, yeah," Sam put in, sounding embarrassed. "The thing is, there wasn't much left in that tank. See, Wade asked me to call the propane guy?"

"But I forgot," Sam admitted. "I had, uh, something else on my mind, and . . . man, I've really been batting a thousand lately, haven't I?"

"Maybe so," said my dad, "but in this case, if you had done what you said you'd do, your mom would be mincemeat now."

"Right," said Bob. "So cut yourself a little slack."

Then: "What about Wade?" My dad's voice turned no-nonsense serious; at the sound of it, it hit me whose voice I *hadn't* heard and a bolt of fright surged through me.

Bob again: "That's what I came to tell you. Wade's out of surgery, and from what they're telling me–"

My eyes popped open. "Surgery? What surgery?"

They all looked at me, pleased that I was awake. But they couldn't hide their worry. About Wade, I realized . . .

"Bob?" I asked, turning to him in appeal. A fat plastic IV bag full of dark red blood hung from the pole by my bed, dripping into my arm. Besides the transfusion I also had enough other tubes, monitors, and high-tech gadgets on and around me to equip a mad scientist's laboratory.

"Wade's fine," Bob assured me soothingly.

I sat all the way up. The room didn't spin, and I didn't pass out. But: "Facts, Bob, I want—"

"Mom, Wade got shot," Sam said. God, he was handsome, just like his father at that age. "In the leg, but they—"

"I want to see him." I swung my own legs out of bed, paused at the wave of faintness that clobbered me. But: "Get me a nurse. A wheelchair, a nurse, and a hot, soapy washcloth."

I got a horrifyingly clear glimpse of myself in the mirror over the washstand, opposite the bed. "And a comb, please." I looked like Dracula's leftovers.

"Mom," Sam said cautioningly, rushing forward, and the nurse who hurried in after I'd hammered on the call button wasn't too pleased with me, either.

But half an hour later—I'd had to threaten to sign myself out against medical advice and take a cab home, which I would have—I'd had my face washed, teeth brushed, hair combed, and a fresh bale of cotton put into my nose with, I guessed, the same device the State of Maine uses to drive highway mile markers into granite bedrock. After that, they helped me into the chair I'd demanded and rolled me down the hall to the recovery room.

Inside, Wade lay still unconscious and hooked to a long tube connected to a respirator; he hadn't woken up yet from the surgical anesthesia.

A sheet covered him to his armpits; his face, half-obscured by tubes and tape, looked like something a house cat had used for a scratching post. "Hey," I said softly.

I rolled myself nearer. "Hey." I put my hand in his. There was an oxygen monitor clipped to his index finger. A transfusion bag like mine hung over his bed.

He looked awful, but he was fine; I could tell by the even rhythm of his EKG tracing, the unhurried whushing sound of his breathing machine, and the atmosphere in the bright, clean room:

Calm. Unworried. A nurse came over to me. "It's going to be

awhile before the anesthesia wears off. We'll take the breathing tube out when it does."

She shot something into his IV. "It was a little dicey for a while, but the surgeons are happy with how he's recovering."

I couldn't say anything. I just felt so . . . grateful, and it struck me then that when he wasn't vying for the title of Worst Husband in the World, Victor had done exactly this for most of his life:

Fixed things, so sick or injured people could get well and other people like me could sit by their bedsides, trying not to weep with relief.

He'd gotten me out from under that burning cottage, too, I felt very sure, in the only way he could: he'd *scared* me out.

But I'd already decided I wasn't going to tell anyone about that, or they'd think I had brain damage. The nurse adjusted the IV running into Wade's arm. "It was a big surgery," she said. "He'll sleep for quite a while."

"Good," I replied, holding Wade's hand. There were tiny gold hairs on the backs of his fingers, a familiar scar at the base of his right thumb where a rope burned it once.

"That's good," I managed to repeat.

And then I did weep.

Harold had Facebook, and LiveJournal, and Twitter. But when the day finally came for him to leave Eastport, he realized he'd never use them again. Over his two weeks here, the real world had captured him, and now nothing else would do.

Eastport captured him: salt and creosote, woodsmoke and the tang of rose hips ripening in red clusters, their perfumes mixing with the good smells of bacon and coffee drifting from the diner. Harold stood on the fish pier by the tubby, bright blue tugboat *Ahoskie,* listening to the rhythmic creak of her side sliding with the wave action along the pier's rubber bumper.

Gulls cried, rising and diving into the foamy white wake of a wooden boat puttering on the bay. In the harbor, diesel engines grumbled wetly, adding their rich stink to the mix as men in boots clomped down ramps, then jumped aboard the idling vessels.

Oh, Harold thought clearly, turning in the scouringly brisk breeze off the water to the row of red-brick commercial buildings opposite the pier. *Oh, I want to stay.*

But he couldn't. Not now; later, maybe. Across the street, Eastport police chief Bob Arnold came out of the hardware store and saw Harold, nodded a greeting.

The chief had been awfully helpful, especially about the gun, which strictly speaking Harold should not have been carrying with him that day in the woods. But now it was all right, and so was Harold's head, only a small scar remaining.

The chief tossed a bag onto the seat of his squad car and drove off in the direction of his new office. Harold happened to know there was a surprise party planned to celebrate the chief's move; he wished he could attend.

Maybe next time there's a party, I can be there, he thought, absently rubbing his shoulder, which was still a bit sore from the birdshot the surgeons at the hospital had dug out of it. *Maybe when I come back.*

Bob would still be the police chief, Harold was sure; the chief's little girl had returned from her doctor's visit with new medications that were working pretty well already. So to his vast relief, the chief wouldn't have to be moving to Arizona soon but only a few blocks down the street.

In the diner, Harold slid into his accustomed booth. When she saw him, the waitress—Heather, her name was; she had two kids, and a husband who was a fisherman, and her mother worked at town hall, where she did the payroll and issued vehicle registrations—poured his coffee and put in his breakfast order of pancakes and a slice of bacon without having to ask.

Eastport's newspaper, the *Quoddy Tides,* lay on the booth's red leatherette seat; on its puzzle page the word jumble had already been filled in but the Sudoku was blank, so he started on it. Behind the counter, the radio played classic hits and public service spots, church supper announcements and local tag sale ads mingling with Rod Stewart and the Beatles.

By the time he finished his meal, he'd discovered that even the easiest Sudoku was still beyond him, and that two of the diner's massive blueberry pancakes were still all he could eat.

"Thanks, Heather." *For everything.*

He left a ten for a tip and went out before she could argue that it was too much, stopped at the flower shop to pick up the big bouquet he'd ordered earlier, then crossed to Dana Street and walked on up the hill between the library lawn's gazebo and the Rose Garden café, its windows full of geraniums and its graveled side yard furnished with a bowl of water for thirsty dogs.

Like me, Harold thought at the sight of the bowl, old white china with a dark blue stripe around the top. *I was thirsty.*

And they gave me water here. From behind him, the big, deep *whonk!* of a departing freighter's horn seemed to vibrate even the granite beneath his feet. He let the sound go through him:

Remember. Oh, I want to remember all this. He watched as the huge vessel made its ponderous way up the bay toward the Cherry Island light, even in daytime a bright blip on the clear blue sky.

Time to go. He turned left past the old Masonic Hall. Ahead, Jake Tiptree's big old house loomed like a massive lighthouse itself.

As it had been, for him. Even now he felt it drawing him in. Stopping before it, he let his eye run up its massive side along its antique white clapboards to the topmost window.

In the window, which was glitteringly clean, a white lace curtain hung motionless. Then . . . it was over before he could be certain of what he had seen . . . the curtain *twitched.*

Just once, slyly and amusingly, like a joke between friends. Or . . . *had* it? Harold couldn't be sure, not of that or of the other strange things he'd seen and heard in the house over the past two weeks, either.

But even if they'd really happened, that was all right. He guessed he was probably a little strange sometimes himself. And in Eastport, that was all right, too.

Right as rain. Whistling, Harold strode up the front walk of the big old white house on Key Street, crossed the front porch, and went in.

"So was he nuts, or what?"

At about the same time as Harold Brautigan was finishing his breakfast at the diner and then buying his bouquet of flowers, Sam Tiptree stood on a rickety stepladder in the front hallway of his mother's house on Key Street, looking up at the tin ceiling through safety glasses that made his face sweat.

Two weeks had passed since the events at the lake. Now, inches from Sam's face, the grapevine-and-maple-leaf pattern pressed into the antique metal flaked gritty white paint bits down onto his dust mask.

"Dewey Hooper, I mean," he added, scraping off more paint.

"I don't know how to answer that," said his mother. "If you mean did he have some diagnosable, treatable illness, something that would explain . . ."

She shook her head. "I don't know. Ellie thinks he must've, to be able to do what he did. She feels sorry for him, but I'm having a hard time with that. Maybe it's just too soon."

"Yeah." Paint bits dusted down. Next he would vacuum it all, to get the last, tiny loose stuff. His mother stood with one hand on the ladder, supposedly to keep it from wobbling.

But he knew the real reason. He'd been quiet—too quiet, he guessed she thought—since it all happened. So sooner or later of course she would ask him about it; he tried forestalling her question with one of his own.

"What's Ellie up to, anyway?"

His mother laughed fondly. "She's rewriting my *Quoddy Tides* col-umn. I gave it to her to read and she told me it was all bass-ackwards and did I want her to—"

She stopped, making a wry face. "Very funny," she said at the way he'd nearly diverted her. Then: "So do you want to talk about it? Whatever it is that's on your mind?"

He glanced down at her. "It's okay, Mom. I've got things to do, that's all. But I've got it under control."

He did, too, with an AA meeting tonight, one tomorrow night, and one the night after. Nothing terrible had happened on account of his problem; the opposite, maybe. Everybody needed a wake-up call now and then, and he'd had his.

But he'd nearly taken a drink. That fact, stark and scary as hell, stood front and center. So he would do something about it.

Simple as that. *Keep it simple,* he thought calmly, taking a deep breath. So far, today was going just fine.

"That's a no, then, huh?" He heard the smile in her voice as she accepted this. When he looked down again, he noticed suddenly that she was pretty, sort of.

A flurry of paint flakes drifted onto her. "Ma, put a dust mask on if you're going to stand there."

She did, pulling the elastic back over her ears. "This other thing, though," she said through it. "About your dad and so on," she added, startling Sam.

Because at that very moment, it was who he'd been thinking about: his father, and how he could see now in his mother's face what must've attracted him: bright, intelligent eyes, good skin, a mouth that looked as if it smiled very frequently—

And most of all, that *interested* expression she always wore. "Yeah?" he said warily, reaching with the whisk broom to brush into a corner where the ceiling met the wall.

"Yeah. Because the thing is . . ." She was laughing now, which he thought was strange. Good, though: it hit him again just how glad he was that she'd survived. Wade too; now he was at the lake planning the new cottage. Everyone was fine.

Bella. His grandfather Jacob. *And me,* he added to himself.

Me too.

"The *irony* is," she went on, "when he was alive, he didn't believe in—"

What? Sam wondered. *What didn't my dad believe in?* Besides honesty, fidelity, a basic sense of decency, the idea that he had ever owed anyone anything at all—

And yet, Sam thought. *And yet, and yet.*

"Ghosts!" She burst out laughing. "He positively *scorned* the notion! Said people who did believe in them were pathetic."

Or as his father would've put it himself, Sam recalled as he listened, such people were "not top-drawer thinkers." Back then Sam hadn't understood, believing that the phrase meant something about not keeping your thoughts with your socks and underwear.

"Oh, Sam, have you ever heard anything so rich? So . . . so . . . *perfect?*" she asked, her face streaming tears.

Sam climbed down from the ladder. He put his arm around his mother, whose shoulders still shook with emotion. He'd tried out a lot of feelings about what he'd seen.

But it hadn't occurred to him to laugh about it. Or cry, as she seemed now to be doing.

"Wade saw him, too," Sam said. "I'm sure he did. Like Dad was . . . *warning* us, or something."

His mother nodded. "So did Bella. It was why she was grouchy all the time. She was terrified, didn't know what to believe, and didn't want to admit it."

But then his mother looked serious. "The thing is, though, Sam, we were all thinking about him. We all knew his . . . his . . ."

"Deathiversary," Sam supplied.

"Yes. We all felt that date looming, in some way. So—"

"So it could've been, like, a mass hallucination? Just our thoughts fooling us? But you don't think so, do you?"

He could see that she didn't. But before he could say more, Harold Brautigan came in, his step by now so familiar across the back porch that the dogs didn't even get up.

"Hi," the young man said shyly. He'd been staying here in the guest room since it all happened. "Just thought I'd say so long."

Tall and stoop-shouldered, with messy brown hair and an odd kind of irresistibly loose-lipped grin, Harold had a backpack in one hand and a big bunch of flowers clutched in the other.

He thrust them at Sam's mother. "And thanks," he added. "You all have been really great to me."

"We've enjoyed getting to know you," Jake replied.

But now the shy young man was going back to Manhattan to quit his terrible job, then apply to the community college in his hometown in upstate New York. His big goal, he'd confided to Sam, was a degree in criminal justice.

They walked to the door, while Sam's mother got a vase for the flowers. "Listen, Sam," said Harold. "The little guest room I stayed in. Anything unusual ever happen in there?"

Not unless you count my dad dying in it, Sam thought. After a short illness, the newspaper obituary had said.

Short but not sweet. "Nothing I know of. Why?"

No sense in getting Harold going on that subject just as he was leaving. Although—the thought struck Sam suddenly—if Harold had seen something, too, without knowing anything about Sam's dad or the deathiversary, then . . .

Harold frowned. "Ah, no reason. Just . . . no. Nothing at all. Forget it." He looked up, smiling genuinely at Sam.

"Take care, buddy." Then he was gone, across the porch and down the front walk, his step jaunty.

From the doorway, Sam watched Harold stride off through the crisp, fallen leaves, downtown to where the cab would get him and take him out to the bus stop. He stood watching for as long as he could stand it. Then—*something unusual*—he called out:

"Hey, wait a minute!" Sam took off running. Harold turned curiously.

"Wait," Sam called, feeling happy suddenly, as light as a feather. "Wait up, there's a question I want to ask you!"

ABOUT THE AUTHOR

SARAH GRAVES lives with her husband in Eastport, Maine. She is at work on the next Home Repair Is Homicide mystery.